Satyricon

Petronius

Translated by Andrew Brown

ONEWORLD
CLASSICS

ONEWORLD CLASSICS LTD
London House
243-253 Lower Mortlake Road
Richmond
Surrey TW9 2LL
United Kingdom
www.oneworldclassics.com

First published by Oneworld Classics Limited in 2009
Translation, Introduction, Appendices and Notes © Andrew Brown, 2009
Front cover image from the first Calder edition of *Satyricon* (1953)

Reprinted 2010

Printed and bound in Great Britain by MPG Books

ISBN: 978-1-84749-116-9

Contents

Introduction

T HE SATYRICON HAS TRADITIONALLY been attributed to a certain Caius Petronius, one of Nero's courtiers, whose ability to set the tone for the Emperor's revels earned him the sobriquet *elegantiæ arbiter*, or "arbiter of elegance". As a result, later generations of scribes and scholars knew him as Caius Petronius Arbiter, or just Arbiter. Tacitus gives a brief but vivid portrait (see Appendix 3, below) of a Caius Petronius who slept all day and worked (or partied) all night; who was known for his frankness but also for his ability to retain imperial favour; whose taste for the high life did not prevent him from being, in that chilling phrase, an able administrator (proconsul and consul); and who returned to Nero's court to indulge (or pretend to indulge) in his taste for vice. The envy of another courtier, Tigellinus, proved his downfall: Petronius, knowing that his arrest on a charge of treason was imminent, committed suicide.

It is uncertain whether this Petronius was the same man who wrote the *Satyricon*. But the life and death of Nero's courtier show how the trend-setter, the arbiter of taste, the "aesthete", can pander to power. Yet the hint in Tacitus that Petronius was merely "affecting" his vices suggests something more complex. Why "pretend" to be a debauchee? Was he being "ironic" in his pleasures? Did he share in the Emperor's depravities in the same way that, a millenium and a half later, Lorenzino de' Medici (known as "Lorenzaccio") with apparent zest (but inward disgust – or so he claimed) joined his cousin Alessandro, Duke of Florence, on his trail of debauchery? Lorenzino later claimed that his collusion was merely a front, so that at the right moment he would be able to stick a dagger into the tyrant. It is highly doubtful whether Petronius had any similar plans. But absolute power creates an atmosphere of dissimulation: nobody can talk straight (hence the ambiguous flourishing of the arts of metaphor and indirection – or sometimes even of art *tout court* – under tyranny); it is wise to put an antic disposition on. The difference between flattery and contempt, between courtly conformism and elegant disdain, is blurred. At all events, Petronius, mimicking his master's power, played the master to his own slaves as he died, rewarding some with presents and punishing others with a flogging, we are not told why: the "Arbiter" (a name which seems to have been associated with slaves) became as arbitrary as any emperor. Petronius remains a tantalizingly strange figure, both typical "decadent" debauchee and someone who raised this whole act to a newly self-conscious and quizzical level.

Later fictionalized accounts of Petronius (notably Henryk Sienkiewicz's great novel *Quo Vadis*, and the 1951 MGM film adaptation of this novel), uneasy with the ambiguity of Tacitus's Petronius, moralize him. Petronius, aloof and supercilious even as he eggs Nero on to new "elegances", toys with his childish, insecure, greedy, but all-powerful master, sounding at times like a Roman Oscar Wilde or Truman Capote, speaking truth to power but only in such sophistical and riddling ways that power does not even notice and simply applauds. Eventually, in these fictions, Petronius is so repelled by Nero's excesses (the burning of Rome, the persecution of the Christians) that suicide is the only noble way out. The Petronius presented by Tacitus sounds altogether chillier and more amoral, and his suicide is both the typical last act of an aristocratic Roman on whom Fortune no longer smiles, and a calculated critique of that whole Stoic ideology. The collapse of Piso's conspiracy against Nero had implicated the philosopher Seneca and the epic poet Lucan, who both duly committed suicide by opening their veins. As Seneca died, he dictated philosophical maxims to his scribes; Lucan died quoting some of his own poetry. This was in AD 64; a year or so later, when Petronius followed them to Hades, he seems to have ensured that his own suicide was a satire on theirs, but one that was just as "staged", just as much of an aesthetic performance, just as much an attempt to master the absolute master, death. He began his suicide in the usual way, but added a typical refinement: instead of slitting his veins and retiring to his bath, he had the incisions made, but then adjusted the tempo of the deadly haemorrhage by allowing the blood to flow, having the slits bound up again, and then the bandages removed, and so on; not discoursing with his friends on immortality or philosophy, but listening as they bantered away, discussing trifles and reciting light verse. His parting gift to Nero was a sealed letter in which he denounced the Emperor's debaucheries, and named the men and women involved, with a detailed account of what they had got up to.

What survives of the *Satyricon* is a fragment, probably from books 14, 15 and 16, of what would have been a substantial narrative. What percentage of the original do we have? Nobody knows. A tenth? A quarter? Some have speculated that the *Satyricon*, as a mock epic, must have had twenty-four books, since both the *Iliad* and the *Odyssey* were traditionally divided into twenty-four scrolls: but it is not at all certain that the *Satyricon* actually was a mock epic. Many authors of antiquity and the Middle Ages quote fragments that can find no secure place in the narrative as we have it, and which must come from lost episodes. The text we have is the product of centuries of scribal devotion and error: lines were inadvertently jumped; obscenities were censored – or, just as probably, eagerly focused on, at the expense of more "routine" passages; glosses became incorporated into the main text. Mice nibbled at parchments stacked in barns, the flickering light of candles in cold monastery cells perplexed scribal eyes, cold numbed fingers scratched away, trying to make sense of a text whose Latin was in turns terse, ornate, colloquial and incomprehensible. Soon it would be time for supper and vespers; you could lay down your quill with a sigh, and stretch your aching back: this pagan Petronius, ah, what times he had lived in... *Cætera desunt.* In more recent centuries, editors have doughtily added, corrected, defended, deleted, distinguished, omitted and transposed. Translation is part of this ongoing process of editorialization: distorting what it would transmit, having to imagine a whole civilization from scraps and shards: an odd item on a menu, a bizarre superstition, a word that exists nowhere else (*tangomenas, matauitatau, oclopeta*). We still do not know with any certainty in what order many of the passages would have come; allusions in the text and commentaries suggest previous (now lost) episodes in Marseilles, and some have speculated that Encolpius was eventually to travel to Egypt, perhaps to tarry in the fleshpots of Canopus or Memphis. Earlier ages were irritated by this incompletion: they fleshed out the beginning and ending of the work, and added whole "further adventures", as in the case of the forgeries of Nodot, Marchena and De Salas. Those of the moderns who are less bothered by fragmentation may read the text as being more modern than it actually is: and yet, there *is* a charm in the bits of scattered mosaic, which stimulate the reader's imagination to read Petronius as if he were the Cortázar of *Hopscotch*, the Eliot of *The Waste Land* or the Pound of the *Cantos*: allusion, pastiche, quotation, brokenness...

The story plunges *in medias res* even more than most epics. (Readers who like a little more background will find, in Appendix 1, a "prequel", so to speak, with some indication of what the Narrator and his associates might have been doing before we meet them, and, in Appendix 2, a list of main characters.) We immediately find ourselves in a talkative, gossipy world, where pompous pundits hold forth about education not being what it used to be, and the latest trendy theories are held up for critical evaluation. The great set piece, the dinner at Trimalchio's, is exquisitely designed. Trimalchio himself is a great comic character, partly Falstaff, partly Molière's *nouveau riche* M. Jourdain, the *bourgeois gentilhomme* aping an aristocratic culture whose own tastelessness he at times unwittingly lays bare (just as the poems scattered through the text are both parodies of and homages to "original" poems whose own bombast, triviality or cack-handedness are mercilessly exaggerated). All his guests are given their own way of speaking, in which coarseness, pretentiousness, flattery, cynicism and simple everyday chatter (together with a love of bizarre stories) abound. The setting is both provincial and cosmopolitan; high culture and low culture rub shoulders (and not only because the latter apes the former); Trimalchio and his guests spout proverbs and clichés, draw inventively on ill-assimilated classics, swap stories, moan about the weather and the cost of living, growl aggressively at each other when the wine goes to their heads; all very commonplace, and yet their conversation, so different from that of some of the classical authors they claim to revere, is imbued with incredible concision and an intense vigour, both intoxicated and intoxicating. They speak in and out of character, put on different voices, quote scraps of other languages; Encolpius too, practically within one sentence, can swing from a relatively dispassionate register to one of drollery, perplexity or irritation. Written and spoken languages flow into one another; sometimes, in this text composed as *prosimetron*, a mixture of prose and poetry, it is difficult to tell where one begins and the other breaks off. Trimalchio's feast, for all its hubbub, has a strange dignity to it: everything seems part of some ritual organized by the host for his own self-aggrandizement, and every apparently realist detail conveys some symbolic meaning, for Trimalchio is, in his own way – like the Nero of *qualis artifex pereo* – an artist. His dinner is a whole cosmology, and everything is a sign which Encolpius, that innocent abroad, that amateur anthropologist, is forced to decipher. Nothing is as it seems in this semiotic kaleidoscope. (We readers are, as it were, Encolpius squared, forced to interpret *his* interpretations, see through *his* bafflement.) One type of food suddenly turns out to be another; accidents are pre-planned; slaves feed their master, not just with dainty titbits, but with the cues for his jokes. There is also a real (or at least silver) skeleton at this feast, and the funereal atmosphere rises to a climax as Trimalchio rehearses his own death and our heroes make their escape from what has amounted to something of a descent to Hades (the god of the underworld, of course, was also the god of wealth...). Trimalchio's dinner is sometimes taken as a showpiece of morbid exhibitionism: it is true that the merriment is constantly tinged with melancholia, and the food "unnatural" and contrived, even by the standards of the ever curious Roman palate. But the *Satyricon* is a work which, thanks to the whims of its textual dilapidation, begins with torn and mangled bodies (albeit exploited for mere lessons in rhetoric) and ends with an account of cannibalism: in the middle, Trimalchio presides over a banquet that is oddly life-affirming, less because of what he offers his guests to eat than because of the marvellously bitchy and human way they gossip about their fare, and many other things besides – and his strained attempts to entertain them (circus acts, tumblers and jugglers, dreadful poetry...) now have an odd and almost mythical grandeur.

And along with death comes love: we discover the narrator Encolpius while he is in pursuit of his young lover boy Giton, who is stolen away by Ascyltos: affections are fickle, and sexuality is polymorphous and perverse, as the protagonists chase both men and women, prepubescent girls are forced into bed with teenage boys, and almost every married man can vary his life of wedded bliss with a slave boy or two on the side. Voyeurism abounds: every door, every wall, may have a convenient crack in it. Above this riot of appetites hangs the spectre of impotence: Encolpius has spied on the rituals of Priapus being celebrated by Quartilla, and is punished by flagging virility (though only with women). He is forced to resort to spells and potions, and prayers to the offended Priapus. Indeed, Encolpius also seems to have misbehaved with the sacred rattle of Isis (ch. 114) – for this is, as the historian Keith Hopkins called it, "a world full of gods": Encolpius shares many of the "superstitions" of his society while sometimes seeming fazed by the more bizarre of them. He is an insider to Roman society, and yet not entirely at home in it. At Trimalchio's, for instance, the oddities he mentions (such as Trimalchio's obsession with the signs of the zodiac) are clearly versions of habitual beliefs and practices that were so "different" as to be worth mentioning even for a contemporary Roman audience.

The *Satyricon* is as satirical as its title suggests. The general taste-lessness of the age, the pretentious windbaggery of rhetoricians, the conspicuous consumption of vulgar parvenus such as Trimalchio, the paltry productions of poetasters such as Eumolpus, the superstition, greed, lust and money-grubbing of almost everyone, are depicted with what seems to be an acutely critical eye. This satirical element also affects the sometimes lengthy poems, especially those devoted to the Fall of Troy and the Civil War. These may be satires on Lucan's *Civil War* (Petronius would have known Lucan at the court of Nero). But if so, we need to identify the aspects in Lucan that Petronius found offensive or ridiculous. There are features in Lucan's treatment of the struggle for power between Julius Caesar and Pompey that set it apart from, for example, the *Aeneid*. One is Lucan's attitude to myth. Lucan was the grandson of Seneca the elder, and nephew of Seneca the younger: he thus belonged to a distinguished circle of Stoics, who tended to mistrust myth or to allegorize it in a rationalistic way. Whereas Virgil, following Homer, had depicted human affairs as directed by the gods, the Stoics thought that an impersonal Fate (or Fortune) held sway; the *Pharsalia* is thus lacking in the supernatural apparatus of earlier epics. The "Civil War" poem in the *Satyricon* puts them back in, but in a baroque, excessive, fanciful way, as if both to criticize Lucan for their absence and to suggest that they were always ideologically problematic. So any satire here may be double-edged: neither the gods *nor* Fate rule human affairs, and it is conceivable that Petronius is criticizing a contemporary critic of the "divine providence" tradition (Lucan) – but only in order surreptitiously to attack that tradition too. In the 1970s, the French scholar Pierre Grimal suggested, pleasingly, that it was actually Lucan who imitated Petronius. The poems may be serious, or seriously satirical ("damn modern Lucan! long live good old Virgil!"), or non-seriously comical (a scatter-shot mimicry of various poetic devices), or all of these at different times. And more generally, while the *Satyricon* clearly does have its satirical moments, these are undercut by something less easy to "place": characters mock others for their own failings (and Encolpius is never a stable moral reference point); the mechanisms of projection – or scapegoating – are never more apparent than in satire, and never is the transcendental *tu quoque* more applicable than to a satirist. What we have is much more modern: irony, or indeed a curious, impersonal objectivity (aided by the fact that, in true modern style, we often do not know "who is speaking" in this text). This most "realistic" of ancient texts (hailed as such by the great Eric Auerbach in *Mimesis*) is also one of the most artificial and mannered; allusions and quotations abound; not "elegance", but a sustained, glittering, deliberate bad taste is found on every page; every sentence may be a parody or pastiche; this is prose as false as Genet's (as described by Sartre), and its proper subject matter is the fake: fake tears, a fake wedding, fake poetry, even, at the end of Trimalchio's party, a fake death and burial. Given this pandemic of fakery, where is true judgement? Some of the best readers of the *Satyricon*, such as Huysmans, have denied that it is a satire at all: another way of putting it would be to say that *everything* is satirized – or rather, that nothing is safe from its salutary corrosions (love, wealth, art, philosophy, heroism…). And yet nothing is finally negated either. This is the fate of the very greatest satires (one shared by *Don Quixote*): they too eventually become epics.

While the *Satyricon* is not really a satire, it certainly is as randy as a satyr (so that when people started to translate it into the European vernaculars from the Renaissance onwards, the naughty bits were usually left in Latin). Actually, the work we have is better called, as in the title of the scholarly edition by Müller, *Satyricon reliquiæ: What Is Left of the Satyrica*. The Greek word *Satyrika* means "stories about satyrs". And satyrs mean sex. The word "*saturion*" occurs early on in the text: it seems to have been used to refer to any aphrodisiac. Indeed, a fully contemporary translation of Petronius's great work should probably be entitled: *The Viagron*. (Admittedly, this might raise, and then dash, too many hopes.) But an aphrodisiac is a paradoxical thing: by heightening sexual responsiveness, it suggests that what comes naturally isn't enough. This is a relevant observation for a novel in which the protagonist, Encolpius, has been afflicted by impotence, and needs to resort to chemical and magical supplements to have his virility restored.

Something missing, says the text: it forces the reader to employ art and artifice in order to fill the gaps (or to open them even wider...). Either way, what we have is leftovers – from a feast like Trimalchio's, or an orgy at Quartilla's. Time has swigged the *satyrion*, and we must make do with the remains. But then, as one of Trimalchio's guests would no doubt say, in his tipsily blasé way, *enough's as good as a feast, I reckon*, and *is my cup half full or half empty? Depends how you look at it.*

The *Satyricon* is a (problematic) satire, a satyr-work and, finally – and paradoxically enough, given the fragmented nature of the text – a *satura*, a plenitude, a work by which we are satisfied and even satiated, a work in which the golden age of Saturn temporarily returns in linguistic fullness. There would be no work of European prose like it until Rabelais, and the sheer density of the dialogue at Trimalchio's banquet anticipates similar "polyphonic" (or cacophonous) passages in James Joyce. This is a world full of gods, yes, but one that is also bursting at the seams with food, wine, sex, flowers, music and jokes. The food is often weird, the wine leaves you with a hangover, the sex is sometimes a flop, the flowers are pinched from Greek pastoral, the music is awful, and as for the jokes... But all these referential failures create a work of queer gravity and grace.

Petronius probably died in AD 65/66. A still relatively obscure man from faraway Tarsus, known as Paul, had been one of Nero's other victims about a year earlier. The "gospels" and "acts" that were gradually coming into existence would include picaresque wanderings, magical potions, offended deities, mixed identities, an unusual washing of feet, lavish banquets, crucifixions, manumissions and a man promising his heirs that they will enter into his possessions if they eat his flesh. Like the *Satyricon*, these works continue to fire the imagination, not least with their notorious textual (and other) cruxes.

*

A work known as *De dictionibus* was long attributed to Petronius. It is a kind of thesaurus, with lists of synonyms. The last entry in it reads: *hilarum, lætum, iocundum, ridens, plaudens, gaudens, gestiens*: "hilarious, merry, jocund, laughing, applauding, rejoicing, desiring".

– Andrew Brown, 2009

Note on the Text

I have generally followed the fourth edition by Konrad Müller: *Petronii Arbitri Satyricon reliquiæ* (Stuttgart and Leipzig: Teubner, 1995), and have mainly adopted his textual divisions, indications of lacunae, etc., but not his paragraphing; occasionally I have preferred other readings, e.g. Otto Schönberger (Berlin: Akademie Verlag, 1992). I have also consulted with great profit the edition of the *Cena* by Martin S. Smith: *Petronius: Cena Trimalchionis* (Oxford: Clarendon Press, 1975) and, especially for their notes, the fine English translations by J.P. Sullivan (1965), P.G. Walsh (1996) and R. Bracht Branham and Daniel Kinney (1996), as well as the 1969 Loeb edition and translation by Michael Heseltine, revised by E.H. Warmington. The punctuation of the *Satyricon* must always be tendentious: I have been pragmatic, without trying to conceal the fractious nature of the text. [...] indicates a textual lacuna. Figures in bold are the chapters into which the work has generally been divided.

Acknowledgements

It is customary to acknowledge the influence of one's main Latin teacher: so thanks to G.J. A reprimand from him could calm an unruly class as effectively as the '*Quos ego...*' of Neptune quelling the waves. Despite assiduous recourse to the dictionary, I was forever "howling" on this word or that (not yet aware that howling is just what translators do), and I forget how many times I was forced to copy out, twenty times over, the phrase *ridiculus sum.*

Satyricon

1. "Crazy! Raving mad like the other lot, don't you reckon?* All those lecturers in rhetoric, I mean, putting it on: 'Look at these scars! I sustained these wounds while fighting for your country's freedom! See the eye I lost! On your behalf I lost it! Now I even need one of you to lead me to where my children await me, for my hamstrung knees cannot support the weight of my body!'* Well, I suppose even that kind of thing would be just about acceptable as a course in *Declamation for Dummies* – if it actually led anywhere, that is. But the only real result of all this turgid claptrap, all this overblown sound and fury, is that when your rookie lawyers arrive in court, they feel like they've landed on another planet. You want my opinion? A college education turns our young men into total morons. They don't get to see or hear anything of everyday, practical use. No, it's

- pirates standing on beaches, chained and manacled, and it's
- dictators dashing off decrees ordering sons to chop off their own fathers' heads, and it's
- oracles in times of plague ordering the sacrifice of three virgins (or more).*

It's great globs of verbosity, smeared with honey: every word, every deed sprinkled with poppy and sesame seeds. **2.** Gollop down this kind of goo, and bang goes good taste. Spend your life in the kitchen and you're bound to stink. Don't mean to be offensive, but you lot are the prime culprits.* You've buggered up the art of public speaking. You blathered on and on, all style and no substance, and the content of your speech fart-fizzled out like gas from a deflating balloon. Students didn't used to be tied down to set speeches like those – not in the good old days, when Sophocles or Euripides could always be counted on to supply the *mot juste*. No hole-and-corner academic had ruined whatever inborn talent there was. In fact, Pindar and the nine lyrical greats shied away from even trying to compete with Homer.* And that's just the poets. I certainly can't see prose writers – Plato, say, or Demosthenes – bothering with this kind of exercise. Let me put it this way: the sublime style doesn't show off like that; no purple passages, no padding – it just grows naturally. It's spontaneous, it's elegant... All that hot air, that pig's bladder of flatulent palaver, has only recently been imported from Asia into Athens, where it gets pumped into the minds of ambitious students...* It's catching, like the flu. There's no benchmark for public speaking any more. The old tradition has stammered and stuttered to a full stop. Anyway, who, since then, has reached the heights of Thucydides? Who comes anywhere near Hypereides?* Poetry too, a pale, sickly reflection of its former glory... If all the arts are fed on such tripe, it's no surprise they've wasted away long before they can reach grey-haired maturity. And don't even get me started on painting: it used to be a great art, but it's gone down the pan ever since those Egyptians started peddling their *Painting Made Simple* approach."*

3. Agamemnon had just been sweating away giving his lecture. He wasn't going to simply stand there in the colonnade while I out-blah-blahed him.

"Listen, young chap," he said, "I can see from what you've just been saying that you're not inclined to pander to the old *hoi polloi*. You admire a real intellectual, too. Don't see that every day. So here's the scam, and mum's the word. It's no wonder lecturers go blue in the face with those textbook exercises. They're mad, but they don't have any choice – their audience is mad too. The teachers have to say what the kids want to hear, otherwise, as Cicero says, they're left 'lecturing to empty halls'.* It's like those two-faced arse-lickers in comedy, trying to cadge meals from the well-off: they spend their whole time working out what'll play to an audience. They know they're going to have to schmooze the ears off their listeners, and sweet-talk their way into getting what they're after. A lecturer in public speaking is like a fisherman who baits his hook with just the right food to tempt the little fishes in – otherwise he just squats on his rock all day long and never gets a bite. **4.** The fact of the matter is, I blame the parents. They won't hear of their children having to knuckle down to a tough syllabus. Right from the start they sacrifice their young hopefuls to their own ambition, the same way they do with everything else. They want results and they want 'em fast, so they push budding lawyers into the law courts when they're still wet behind the ears, and wrap the art of public speaking – the noblest profession of all, as they freely admit – like a gown round the shoulders of boys who are still practically babes in arms. Why oh why won't they let their kids take it step by step? The lads would have time to study properly, do some serious reading, soak up the facts; they'd fill their minds with words of wisdom; they'd chisel around with their styluses for a neat Attic turn of phrase; they'd listen long and hard, and imitate only the best examples; they'd come to realize that what they'd admired as boys was actually a load of crap... Ah, *then* the grand style of speaking would get back some of its dignity and clout! But these days, the lads just waste their time at school, and then get laughed out of court when they start their careers. And the biggest scandal of all is that, even in their dotage, they won't admit they've learnt it all wrong. Anyway, don't go thinking I've got anything against the occasional off-the-cuff sally into verse. Lucilius,* for instance. It's a good way to get things off my chest. So:

5. "If you want your art
To have weight and clout,
The Big Themes are what
You must write about –

And for this you need
A life that's austere,
Precise and frugal.
Follow rules. Don't fear

The tyrant's grim frown,
Or cadge meals from the swine.
Stay aloof: don't drown
Your bright wit in wine.

Don't sit with the *claque*
Or give your applause
To idiots on stage,
Theatrical bores.

No!

Maybe the battlements of fully-armed Tritonis*
Smile upon you,

Or the land where the Lacedaemonian settler lives,
Or the sea where the Sirens sing.*
Either way, devote your youthful days to poetry;
Drink deeply, gratefully, of the Maeonian spring.*
Then learn by heart the lessons of Socrates's school;
Give free rein, like a free man – shake the weapons
Of giant Demosthenes.
Then stand amid a host of Romans,
Free at last of the shackles of Greek modes,
And imbue your language with a new savour.
Meanwhile turn your back on the law courts,
Con the pages of history instead
And listen to its story of rises and falls.
Take your seat wherever a poet sings
His awe-inspiring tales of arms and the man,
And let the rhetorical flourishes
Of brave-hearted Cicero resound.*
Gird up your loins! It is a worthy task!
Pour out your heart
In a rolling river of words
        From the Pierian stream."

6. I was all ears, so I didn't notice Ascyltos slipping off [...] I was still walking along, absorbed in our heated discussion, when a big crowd of rhetoric groupies came charging into the colonnade. Apparently they'd been listening to some professor or other improvising a speech, just after Agamemnon's set piece.* They were taking the piss out of the pompous old fool and basically trashing his whole style. So I saw my chance and scarpered off in pursuit of Ascyltos. But (a) I kept getting lost, and (b) in any case I didn't have the foggiest where our lodgings were.* I'd walked my legs off and the sweat was pouring down me when I spotted this old woman in from the countryside sitting there selling fresh vegetables.

7. "Excuse me, madam," I said, "but you don't happen to know where I'm staying, by any chance, do you?"

She chortled: my politeness must have sounded silly.

"Oh, but of *course* I do!" she replied, and got up and proceeded to lead the way. Hmm, she must have second sight, I thought to myself, and [...] when we came to some godforsaken part of town, the sly old biddy invitingly opened the patchwork door hanging.

"This must be your place," she said. I was just starting to tell her I'd never set eyes on the house before, when I suddenly saw some blokes prowling up and down between lines of naked whores with names and prices on display. It gradually dawned on me – too late! – that I'd been brought to a whorehouse. The old cow had really pulled a fast one on me. I yanked my cloak across my face and dashed through the brothel. And who should come running into me at the back entrance but Ascyltos, looking just as dead on his feet as I felt. I imagined he'd been brought here by that same old biddy. I burst out laughing. Well, hello, I said, and I asked what a nice boy like him was doing in a nasty place like this.

8. He wiped the sweat off his face with both hands.

"You just don't want to know what I've been through," he gasped.

"Oh? And?"

He could barely speak.

"I was traipsing all over town, trying to find where I'd left our lodgings. This bloke came up and offered to lead the way. Very kind he seemed, too. A decent, respectable chappy. Anyway, he took me down some dark, winding alleys, and brought me here – and then offered me a few coppers and started badgering me to do it. The madam here had already been given a few quid for the room, and he was already feeling me up. Good thing I was stronger than him, or I'd have had it [...]"

It looked to me as if they'd all been swigging down the *satyrion**

*

We joined forces and managed to see off the randy old sod

*

9. Peering through the gloom, I spotted Giton standing on the kerbside. I trotted up to him [...]

I asked if my bro* had managed to pick anything up for supper. But the boy plopped down on the bed and with his thumb wiped away the tears trickling down his cheeks. I was alarmed at the state he was in, and asked him what was up. He wouldn't say. I persisted. Eventually I really lost my rag with him and he finally told me.

"This bro of yours, or mate, or whatever he is,* came running in here just now and tried to have his filthy way with me. I started screaming, and he pulled out his sword. 'Think you're Lucretia?' he said. 'Well, meet Tarquin!'"

When I heard this I nearly punched Ascyltos in the eyes.

"What's all this about then?" I roared. "Slut! Bum bandit! Smeg-breath!"

Ascyltos played all sweet and innocent, but soon he too was waving his fists around, and roaring even louder than me.

"Shut your face!" he spat. "You freaking filthy gladiator! You even got kicked out of the arena!* Shut your face! A quick stab in the dark – that's all you can manage. Even in the days when you'd got a bit more stuffing in you, you couldn't even handle a woman. I was your bro in the park, wasn't I? The kid's the same, here in our digs."*

"You soon snuck off instead of talking to the Prof," I retorted.

10. "And *what*, you great moron, was I *supposed* to do, exactly? I was starving! Oh sure, I should just have gone on listening to him droning on and on… 'shattered glass' this… *'Interpretation of Dreams'* that… You're a worser bastard than me, much worse, damn you, licking some poet's arse 'cos there's a free dinner in it." […] That made us giggle. It had been a vicious little tiff, but we finally kissed and made up and settled down to business

*

But the way he'd treated me, I couldn't get it out of my head. It was… disrespectful.

"Look, Ascyltos, it's just not working between us," I said. "We haven't got much stuff to share: let's split it fifty-fifty. We may be skint, but if we each do our own thing, we can try and scrape together enough to get by. You're an educated bloke. Me too. I don't want to get in your way, I promise not to stray onto your turf. Otherwise, we'll be at each other's throats all day over this, that and the other. The whole town'll be talking about us."

Ascyltos didn't object.

"But," he said, "we've accepted that dinner invite for tonight. We're there to add a bit of culture. Let's not waste the evening. And then tomorrow, since that's what we've agreed, I'll look for a new place to stay. And a new bro."

"Why wait?" I retorted. "Never put off till tomorrow"

*

I'd decided on this sudden split because, basically, I'd got the hots for someone else. That possessive old fart had been dogging my steps for too long. I wanted Giton back

*

11. I had a good mooch round town, and went back to my room. At last I could kiss him, again and again, he was all mine. I put my arms round my bro, held him tight, had my desire, you should have seen us. Bliss… And we hadn't even finished when Ascyltos crept up to the door and forced it open to find me *in flagranti* with my bro. The room echoed to his cheers and guffaws; he clapped his hands and pulled me out of the cloak I was wrapped in.

"What*ever* were you up to, bro? Butter couldn't melt in your mouth, eh? Sharing tents, soldier boy?"

And lo, he matched his deeds to his words. He loosed the belt from his knapsack and treated me to a regular thrashing.

"That's *not* the way to share things with a bro!" he sneered

*

12. By the time we reached the marketplace, evening was drawing in. There were plenty of items for sale, mainly junk, but in the twilight it wasn't easy to see that they'd probably just fallen off the back of a cart. We'd brought along the cloak we'd nicked, and decided to grab this opportunity, so we hung around in one corner, displaying the cloak by its edge, hoping that such a lovely piece of work would tempt a buyer. We didn't have to wait for long. A peasant – he seemed oddly familiar – came right up to us with a young woman in tow, and started to examine the cloak carefully. Ascyltos in turn stared at the shoulders

of our customer from the countryside, and suddenly froze and turned pale. Gobsmacked he was. And when I looked at the man more closely, I too gave a start; he looked just like the guy who'd found our little shirt out in the empty fields. Yes: it was him all right. But Ascyltos couldn't believe his eyes. Not wanting to do anything he might regret, he first went up close as if he wanted to buy, tugged at a corner of the garment hanging from the man's shoulders, and felt it all over with great care. 13. What a bloody great piece of luck! The peasant's meddling fingers hadn't even touched the seam, and now he was touting it round for sale with an air of disdain, as if he'd picked it up from some beggar. As soon as Ascyltos had assured himself that the treasure we'd stashed away in it was untouched, and that the man selling it was a nobody, he pulled me away from the crowd.

"You know what, bro? We've got it back – our treasure, the one we lost and I was so pissed off about! That's our little shirt all right – and it seems like all our gold's still intact. So now what do we do? It's ours – but how're we going to claim what's ours by right?"

I was over the moon with relief: not only had our loot turned up again, but this twist of fate had relieved me of a nasty suspicion. I said we shouldn't use any underhand methods, but fight for our property fair and square – take the case to court and, if they wouldn't return the stolen property to its rightful owner, ask the local magistrate to decide.

14. But Ascyltos was nervous about going to law.

"Does anybody here know us?" he said. "Who'll take our word for it? I really prefer just to buy the thing back now we've spotted it, even if it *is* actually ours... That way we can get our little treasure hoard back cheap, rather than running the risk of a lawsuit. After all:

"What use the law, when hard cash reigns supreme,
When poverty can never win its case?
Some ape the Cynics with their begging bowl* –
But even they will sell truth at a price.
A lawsuit's nothing but a public auction:
The juror turns a blind eye to injustice."

But apart from a twopenny coin, which we'd been saving to buy lupines with,* we were broke. Our quarry might walk off any minute, so we preferred to sell the cloak for less than we'd planned. Swings and roundabouts. But as soon as we'd unrolled our item, the bareheaded woman next to the peasant took a closer look at the markings on it and then pulled at the edge with both hands.

"Thieves!" she shrieked at the top of her voice. "Gotcha!"

We were startled out of our wits, but we couldn't just stand there: we in turn started tugging at the filthy, ragged shirt, yelling just as angrily that *they* had stolen it from *us*. But the two sides weren't equally matched: the traders who came running up at the commotion just laughed, as you might expect, and thought we were completely nuts, since one party (them) was laying claim to a very expensive cloak, while the other party (us) was after some raggedy old shirt scarce worth the patching.

Ascyltos called for silence and, when the laughter had died down, explained:

15. "People far prefer to keep what's theirs. 'S obvious. So if they'll give us our shirt back, they can have their cloak."

The peasant and the woman were happy to do a straight swap, but by now the nightwatchmen had been summoned – and they in turn spotted a chance to make off with the cloak. We were told to hand over the disputed items; in the morning, a magistrate could settle the case. It wasn't just a matter of who owned what, apparently; something much more serious was at stake, since both parties were now under suspicion of theft. It had already been agreed who'd take custody of the items: one of the traders – I didn't know him, some bald guy with warts all over his forehead, apparently did a bit of legal work now and again – picked up the cloak and declared he'd bring it along to court next day. Of course, the real reason was that once the cloak was in the safekeeping of that pack of thieves, they'd never let go of it – and we wouldn't dare show up for the appointment, in case we were charged [...]

But of course, that was exactly what we wanted. And things turned out so that each party was satisfied. The peasant flew off the handle when we insisted on the old rag being handed over. He flung the shirt into Ascyltos's face and said he was welcome to it; we should just hand over the cloak that was the real bone of contention [...]

So we'd got our stash of gold back – or so we thought. We rushed back to our lodgings, slamming the door behind us, and started to laugh our heads off at those clever-dick traders, those con artists who'd tried to lay false accusations against us! So very clever, in fact, that they'd simply ensured we got our money back.

Don't hand me victory on a plate:
I want to win, but I can wait.

*

16. Giton had done his job and we found dinner all ready for us. We were just tucking in when somebody started hammering at the door [...]

We all turned pale and asked who was there.

"Open!" came the reply. "You will see soon enough."

At these words, the bar slipped and fell of its own accord, and the door swung wide open to reveal a woman, veiled.

"So!" she said. "Did you all really imagine that you had fooled *me*? I am the personal maid of Quartilla – of she whose ritual you desecrated at the entrance to the grotto! She herself has come hither to your dwelling. But fear not! She will not wax wroth at your misdeeds, neither will she punish you for your iniquities. Nay!... Actually, she just can't help wondering what god has brought such nice, streetwise young chaps to her part of the world."

17. We sat there in silence, wondering what the hell to say. Then Quartilla herself came in, with a young girl in attendance. She sat down on my bed and burst into tears. She wept and wept. We still said nothing, but waited in consternation for her to turn off the waterworks. When this shower of crocodile tears had finally subsided, she unveiled her haughty head and wrung her hands until the joints cracked.

"It's outrageous!" she moaned. "How *could* you? Wherever did you learn to behave worse than common-or-garden thieves? Oh, but I pity you, by heaven I do. Nobody sets eyes on forbidden things and gets away with it.* You know, this area is so full of divine presences that it is easier to bump into a god than a man. But don't imagine I'm here to exact vengeance: no, it's your tender years that I'm really sorry about, not the insult to me. Sure, you didn't mean to do it; I still think that your crime, though unforgivable, was an accident. That night I lay there in torment, shivering so much at what had happened that I was afraid

I'd gone down with malaria. So, in my dreams, I asked for a remedy. I was ordered to seek you out and allay the attacks of my fever by a method shown me, secret and subtle. But finding a cure is not my first priority. No, deep within my heart I feel the smart of an even fiercer pain, luring me downwards, tempting me with the thought that death is the only answer. You are still young; I am terrified that you will be so indiscreet as to blab out what you saw in the shrine of Priapus, and divulge the mysteries of the gods to ordinary folk. And so I hold out my suppliant hands to your knees, I beg you and implore you: do not turn our nocturnal rites into an object of derision, do not betray the secrets of the ages, known to scarcely three people."

18. After uttering this tragic plea she again wept bitterly, shaking with sobs and burying her face and breast in my bed. Meanwhile I was all torn up with pity and fear; I urged her to cheer up, and told her she could rest assured about both her anxieties. None of us would betray her rituals to the public, and if a god had shown her some other way of curing her fever, we'd give divine providence a helping hand, at whatever risk to ourselves. This promise made her brighten considerably. She kissed me again and again; her tears turned to laughter; she gently stroked my hair where it fell below my ears, and then she said:

"Let's call it quits; I'll drop the charges I was going to bring. Actually, if you hadn't agreed to provide me with the proper remedy, there was an angry mob ready to come round tomorrow, avenge the insult to me and defend my honour. You know:

> "Losing face is a disgrace:
> No one puts *me* in my place!
> I love going my own way.
> Tooth for tooth and eye for eye –
> But bring your quarrel to an end
> And you'll have found a grateful friend."

*

Then, clapping her hands, she burst out into such a loud, sudden peal of laughter that it scared us. So did the maid in the other corner, and so did the little girl who'd come in too. **19.** The whole room echoed to the sound of their hysterical hilarity. But we were aghast at this farce and had no idea what had brought about such a change in the mood of these women – we just kept staring first at them, and then at each other

*

"The reason why I've given orders not to admit a mortal soul into this hostelry today is this: I *need* that cure for my malaise, and I need it from you, without anyone else interfering." When he heard Quartilla say this, Ascyltos was dumbstruck for a few moments – and I turned colder than a winter in Gaul, and couldn't utter a single word. But I was among friends, and this stopped me feeling too pessimistic. After all, on the one side there were just three women, and if they decided to try their hand against us, they'd be a bunch of big girl's blouses, and on the other side there was us: not much, perhaps, but real men. And after all, our loins were girded and our sleeves rolled up. Oh yes, I'd already mentally paired us off: if we did have to fight for our lives, I'd square up to Quartilla, Ascyltos would have the maid, and Giton the little girl

*

But then our morale collapsed. We were dazed and terrified by the prospect of imminent death. Everything swam before our eyes. No escape

*

20. "Madam," I groaned, "please, *please*: if you've got anything worse in store for us, just get it over with. We haven't done anything so very wrong; we don't deserve to be tortured to death"

*

The maid – Psyche, that was her name – carefully spread a blanket out on the floor tiles

*

14

She started tickling and teasing my prick, but it had already died a thousand deaths and just lay there limp and cold

*

Ascyltos had covered his head in his cloak. I guess he'd learnt it's dangerous to play Peeping Tom

*

The maid produced two strips of stiff fabric from inside her dress and used one to tie up our feet and the other to tie up our hands

*

We'd rather lost the thread of our conversation; then Ascyltos piped up:

"Come on now! What's wrong with *me*? Don't *I* deserve a drink?"

I chortled, and my laughter brought the maid across. She clapped her hands and retorted, "But I already put one down for you... Oooh, you young devil! Have you pigged down all the medicine by yourself?"

"No kidding? You mean to tell me," exclaimed Quartilla, "that there's no *satyrion* left? Encolpius has swigged it all?"

*

Her sides shook with laughter. Sexy thing

*

Finally, even Giton couldn't help laughing – especially as the little girl flung her arms round his neck and plastered him with kisses. Can't say the kid put up much resistance

*

21. We felt like yelling and screaming for help – but nobody would have come, and every time I tried to call out for reinforcements ("Friends!

Romans! Countrymen!"), Psyche just stuck a sharp hairpin in my cheek. Meanwhile the girl kept trying to shove a sponge soaked in *satyrion* into Ascyltos's mouth

*

Last of all, a drag queen swanned in, wearing a myrtle-green woollen robe hoicked up with a belt [...] One minute he was grinding his buttocks down on us, the next minute he was slobbering foul-smelling kisses all over us. Eventually Quartilla, skirt hitched high round her waist, came over with her whalebone rod in hand and ordered him to let us poor sods off

*

Both of us swore the most solemn oath imaginable: such a vile secret would go to our graves with us

*

Several masseurs came in and gave us a rub-down with some proper oil. That revived us. At all events, we managed to drag ourselves out of our exhaustion and get dressed again for dinner. We were ushered into the next room, where three couches had been arranged, together with a full dinner service: everything you need for a spot of haute cuisine. We took our places as requested, and started off with some tasty hors d'oeuvres, washed down with plenty of wine – Falernian,* no less. Course followed course until we were starting to drift off to sleep.

"Whatever are you thinking of?" cried Quartilla. "Sleeping on now? Taking your rest? You know perfectly well you need to watch and wake, to celebrate the cult of mighty Priapus!"

*

22. Ascyltos was worn out by all these exertions, and he was just dozing off when the maid he'd cold-shouldered started rubbing soot all over his face. Then, while he was still lying there unconscious, she daubed phallic symbols onto his sides and shoulders. I was shagged out too, and had taken a quick sip of the waters of sleep, as you might say. All the slaves, inside and outside the room, had done the same; some of them lay sprawled out at the feet of the guests lying on their couches, some were slumped against the walls, while a couple were propping up the doorway, their heads leaning together. The oil in the lamps had almost dried up, and the light they shed was faint and wavering. Just then, two Syrians stole into the dining room hoping to filch whatever they could. But they started brawling greedily over the silverware, and as they each tugged at a wine jug, they broke it. The table and the silverware came crashing to the ground. One big cup was knocked from a shelf and smashed down onto the skull of a maid lolling over a couch. She screamed, and her scream alerted some of the drunks to the would-be burglars. The Syrian intruders realized they risked being caught – so they simply flopped down next to a couch together, as if this had been part of their plan all along, and proceeded to snore as if they'd been asleep for ages.

By this time the butler had roused himself and topped up the oil in the guttering lamps, while the slave boys rubbed their eyes for a few moments and returned to their duties. Suddenly a girl cymbal-player came in, and with a steely ringing of bronze woke everyone else up. **23.** This breathed new life into the proceedings, and Quartilla summoned us all back to our places for another drink. The cymbal-player had put her back in party mood with her songs

*

In came a prancing queen. You've never seen such a repellent specimen: he was obviously in his element here. He waggled his limp wrists, snapped his fingers and launched into a song, something like this:

"Come, oh come, bend-over-boys!
Shake a leg and mince along,
Spread your legs and wiggle your bums,
Poke and prod with eager hands,
Molly boys and ageing pros,
Balls snipped off by Apollo's
Knife – capons of Delos!"*

After this little ditty, he planted a dribbling slobber of a kiss on me. Soon he was on top of my couch and pulling the blanket off me, though I tried desperately to push him away. He ground away at my groin for ages, but nothing stirred. Streams of greasy acacia-sap make-up trickled down his sweating forehead, and his wrinkled cheeks were so heavily powdered that he looked like a peeling wall pitted by the pelting rain. **24.** The whole thing made me feel as depressed as hell, and I couldn't hold back my tears any longer.

"Madam, one quick question: I thought we were going on a bender. Why's the bender* coming on us?"

She clapped her hands softly.

"Oh!" she exclaimed. "I adore jokes like that! Very witty! But do you mean to say you hadn't realized that *bender* meant our prancing queen here?"

I suddenly decided it was time for some of this treatment to be meted out to my dining companion.

"Honestly, madam, just look at Ascyltos! Is he the only dining guest to be allowed time off?"

"You're quite right," said Quartilla. "Ascyltos's turn for a bender!"

So Prancing Queen obediently changed horses in mid-stream, and climbed onto my friend – and worked away with wiggling arse and avid lips. Giton just stood there, pissing himself with laughter. Quartilla darted a glance at him. Her curiosity was aroused, and she started asking whose boy he was. I told her he was my bro.

"Really?" she retorted. "In that case, why hasn't the silly lad given me a kiss?"

She beckoned him over, and pulled him down to her for a kiss. Before long she'd slipped her hand under his tunic and started to fondle his fresh young tool.

"This wee man can stand to attention for us tomorrow. He'll provide a spicy little *amuse-bouche*. But not today. I've no use for an anchovy when I've filled myself with a lovely piece of cod already."

25. As she was speaking, Psyche came over, giggling, and whispered something in her ear.

"Oh yes! Thanks for reminding me!" said Quartilla. "This is *such* a fantabulous opportunity! And why not? Our little Pannychis can finally get her cherry popped."

Immediately the girl was brought in; pretty little thing, didn't seem above seven years of age. Everyone broke into applause and started clamouring for a wedding – everyone except me, that is: I froze in horror. Then I started protesting: Giton, the shy little lamb, was just not up for this kind of shenanigans, and the girl was underage, too young to be treated as a grown woman.

"Excuse me?" retorted Quartilla. "And is she any younger than I was when they first shoved me under a bloke? May my Juno* damn me if I can even remember being a virgin. I was already doing it with kids my own age when I was still a toddler. As the years went by I got more of a taste for older boys, until I reached woman's estate. Actually, I think that's the origin of the proverb, you know: *if you've carried a calf you can carry a bull.*"

That got me worried: maybe my bro might end up in a worse scrape if I left them to it. So I got up to join the wedding party. **26.** Psyche had already draped the girl's head in a flame-red wedding veil; Prancing Queen was already leading the way, holding a torch; a gaggle of drunken women, clapping and cheering, had already formed a long procession – they'd decorated the bridal suite with highly suggestive drapes. Quartilla too had caught the mood of randy indulgence; tingling with glee, she grabbed hold of Giton and dragged him into the bedroom.

I can't say the boy had seemed all that reluctant. And even the girl hadn't blinked at the word "marriage". And so, once they were in bed together and the door was shut, we hunkered down outside the bridal suite. Quartilla didn't hesitate to make a little peephole in the wall. She immediately applied her eager eye and, positively panting with excitement, spied on the kiddies' love-play. She gently pulled me over so that I could watch the show too; peering through the hole, we were cheek to cheek; every so often she would turn away from the goings-on inside, and her lips would wander towards me, and she would kiss me with darting, furtive kisses

*

We fell into bed, and spent the rest of the night with not a care in the world

*

So the third day had come, and with it the promise, or threat, of our last supper.* But we'd taken so many hard knocks recently that the idea of just clearing out seemed preferable to hanging around. We were glumly trying to work out how to escape the gathering storm when along came one of Agamemnon's slaves.

"Hey," he said, seeing we were acting kind of jumpy, "don't you know where it's all at today? Trimalchio's place. You know, the dedicated follower of fashion [...] there's this water clock in his dining room, and a trumpeter in uniform to keep him informed of exactly how much *temps* he's *perdu*."*

We forgot all our troubles and found some decent clothes to wear, and told Giton, who'd happily been playing the part of our servant, to come along with us to the bathhouse [...]

27. We didn't undress, but wandered round in our glad rags... Laughing and joking, we walked over towards the people playing different games,* when all of a sudden we saw this old bald guy wearing a red shirt, tossing a ball to some long-haired boys. They deserved a more appreciative look from us, but what really caught our eye was the spectacle of their master, this old codger exercising in his bedroom slippers, throwing a pea-green ball around. He didn't bother to pick the ball up if he dropped it, as there was a slave standing nearby with a whole bagful of balls, and chucking them out to the players whenever necessary. We also noticed several other unusual features to the game: for instance, there were two eunuchs standing on opposite sides of the circle, one of them clutching a silver piss pot while the other was counting the balls – but not the ones flying to and fro from hand to hand, just the ones that fell to the ground. Quite a nice variation on the usual game. Anyway, we were standing there staring when Menelaus* trotted up.

"See him? He's the guy whose couches you'll be propping your elbows on at dinner. What you have here is actually the overture to the proceedings."

No sooner had Menelaus finished speaking than Trimalchio snapped his fingers. This was the signal for the eunuch to come and hold the piss pot out for him while he continued playing. He relieved his bladder, called for a basin of water, dipped his fingers in and wiped them on a slave boy's hair [...]

28. It would take too long to mention all the details, but anyway, we went into the hot bath and stayed there until we were baked in sweat, before jumping straight into the cold bath. Trimalchio, dripping with scented oil, was already being given a rub-down, not with ordinary linen towels but with nice thick ones, woven from the softest wool. Three masseurs were sat there drinking Falernian, right in front of his eyes, and they started brawling and spilt most of it – but Trimalchio just said they were drinking a toast in memory of him.* Then he was wrapped up in a rather nice shaggy scarlet gown, and lifted into a litter. Four runners wearing military-style medals ran ahead of him,* and a little four-wheeled go-kart with his darling boy in it – a wrinkled, bog-eyed little oik, even uglier than his lord and master Trimalchio. And as he was being carried off, an expert musician with a set of miniature pan pipes walked along level with him and played him all the way home, leaning over towards his head as if whispering secrets into his ear.

We tagged along, bursting with admiration, and arrived at the door together with Agamemnon. On the doorpost was fixed this notice:

NO SLAVE TO LEAVE THE PREMISES
WITHOUT THE MASTER'S PERMISSION.
PENALTY: ONE HUNDRED LASHES.

Right at the entrance, the hall porter was standing, dressed in a light-green uniform and a cherry-red belt; he was shelling peas in a shallow silver dish. And a golden cage was hanging in the doorway; inside it a black-and-white magpie greeted visitors. **29.** I was staring round in disbelief at all these things when, whoops! – something almost made me fall backwards and break my legs. On the left-hand side going in, right next to the porter's little lodge, was the most enormous dog on a chain, painted on the wall, and above it was written, in block capitals:

DANGER! DOG!*

Of course, my old mates really took the piss out of my panic. But once I'd got over my funk, I went across to examine the whole wall. The mural depicted a slave market, with placards showing the names and prices of those up for sale. Trimalchio himself was there, with flowing locks, holding a caduceus,* as Minerva led him in triumph into the city of Rome. Then you saw him learning how to keep accounts, and finally being promoted to steward – all depicted in careful detail by the painstaking painter, with captions, just to make it all as clear as possible. Just where the wall space ran out, he'd painted Mercury benevolently lifting Trimalchio by the chin* and sweeping him aloft onto the raised dais. Fortune sat near by with her overflowing cornucopia, and the three Fates, spinning their golden threads.

In the colonnade I also saw a team of runners in a practice session with their trainer. And in the corner I saw a large cabinet-like shrine: it held the silver figures of the Lares,* with a marble statuette of Venus, and a golden casket, rather impressive in size – this, I was told, was where His Nibs's first beard had been deposited* [...]

So I asked the hall steward what other pictures they had around.

"*The Iliad*," he said, "and *The Odyssey*. And *The Gladiatorial Display Provided by the Munificence of Laenas*."*

30. We just couldn't take it all in [...]

We'd almost reached the dining room. In the antechamber, the bookkeeper was sitting, checking over the accounts as they were brought in. And what really made me stare were the rods and axes* fixed to the dining-room doorposts and tapering down below so as to resemble the bronze beak of a ship,* with this inscription:

PRESENTED TO CAIUS POMPEIUS TRIMALCHIO,
SEVIR IN THE COLLEGE OF AUGUSTUS,*
BY CINNAMUS HIS STEWARD

Under the same inscription, there was also a two-branched lamp hanging from the ceiling. And two tablets were fixed either side of the door: one of them, if I remember rightly, had these words written on it:

II DAYS AND I DAY BEFORE KALENDS OF JAN.,
OUR CAIUS IS DINING OUT*

– while the other had paintings showing the phases of the moon, together with the seven stars,* and lucky and unlucky days were also indicated by different coloured studs.*

All of this had been a feast for the eyes. But when we tried to enter the dining room, one of the slave boys, stationed there for this very job, suddenly yelled, "Right foot first!" Naturally, we stood stock-still; nobody wanted to break the rules as we crossed the threshold.* Anyway, our right feet were all raised and ready to step in when a slave flung himself at our feet. He'd been stripped bare for a flogging and was begging us to get him let off. He hadn't done anything all that wrong, he moaned, he didn't deserve this kind of treatment, he'd been supposed to keep an eye on the steward's clothes in the baths and they'd been nicked, but they weren't even worth ten sesterces. So we withdrew our right feet and went back to where the steward was counting the gold pieces in his little office, and pleaded with him to let the slave off.

He looked down his nose at us.

"I'm not so bothered," he said, "about the loss of my clothes. But that slave is crap at his job. My best dinner clothes, they were. Just went and lost the lot. Birthday present from a client of mine. Tyrian purple they were, of course: but I suppose they *had* been cleaned once... Whatever. You can have him."*

31. That was really big of him. We trotted back to the dining room, and the slave on whose behalf we'd asked for indulgence came running up to us and, as we stood there not knowing where to put ourselves, showered kisses on us and thanked us again and again for our kindness.

"A nod's as good as a wink," he said, "but you're going to find out before long that I'm the sort of chap as repays a favour. It's the master's wine, but it's the waiter who pours it."

We finally took our places. Slave boys – Alexandria's finest! – poured snow-cooled water onto our hands; then others followed and knelt down at our feet and started to pare our hangnails. Extremely good at their job they were, too. Not the most pleasant profession, but they didn't do it in sullen silence, but kept right on warbling away. I suddenly decided to find out whether all the slaves could sing, so I asked for a drink. A slave boy was ready and waiting, and treated me to a shrill little melody, and so did they all whenever they were asked to fetch anything... It was like being at a song-and-dance act rather than in the dining room of a respectable gent.

Anyway, some delicious hors d'oeuvres were brought in, as everyone had taken their places except for Trimalchio himself, who, quite unusually, had reserved the top place for himself.* The entrée dish had a donkey made of Corinthian bronze on it, with a double pannier holding white olives on one side and black on the other. On either side of the donkey there were two shallow dishes with Trimalchio's name engraved on their rims, plus the weight of the silver they contained. There were little bridges soldered onto the plate, and on these bridges lay dormice, rolled in honey and poppy seed. And there were hot sausages sizzling on a silver grill and, under this, damsons with pomegranate seeds.*

32. We had settled down to enjoy these delicious appetizers, when Trimalchio himself was carried in to the sound of musicians playing. The sight of him propped up on a mound of tiny cushions made some people forget where they were and start to snigger. His shaven head* seemed to protrude from a tight scarlet cloak, and round his neck, swathed in its thick folds, he'd tied a table napkin with a broad purple stripe* and tassels dangling from either side. He was also wearing, on the little finger of his left hand, a heavy gilt ring, and on the top joint of his ring finger a smaller one – it looked to me like solid gold at first, but then I saw that small iron stars had been soldered on.* And his ostentatious display of wealth didn't stop there: he'd bared his right arm, on which a gold bracelet gleamed, and an ivory bangle with a glittering metal clasp.

33. He started to dig away at his teeth with a silver toothpick.

"My friends!" he said. "I wasn't actually in the mood to come into dinner just yet. But I didn't want to stay away and keep you all waiting even longer. So I put my own pleasures last. Still, with your permission, I will just finish my game."

A slave boy had followed him in, with a board made of terebinth wood, and some glass dice. And then I noticed that, instead of black and white counters, he was using gold and silver denarii. Talk about stylish! He chattered away brightly, regaling us with weavers' proverbs as he wiled away the time playing, and, as we were still dipping into the hors d'oeuvres, a big tray was brought in. On it there was a basket with a hen, a wooden hen, its wings spread out in a circle as if brooding a clutch of eggs. Two slaves immediately ran in and, as the music blared out, started to rummage round in the straw and quickly pulled out some peahen's eggs, which they handed out among the guests. Trimalchio turned his slow gaze to the scene.

"Friends!" he said. "I ordered some peahen eggs to be popped under that chicken there. And I bet the damn things are already about to hatch! But let's give them a go: they might still be good to suck."

We were given special egg spoons (at least half a pound each they weighed) and cut the tops off the eggshells, actually made of rich pastry. Personally, I nearly threw my one away. I thought there was already a fully formed little chick in there. But then I heard an old habitué of these parties saying, "I bet there's something nice inside, as usual!" So I prodded and poked my finger right through the shell and found a really juicy fig-pecker bird, all coated in peppered egg yolk.

34. Just then, Trimalchio broke off from his game and, seeing what we were eating, said he'd have the lot. And he shouted out loud and clear that if any of us fancied another glass of mead, we could have one. Suddenly a fanfare pealed out, and at this signal the hors d'oeuvres were whisked away by a troupe of singing slaves. However, in all the hubbub, one of the dishes crashed to the ground and a slave boy picked it up. Trimalchio noticed. He ordered the slave boy to be given a clip round the ear, and made him throw the dish back down on the floor. One of the litter bearers came up and started to sweep away the silver, and the other mess on the floor, with a broom.

Just then, two long-haired Ethiopian slave boys* came in with little skin pouches like the ones used to sprinkle water on the sand in an amphitheatre, and poured wine over our hands. Nobody offered us water.

Our host was praised for his taste and refinement.

"Mars loves a fair fight," he remarked. "That's why I ordered everyone to be assigned to a table of their own.* It also, by the way, means that those bloody stinking slaves won't get us all hot and bothered barging past us."

Next, some large glass jars were brought in, carefully sealed with gypsum. Onto their necks, labels had been stuck, reading:

FALERNIAN. VINTAGE OPIMIUS.
ONE HUNDRED YEARS OLD.*

As we scrutinized the labels, Trimalchio clapped his hands.

"You know, it really grieves me," he exclaimed. "Wine lives longer than us poor mortals! So cheers, chin chin and down the hatch!* Wine is life. That's real Opimian I'm serving up to you. Yesterday I laid on some stuff that wasn't half as good, even though my dinner guests were a much nicer class of person."

Thus we caroused, taking care to admire every splendid detail of this marvellous banquet. Just then a slave came in carrying a skeleton, a silver skeleton, put together so skilfully that its joints and its backbone could be easily bent every which way. Trimalchio plonked it down on the table a couple of times, to show how its limbs were so supple that it could fall into different postures. Then he declaimed:

"Astride of a grave...
We'll all be nought
like this manlet here
when to Orcus* we're brought,
so let's live and let's eat:
Bon appétit!"

35. Our applause was followed by a new dish, not as big as we'd all been hoping... but still, there was something unusual about it, and we stared. There was a deep round plate with the twelve signs of the zodiac arranged in a circle on the lid, and the chef had placed symbolically suitable food on each sign. So:

on Aries the Ram, a ram's-head chickpea;

on Taurus the Bull, a slice of beef;

on Gemini the Twins, two testicles and kidneys;

on Cancer the Crab, a garland;

on Leo the Lion, an African fig;

on Virgo the Virgin, the uterus of a barren sow;

on Libra the Scales, a balance: in the one pan there was a slice of quiche and in the other a little cheesecake;

on Scorpio the Scorpion, [...] a little sea fish;

on Sagittarius the Archer, a sea horse;

on Capricorn the Goat, a lobster;

on Aquarius the Water Carrier, a goose;

on Pisces the Fishes, two mullets.*

And in the middle lay a freshly cut clod of turf with a honeycomb nestling in the grass. An Egyptian slave boy brought round bread in a silver bread-baking dish [...]

Mine host croaked out a song from the hit musical comedy *The Silphium Gatherer.**

We suddenly lost our appetites at the sight of this unappetizing fare.

"Please, let's eat!" exclaimed Trimalchio soothingly. "It's only polite. You'll soon be getting your just desserts."

36. As he spoke, the music struck up and four ceremonial dancers skipped in and swept away the lid of the dish – whereupon we saw some fattened fowls and sow's udders, and in the middle a hare decorated with wings to make it look like Pegasus. Our eyes were also drawn to four figurines of Marsyas* at the corners of the dish; from their miniature wineskins they were pouring a peppered garum sauce* over fish that seemed to be swimming in a kind of channel. The slaves gave a big round of applause; we all joined in, and laughed, and tucked into these choice morsels.

Trimalchio was beaming with delight. His clever little joke had worked. Then, all at once, he said:

"Hackett!"

The meat-carver was there in a flash; brandishing his knife in time to the music, he slashed at the meat so viciously you'd have said he was a chariot fighter, aiming his blows to the accompaniment of a water organ.

Trimalchio kept on and on at him, droning away remorselessly: "Hackett, Hackett..."

He went on for so long that I started to suspect I was missing a joke. I swallowed my pride and decided to learn the truth from the horse's mouth; so I turned to ask the man next to me.

He'd witnessed this kind of prank before, on many occasions.

"See the guy who's hacking away at the meat?" he asked. "Name's Hackett. So whenever he says 'Hackett', he means 'hack it!' It's a vocative and an imperative, see."*

37. I couldn't eat another thing. I turned back to my neighbour, hoping he could fill me in on a few details; I wanted to catch up on all the gossip, and enquired who that woman was who kept running all over the place.

"Her?" he replied. "Oh, she's Trimalchio's wife. Fortunata, that's her name. Suits her. Sackloads of dosh she's got. And until just recently, what was she? I hope your guardian spirit won't mind me saying this, but you wouldn't have accepted a piece of bread from her hand. But now – dunno how, dunno why – she's a real star, she's Trimalchio's one-and-only. Point is, she can tell him it's darkest night when it's really high noon, and he'll believe her. He doesn't even know how much he's worth. He's mega-rich. But that minx keeps a close eye on everything... You'd never believe it; eyes in the back of her head. She's sober, she's thrifty – no nonsense about her; you can see how much gold she's got, but what a sharp tongue: shrewd, but shrewish. If she likes you, she likes you, if she doesn't, she doesn't. Old Trimalchio's got estates all round for as far as a hawk can fly. *Crème de la crème* he is: a billionaire. There's more silverware in his porter's little lodge than there is in some people's entire fortunes. And the slaves – *mon Dieu*, I don't think a tenth of those slaves has ever even clapped eyes on his lord and master. Point is, those other fat cats with the cream, he could beat any of 'em into a cocked hat,* no sweat. **38.** And does he ever have to buy stuff from outside? Don't make me laugh! All home-grown: wool, bitter oranges, pepper; ask him for hen's milk and you'll get it. Point is, he decided the wool he was getting wasn't up to scratch. He bought some rams from Tarentum, and let them loose to screw his ewes. He fancied a little home-made Attic honey. *Pas de problème*; he just ordered bees from Athens. The little Greek buzzers improved his local stock quite a bit, too. You'd never guess, but just a day or two ago he was writing off for some mushroom spores from India. Every single one of his mules was born from a wild ass. Look at all that pile of cushions: stuffed with purple or scarlet wool, every one. No wonder he's as happy as Larry. But don't you go looking down your nose at the other freedmen either. Dripping with cash they are. See that one down there, end couch? Eight hundred grand* he's worth nowadays. Came from nothing. Not long ago he was schlepping wood round on his back. But they do say – I dunno for sure, I just heard – he pulled off Incubo's hat and found a hidden treasure.* Jealous, *moi*? God helps those and all that... But now he's been slapped free,* he thinks pretty highly of himself. Actually, he's just put his little place on the market.

"TO LET
ONE SMALL UPSTAIRS ROOM
STARTING KALENDS JULY*
APPLY TO CAIUS POMPEIUS DIOGENES
(OWNER RELOCATING TO HOUSE BELOW)

"Then take that other guy, lying in that freedman's place.* Really done well for himself, he had. I don't mean to be critical, either. He'd got it made. A million sesterces, but then it all fell apart. If you ask me, he's mortgaged up to the hair on his head. None of his goddamned fault, though. You won't find a better bloke around. It was the bloody freedmen. Just helped themselves. You know how it is: a shared pot's neither cold nor hot, and a friend in need is a friend to avoid. Nice little business he had, too – and now look at him! Undertaker he was. Used to feast like a king: boars served up in their skins, fancy patisserie, fowl [...] chefs, pastry cooks. There used to be more wine spilt under his table than some men have in their cellars. A legend in his own lunchtime. Once business started going downhill, he got worried his creditors might guess he was going bust, and advertised an auction. The sign read:

"TO BE SOLD AT AUCTION
PROPERTY OF CAIUS JULIUS PROCULUS
(NOW SURPLUS TO REQUIREMENTS)"

39. This stream of juicy anecdotes was interrupted by Trimalchio; the latest course had been cleared away, and the merry throng had proceeded to turn their attention to the wine, and to general conversation.

He propped himself up on his elbow.

"Do this wine a favour," he said, "and drink it. Fish must swim. I ask you: do you really think I'd be happy with that meal you saw on the dish lid? 'Is that the Ulysses you know?'* So what d'you reckon to that, then? Mustn't forget our classix, eh, even at the dinner table! May my old patron's bones rest in peace! He wanted me to be a man among men. There's nothing new under the sun, as far as my table's concerned. The proof of the pudding was in that last dish. Look, there's the sky, where the twelve gods live; see how it turns into twelve pictures. Aries the Ram, for instance. Anyone born under the sign of Aries has plenty of sheep, plenty of wool, a rather hard head, a brazen face and a sharp horn. So under this sign there are many highbrows, always ramming their lessons home. Muttonheads too."

Quite the astrologer. And witty with it! We applauded.

He went on:

"Then the whole sky turns into young Taurus. Under this sign are born bullish men, the sort who like to kick out, and ploughmen, and all those who can fill their own bellies. Under Gemini are born things that are paired or yoked together, bullocks, and bollocks, and those who smear both the front door and the back passage. Then Cancer: well now, I'm a Cancer! So I have many legs to stand on and possessions everywhere, on land and sea; a crab's at home in either element. That's why, for quite a while, I didn't put anything on that constellation, in case I weighed down my own birth sign. Under Leo, greedy guzzlers are born, and bossy-boots characters; under Virgo, women both male and female, and runaway slaves, and chain-gang convicts.* Under Libra, it's butchers and perfume-sellers and anyone else who has to weigh things out for dispatch; under Scorpio, poisoners and back-stabbers; under Sagittarius, those cross-eyed types who look at your beans but filch your bacon;* under Capricorn, those poor sods who worry so much that horns grow onto their heads.* Under Aquarius, innkeepers* and people with water on the brain. Under Pisces, fish-fryers and rhetoricians.* So the great sky turns round and round like a millstone, always bringing trouble, people being born, people dying. That green turf in the middle, with the honeycomb on top of it – well, there's a reason for that, like everything I do. Mother Earth lies in the middle, smooth and round as an egg, and she contains all good things within her, like a honeycomb."

40. "Bravo!" we all yelled, raising our hands to the ceiling as in prayer and swearing that Hipparchus and Aratus* were nobodies compared to him. Eventually servants came in and spread covers in front of the couches, with nets painted on them, and hunters lying in wait with spears, and every kind of hunting equipment. We suspected something was about to happen, but didn't know what shape it would take... when lo and behold, a terrible din was heard outside the dining room, and in charged a pack of Spartan hunting dogs, and started to run round and round the table. They were followed by a big tray on which lay an absolutely gigantic wild boar. To our surprise it was crowned with a cap of liberty, and from its tusks hung two little fruit baskets woven from palm twigs, one full of juicy Carian nut-shaped dates, the other full of dry Theban dates. And round about it lay little suckling pigs made of crusty pastry, with their mouths at the teats, showing that this "boar" was supposed to be a mother sow. These little piglets were for us to take away in our party bags. Anyway, it wasn't Mr Hackett, the one who'd cut up the fattened fowls, who now stepped up to carve the boar, but a bearded giant of a man; he was wearing hunter's leggings and a short, tight-woven hunting dress; he drew out his knife and plunged it with gusto into the boar's paunch. Out of the gash came flying a flock of thrushes. They fluttered round the dining room, but there were bird-catchers with limed reeds ready and waiting, and they'd soon caught them. Trimalchio ordered that one bird be given to each guest. And he added:

"Now take a look at the fine acorns that old porker from the woods has been guzzling!"

Some slave boys quickly went up and took the baskets hanging from the sow's tusks, and shared the juicy and dry dates out evenly among the guests.

41. Meanwhile I'd become absorbed in my own thoughts, and had wandered off into a train of speculation. I couldn't work out why the boar had been wearing a cap of liberty. I tried out one wild guess after another, but rejected them all. Eventually I made up my mind to ask my very own informant to put me out of my misery.

"Oh," he said, "of course; even your humble servant can tell you that! It's not that much of a riddle, actually. Pretty obvious, you know. The boar was meant to be the *pièce de résistance* yesterday – but the dinner guests let him off. That's why he's back in the dining room today – this time as a freedman."

I cursed myself for being so dim. That was the last time I asked any questions. Didn't want to look as if I'd never dined out in sophisticated company before.

As we were speaking, a handsome young slave boy with a garland of vine leaves and ivy on his head started bringing round grapes in a small wicker basket. He first said his name was Bromius, then Lyaeus and Euhius,* and he warbled his master's poems in a shrill descant voice. At the sound, Trimalchio turned round and said:

"Dionysus! Be Liber the Liberator!"

The slave boy took the cap of liberty from off the boar's head and put it on his own.

Trimalchio went on:

"None of you will deny that I have a Father Liber here. *Viva la libertà!*"

We cheered Trimalchio's joke, and as the boy came round the room, we kissed him hard.

After this course Trimalchio had to go out to use the pot. The boss was away! Now we could enjoy our freedom, and we started to chat to all the other guests [...]

Dama first called for bigger and better wineglasses and then launched into a monologue.

"A day's nowt," he said. "Turn round and it's night. So there's nowt better than to 'op out of bed and straight into dinner. And it's bin pretty nippy, like. Even the 'ot bath didn't really warm me up. Still, nice 'ot drink's like a snug cloak, intit lad? Eeh, I've 'ad a few jars and I'm right plastered. Wine's gone to me 'ead."

42. Seleucus picked up the thread.

"Me, personally speaking now, I don't wash every day. The bath wears you away like a rub-down from a fuller. Water has teeth – so, every day, our hearts dissolve a little more. But when I've necked a few jars of mead, I can tell the cold weather to fuck off.* 'Course, I couldn't have a bath today anyway. Had to go to a funeral. Thoroughly decent bloke he was, a really nice chappy, Chrysanthus. Bubbled out his soul.* Seems like only yesterday he popped over for a chat. I can still see myself chewing the fat with him. Damn shame. We go strutting round like bladders of hot air. But like flies we are – no, less: at least there's a bit of a buzz to a fly, but we're just bubbles. If only he hadn't tried that nil by mouth regime. Five days with not a sip of water or a morsel of bread. Didn't help: he's joined the silent majority. It was the doctors that did for him... No, actually it was just his bad luck; a doctor's only there to try and cheer you up a bit. Anyway, the funeral was a really nice do, with a lovely bier, top-quality pall, too. He got a first-class send-off from the mourners; he'd freed quite a few slaves* – everyone in tears except maybe not his missus. Old crocodile. And him a model husband, eh! But women, don't even get me started on women... Flock of vultures. Just ain't worth being nice to any of 'em. Might as well chuck your kindness down the well. But love past its prime pinches tight like a crab."

43. He was starting to get on our nerves and Phileros suddenly yelled:

"Look, life's for the living, all right? He got what was coming to him: he lived a decent life, and he died a decent death. What's he got to grumble about? When he started he just had tuppence, and he was always ready to pick a farthing out of a pile of shit with his own teeth. Result: whatever he touched just grew like a honeycomb. Damn me if he didn't leave a good hundred grand, all in hard cash. I may be a cynical old dog,* but to be perfectly honest with you, he was always shooting his mouth off, wagging that vicious tongue of his: snappy old chappy. Now his brother, he was your solid man, a friend to a friend, generous with his help, always asking you round for a meal. But Chrysanthus was just getting started when he went and bought a dead parrot.* Still, the first vintage he produced put him back on his feet; he could charge as much for that wine as he wanted. And he could really keep his head above water once he came into an estate – he managed to pocket more than he'd actually been left. And then the great blockhead got mad with his brother and bequeathed the family property to some nobody from nowhere. If you run from your family, you've got to keep running. But he used to trust those slaves of his as if they were oracles – and they scuttled him. You shouldn't be too quick to believe what people say: you'll always screw up, leastways if you're in business. Still, true enough: he enjoyed life while he could. We don't always get what we deserve. He was Fortune's blue-eyed boy; in his hands lead turned to gold. Oh, it's easy enough all right when things run along fair and square. And how many years did he have on his back? Seventy and more. But he was tough as horn, carried his age well, hair as black as a crow. I'd known him for ages and ages and he was still a randy old sod. For God's sake, I don't think even his pet dog was safe! Always after boys, too. He liked trade of every sort. Can't say I blame him, of course. It's all he could take with him."

44. Phileros had finished, and up piped Ganymedes.

"'Tain't got nothing to do with nothing in heaven or on earth, what you lot are chuntering on about. Nobody seems to worry a tap about the price of corn in the shops. It's really starting to bite. I don't think I'd managed to get hold of a single frigging mouthful of bread today. And the drought – it just goes on and on. We've been starving for a whole year. Bloody market officials.* Just hope they get what's coming to them. All in cahoots with the bakers. It's 'you scratch my back and I'll scratch yours'. So your little man in the street gets ground down, while your better-off chomp away like every day's party day. Ah, now if only we had those blokes I found here when I first came over from Asia. Lions, they were. Those were the days! They'd put the fear of Jupiter into those slobs if the flour from Sicily wasn't up to standard.* Reminds me of Safinius: in those days – I was still a boy – he used to live by the Old Arch. Bad-tempered bastard. Left scorch marks behind him wherever he went. But he was straight, reliable, a friend to a friend, someone you could play guess-how-many-fingers* with in the dark. And in the town hall! He used to give them a right bollocking, every one of them in turn, no beating about the bush, just launching straight in. Plus, when he was arguing a case in court, his voice used to get louder and louder, like a trumpet. Never sweated, never spat; a dry old stick, just as the gods had made him. If you said hello, he very nicely said hello back – knew everybody by name. He was just like one of us, he was. So, in those days, bread was dirt cheap. Tuppence, that was all you paid – for a loaf so big even two people couldn't eat it all. I've seen a bull's-eye bigger than the loaves you get nowadays. Oh my god! Gets worse by the day! This town's growing – yes, growing backwards like a calf's tail. But why, I ask you, do we put up with a market official not worth three Caunian figs,* too interested in making a bit of money on the side to care whether we live or die? He sits at home laughing, and pockets more ready cash per day than most people can ever expect to get their hands on. I happen to know how he came by his hundred grand.* But if we were men with balls, he wouldn't be so pleased with life. Nowadays people are lions at home and foxes outside. As far as I'm concerned, I've already sold the shirt off my back just to feed myself, and if the price of bread stays as high as it is now, I'm going to sell my little cottage too. What kind of future do we face, if neither gods nor men will turn a sympathetic eye on this town? I swear on my kids' lives, I really do believe all this is the gods' doing. Just think about it: nobody thinks heaven is heaven, nobody observes the fasts, nobody gives a hair off his head for Jupiter. When people close their eyes, it's to tot up their profits. In the good old days, women used to put on their best robes, let their hair hang modestly down, climb up the hill, their feet bare, their hearts pure, to pray that Jupiter would send rain. Whereupon down it came, bucketfuls of the stuff, like it was now or never, and they all went home as wet as drowned rats. But now the gods pad around in slippers of wool, and it's because we don't worship them as we should. So our fields lie…"

45. "Mind what you say, if you please," said Echion, the second-hand clothes dealer. "'Need to take the rough with the smooth', as the farmer said when he'd lost his spotted pig. If it be not now, yet it will come: so life trundles along. Damn it all, I bet you couldn't name a nicer part of the world than this, if only it had some decent men living in it. OK, it's going through a rough time right now, but it's not the only one. We mustn't be too pernickety; the same sky rests over us all. If you lived anywhere else in the world, you'd say that the pigs here walked the streets ready-roasted. And you know what we've got to look forward to? Three days' time and we've got the holiday, with a gladiatorial show laid on. Not just your ordinary fighters – no, a team of freedmen. Old Titus likes to splash out. Headstrong bloke, he is; whatever he lays on, it'll be really, like, *wow*! I'm a regular at his place, and he doesn't do things by halves. You'll see the best display of swordsmanship ever, none of the fighters turning tails and running off – no: a real slaughterhouse out there, bang in the middle where the whole audience can see it. He's got the wherewithal, you know: picked up thirty million when his old man kicked the bucket. Phew! He could spend four hundred grand, and not make a dent in his estate, and his name will live for ever. He's got some dwarves, and this girl charioteer, and Glyco's steward – *he* got caught having fun with Glyco's wife. You'll see the audience split down the middle over him: jealous hubbies versus the ladies' men. Glyco's hardly got two coins to rub together, you know, but he's thrown his own steward to the beasts. Rather gives the game away, doesn't it? Was it really his slave's fault? He had to do as he was told – by Her Ladyship. She's the one that ought to be gored by the bull. She's a filthy piss pot. But if you can't thrash your donkey, you have to thrash the saddle. How did Glyco think that Hermogenes's soppy daughter would ever turn out right anyway? And Hermogenes – now there was somebody who could trim the claws of a hawk on the wing. You don't get a rope from a viper. Glyco? Glyco's dumped his own family in it. He'll be a marked man as long as he lives, until death wipes away the shame of it. But nobody's perfect, and we pay the price. Still, I can already practically smell the feast Mammaea's going to lay on for us. Two denarii each for me and my folks it'll cost him.

And if he does, he's going to win more votes than Norbanus* all right. Take it from me: he'll walk all over him. And when you think about it, what's that Norbanus ever done for us? The gladiators in his shows are barely worth tuppence, so decrepit you only have to blow on them and over they topple. I've seen better beast-fighters in my time. He had a bunch of pint-sized little horsemen killed off,* ran around like headless chickens, they did; one was as thin as a rake, his opponent was bandy-legged, and the reserve who took on the winner was a dead loss just like the other dead loser – hamstrung, he was. The only one with any fight in him was the Thracian.* But he just fought by the rulebook too. Anyway, they all got a flogging in the end. The crowd roared, 'Let 'em have it!' So they got it. Bunch of yellow-bellies. 'Well,' he said, 'I *did* give you a show!' Yeah – and I gave you a round of applause. But tot it all up and I still reckon I was ripped off. One good turn.

46. "Hey! You! Agamemnon! I can see from your face what you're thinking. 'Boring old fart, can't he shut it for once?' But you've got a tongue in your head, ain't you? Why not use it? Too hoity-toity for us, eh? Making fun of the way us poor blokes talk. All right, we know all your book-learning's addled your brains. Never mind: tell you what. One of these days, do you think I might persuade you to come out to our little place? See our humble abode? We'll provide a snack: a chicken, some eggs – it'll be nice, even if the weather's ruined everything this year... we'll still find something to fill our faces with. My young nipper's* already growing up to be a potential pupil of yours. Knows his four times table already. If he lives, you'll have a little devotee at your side. Just give him a few spare minutes and he's, like, heads down over his writing slate. Bright boy, got a good brain in him, even if he does have this thing about birds. I've already killed three of his goldfinches. Told him a weasel had eaten 'em. But he's picked up some other odd hobbies too. Loves painting, for instance. He's already given Greek the boot, and he's really taken to Latin in quite a big way,* even if his teacher thinks a bit too highly of himself and keeps jumping from one topic to another. Knows his letters all right. But he won't work. And then there's another teacher, he don't know so much, but he *does* take a bit of trouble, and teaches the lad more than he actually knows hisself. Even comes round ours on days off, and doesn't mind what you pay him. So I've bought the lad a few books. Red-letter books, 'cos I want him to pick up a smattering of law so's he can help run things at home.

That's a profession that brings in the bread. He's messed around with literature quite long enough. Any objections from him and I'm minded to get him trained up as something: a barber, or an auctioneer, or at least a barrister. If you've got a decent job like that, nobody can take it away except Orcus. So I yell at him every day: 'Primigenius,' I says to him, I says, 'just you take my word for it: whatever you learn, it's for your own good you're learning it. Look at Phileros the lawyer: if he hadn't slogged away, he wouldn't be able to keep body and soul together today. You know, it was only yesterday as he was hawking stuff round on his back; now he can show Norbanus a thing or two. Being educated, like, is worth its weight in gold. A trade lasts for ever.'"

47. While the air was abuzz with the hum of conversation, Trimalchio came in, mopping his brow. He washed his hands in scent and paused briefly before speaking.

"Friends!" he said. "You'll have to forgive me! My digestion hasn't been doing a thing I ask it these past few days. The doctors are stumped. But I've found that pomegranate rind and pinewood boiled in vinegar helps. And I hope the old tum's starting to do the decent thing again. Otherwise I have this rumbling in my belly like a roaring bull. So if any of you needs to pay a visit, don't feel in the slightest bit embarrassed. We're leaky from the day we're born. Better out than in, I always say: otherwise it's pure torment. It's the one thing Jove can't forbid. You laughing, Fortunata? But it's you that keeps me awake night after night. When people are in my dining room, they can do anything they like, as far as I'm concerned: and doctors expressly forbid you to hold it in. And if anyone needs to do a big job, they've got all they need right outside: water, chamber pots, all the other little necessaries. Take my word for it: a touch of wind soon goes straight to the brain and then floods through the whole body. I know there's been many people who've died that way – they couldn't admit the truth to themselves."

What a broad-minded, considerate man... We thanked him profusely – and tried to drown our sniggers by drinking hard and fast. We hadn't yet realized that we were still only halfway up the hill, as the saying has it. The tables were cleared while the music played, whereupon three white pigs were driven into the dining room, decked out with muzzles and little bells: one of them, as the master of ceremonies* told us, was two years old, the second three years and the third was already an old man.* So I started to think that some acrobats had come in, and that the pigs were going to perform a few tricks, like they do in sideshows. But Trimalchio soon disabused us.

"My friends! So which one of these would you like to be served up right now for dinner? A farmyard cock, mincemeat *à la Pentheus*...* any peasant can throw a rubbish meal like *that* together: but *my* chefs are in the habit of serving something a bit more special – whole calves, pot-boiled."

Then he ordered the chef to be summoned and, without waiting for us to make our choice, told him to slaughter the oldest of the pigs.

"Which division* are you from?" he asked him in a loud clear voice.

The chef replied that he was from the fortieth.

"Bought," he asked, "or born into the household?"

"Neither, actually," said the chef. "I was left to you in Pansa's will."

"So just you take care," said Trimalchio, "that you serve this meal properly; otherwise, I'll have you demoted to the messenger boys' division."

The chef was duly intimidated by this display of power, and followed the pig as it was taken into the kitchen, to prepare it as the next course.

48. Trimalchio turned to us, all smiles.

"If the wine doesn't meet with your approval," he said affably, "I'll replace it; I'm sure you can do it justice... Thank the gods I don't have to buy it in, and the pleasant quaffing stuff here comes from an out-of-town estate of mine. I haven't even been there yet, actually. I gather it extends between Tarracina and Tarentum.* My latest plan is to add Sicily to my modest collection of properties, so when I fancy a trip to Africa, it'll all be my own territory I sail through en route! Anyway, Agamemnon, tell me now, what was the subject of your casebook speech* today? Personally, I don't do any legal work, but I have learnt to read and write. Helps with running my little estate. And don't think I'm a Philistine. Oh no, two whole libraries I've got, one in Greek and the other in Latin. So I'd love you to just run over your speech for me."

Agamemnon had just started: "There were once a rich man and a poor man who had quarrelled..." when Trimalchio interrupted him.

"A poor man?" he queried. "Whatever's that?"

"Er... yes, most amusing," said Agamemnon, and continued to describe his fictitious legal argument; I forget the details.

Trimalchio jumped in again.

"If it really happened, it's not a real fictitious argument, and if it didn't really happen, then it's not worth mentioning."

We fell over ourselves to express our admiration at this and other witty remarks.

"Agamemnon," he continued, "my dear friend, the Twelve Labours of Hercules – you've heard of them, I take it? Or the story of Ulysses, and how the Cyclops twisted his thumb out with a pair of tongs? Personally, I was already reading these stories in Homer when I was still just a lad. Oh yes: I was in Cumae once, and I saw the Sibyl with my own eyes, just hanging there in a bottle. Some kids kept asking her, 'Σίβυλλα, τί θέλεις;' And, each time, she answered: 'ἀποθανεῖν θέλω.'"*

49. He had plenty more hot air where that came from... but then the next course was brought in: the giant pig. It completely filled the table. We were amazed it had been served up so soon – and we swore that not even a plain rooster could have been cooked in that short time, especially as this pig seemed a good deal bigger than before. But Trimalchio started looking at it more and more intently.

"What?... What the?... This pig hasn't been gutted, has it? No. It. Has. Not. Fetch me the chef. I want him here. *Now!*"

The chef came in and stood by the table looking crestfallen. He said he'd forgotten to gut it, and...

"What? *Forgotten?*" roared Trimalchio. "You'd think, to hear him talk, he'd just forgotten to season it with pepper and cumin. Strip him!"

They jumped to it, and the chef was soon stripped naked and standing there despondently between two executioners.* But everybody started to plead on his behalf.

"These things *will* happen. Please, please let him off. If he does it again, *then* he'll get no mercy from us."

But I'm inclined to be strict. Bit of a sadist, actually. I couldn't keep my thoughts to myself, but leant over and muttered in Agamemnon's ear:

"This slave is obviously useless. Who else would forget to gut a pig? I wouldn't let the stupid bugger off even if it was just a fish."

But not Trimalchio; *his* face melted into a broad grin.

"Oh well," he said, "if your memory's that bad, gut Mr Pig right here in front of us!"

The chef slipped on his shirt again, grabbed a knife and, his hand trembling, made incisions on both sides of the pig's belly. Straight away the slits widened and burst open under the pressure from inside, and out tumbled sausages and black puddings.

50. All the household slaves burst into a round of applause at this trick.

"Bravo, Caius!" they shouted in unison. The chef was naturally given a drink and a silver crown as a reward; a goblet was presented to him on a dish of Corinthian bronze. Agamemnon peered at the dish curiously.

"Nobody except me has real Corinthian plate," intoned Trimalchio.

I was waiting for him to boast, as per usual, that his drinking cups were imported from Corinth. But he went one better.

"You're probably asking," he said to Agamemnon, "*why* exactly nobody except me has real Corinthian plate? The reason is… the coppersmith I buy from is a man called Corinthus. Only Corinthus's stuff is your real Corinthian… And don't think I'm a total hignoramus. I know perfectly well how and where Corinthian bronze actually originated. When Troy was captured, Hannibal – an old snake in the grass he was, a right slippery customer – collected all the statues, bronze, gold and silver, into one pile and set fire to the lot; they fused into a lump, a kind of bronze alloy.* The smiths took bits out of it and made bowls and dishes and figurines. That's how your Corinthian-ware came into being, from a mixture of all sorts, a bit of this and a bit of that. I have to say that, no offence, personally I prefer glass. It doesn't smell. It's a bit fragile, otherwise I'd even prefer it to gold. But as it is, not worth having. 51. Actually, there was this craftsman once who made a glass drinking bowl that was unbreakable. So he was granted an audience with the Emperor to show him his invention* […]

"Then he asked Caesar to hand the bowl back to him – but immediately flung it to the ground. Caesar almost fainted dead away with shock! But our man picked up the bottle; it was merely dented like a bronze vessel; so he took a little hammer out of his tunic and tapped it all smooth again, no sweat. By this time he thought he was practically sitting on Jove's throne – especially when Caesar asked him:

"'Does anyone else happen to know how to make glass like this?'

"Now comes the good bit. He said 'no' – and Caesar ordered him to have his head chopped off: the reason being that, if word of his invention got around, gold would be dirt cheap. 52. I'm actually a connoisseur of silver. I've got some really big wine cups – maybe a hundred they contain, more or less [...] The design shows Cassandra killing her sons, and the kids' bodies are lying around, looking so dead you'd swear they're alive. I've got a sacrificial bowl that a patron of mine bequeathed me, you can see Daedalus shutting Niobe up in the Trojan horse.* And I've got goblets showing the fights between Hermeros and Petraites,* *and* you should just feel the weight of the silver! Talk about taste – I wouldn't sell my expertise for all the money in the world."

As he held forth, a young slave dropped a cup. Trimalchio turned and glared at him.

"Go and top yourself, you stupid little bugger. Go on – just do it!"

The boy's lips started twitching and he begged for mercy.

"What are you begging me for?" retorted Trimalchio. "*I* ain't the problem, am I? Take a word of advice: just beg yourself not to be such a stupid little twat."

Eventually he listened to our pleas and let the boy off – whereupon the latter started running round and round the table [...]

and he yelled, "Out with the water! In with the wine!" We roared at his brilliant joke – especially Agamemnon, who knew how to get himself invited back for another dinner. Trimalchio glowed with pleasure at our praise, and cheerfully knocked back the drink; by this stage he was quite sozzled.

"Isn't any of you going to ask my dear Fortunata to do her dance? You take my word for it: she can get down and dirty and *cordax** away like nobody else."

He lifted his hands to his forehead and did an impression of the actor Syrus, while all the slaves chanted: "*Μάδεια, περιμάδεια.*"* And he'd have taken to the middle of the floor himself, if Fortunata hadn't whispered in his ear, probably telling him not to make a bloody great fool of himself. But he was always changing his tune; one minute he was cowed by Fortunata, while the next he'd reverted to his real self.

53. Anyway, his longing to do a bit of vulgar dancing was interrupted by a clerk who started reading as if it was the local *Town Gazette*:*

"**VII sextile Kalends;*** on the estate at *CUMAE*
(prop. *TRIMALCHIO*):
- **births**: 30 boys and 40 girls;
- **wheat** brought into the barn from the threshing floor: 500,000 pecks;
- **oxen** broken in: 500.

Today: the slave Mithridates was crucified for insulting the guardian spirit of our master Gaius.

Today: returned to the treasury, for lack of investment openings: ten million sesterces.

Today: a fire broke out in the gardens at Pompeii, starting in the mansion of Nasta, the bailiff."

"Erm, hang about a bit," said Trimalchio, "when exactly were these gardens in Pompeii bought, then?"

"Last year," replied the accountant. "That's why they haven't shown up in the books yet."

Trimalchio flared up.

"If any property is bought in my name, I want to know about it within six months straight. Otherwise it is *not* to be entered in my books!"

Then the reports of the *ædiles* were read out, and the wills of some gamekeepers, in which Trimalchio was politely disinherited. Then came the names of some bailiffs, and of a woman freedman who'd been divorced by her husband when she was caught in the bedroom of an attendant from the baths. Then a porter who'd been banished to Baiae,* then a steward who was being indicted and a lawsuit between some valets.

By now the acrobats had finally turned up. Some hulking great oaf stood there holding a ladder and made a boy hop and skip up the rungs and dance a jig at the top while singing a song. Then he had to jump through burning hoops and pick up a wine jar in his teeth. The only person to be impressed by any of this stuff was Trimalchio, who kept saying what a thankless profession it was. In fact he proclaimed that there were only two types of performers that he really enjoyed watching: acrobats and trumpet players. Any other kind of show was a waste of space.

"You know, I even bought a troupe of actors once," he told us, "but I preferred them to put on Atellan farces* and I ordered my flute-player to perform some local Latin tunes."

54. Just as he was speaking, the boy slipped and crashed into Trimalchio [...] All the slaves cried out in dismay, and so did the guests. Not that they could have cared less about the stupid little acrobat – they wouldn't have minded seeing him break his neck; no, it would just have brought the whole dinner to a gloomy end if they'd had to shed tears over the death of a complete stranger. As for Trimalchio, he was groaning in pain and nursing his arm as if it had been severely injured. The doctors came running in, Fortunata leading the way, with her hair flying, clutching her cup and screaming blue murder at this terrible accident. The lad who'd crashed into him was crawling round at our feet, begging to be let off. I had a terrible feeling that all his pleadings were the prelude to some unexpected practical joke or other. I hadn't forgotten that chef who'd forgotten to gut the pig. So I started to look all round the dining room, half-expecting some wonderful contrivance to come bursting out of the walls – especially when they proceeded to thrash a slave just because he'd dressed the bruise on his master's arm with white wool rather than purple. And my suspicions weren't far off the mark; instead of having him punished, Trimalchio ordered the slave who had crashed into him to be freed... just in case anybody dared to suggest that such a Great Man as himself had been wounded by *a mere slave*.

55. We voiced our approval and chattered on brightly, observing, in our different ways, how fickle fortune could be.

"You know," said Trimalchio, "we really shouldn't let this turn of events go unrecorded for posterity."

He immediately called for his writing tablets. And, without racking his brains for very long, he recited these verses:

> "Life always throws up some surprise,
> And Fortune rules us from the skies.
> So, pour it out, boy, if you please!
> A glass of nice Falernian! Cheers!"

This epigram was the signal for a discussion of poets. To begin with, Mopsus of Thrace* was generally reckoned to be the best... until Trimalchio weighed in.

"Tell me, Professor," he asked, "how would you compare Cicero and Publilius?* Personally, I find the former has more aesthetic refinement, while the latter has more moral substance. What could possibly be better than the following example? Listen:

"Lust for luxury makes the city walls of Mars crumble.
To pamper your palate the peacock's imprisoned and
plumped up amid the gilt plumes of Babylon;
the Numidean guinea fowl too, and the gallinaceous capon.
Even the white stork, our welcome guest from abroad,
the piety-cultivating, slender-legged clatterclatterclatterbeak,
exile-bird of winter, harbinger-of-warm-winds,
has recently built a nest in the cooking pot of iniquity.
Why is the pearl, that Indic fruit, so dear to you?
Is it so that your wife, adorned with sea-born jewels,
may really let her hair down and part her thighs on a stranger's bed?
Why do you select the emerald, green-gleaming, or precious glass,
or the fire gems of Carthage?
Is it so
        that probity will shine
from amid the bright-red-burning stones?
Is it right for a young bride to dress herself in the weave of the winds?
A see-through garment?
Or stand there in public, wearing a thin veil of misty, wispy gauze, and
no underwear?

56. "And now," he went on, "what do we think is the most difficult profession – after being a writer, of course? I think it's a doctor, or maybe a money-changer. The doctor, because he has to know what's going on behind those poor old ribs of ours, and when we're likely to go down with something nasty... though I have to say I really can't stand those medics – they're forever prescribing duck meat* for me. And the money-changer's life is tough because he sees the copper concealed under the silver. And among the dumb beasts, the ones that work hardest are oxen and sheep. Oxen because it's thanks to them we get to eat bread; sheep because their wool provides us with our splendid attire. You know, it's outrageous to eat lamb *and* wear its shirts. And I think bees are divine little creatures; they puke honey... even though people do say they get it from Jupiter. And if they sting, well, that's because there's no sweet without sour."

On and on he went, putting all the philosophers onto the dole queue. Then a cup came round with some little tickets inside it, and the slave in charge read out the names of the presents for the guests' party bags.*

"Tubby or not tubby?" he shouted; in came two hams, one large, one small.

"Headrest!" – a scrap of neck-end was brought in.

"Snooty and smelly!" – a toffee apple and rotten eggs.

"Leeks and peaches!" – peas and leeches.

"Flour and flypaper!" – raisins and a honey pot.

"Sunday roast, reporter's boast!" – a slab of meat and some notebooks.

"Go on foot to the dogs!" – a hare and a slipper.

"He's hit the jackpot!" – a bedpan with a bundle of beetroot.

We couldn't stop laughing: there were hundreds of these joke presents, so many I can't remember them all.

57. But Ascyltos went too far, putting on an act, reeling with hysterical mirth. He threw up his hands and laughed till he cried. Eventually one of Trimalchio's fellow freedmen – the one lying in the dinner place next to mine* – flared up.

"What you laughing at, mutton-head?" he snarled. "The boss has done us all proud here. But not good enough for you, eh? Got more money than us? Used to better company – is that it? I hope the lady spirit of this house is listening to me, 'cos if I were lying next to him, I'd soon shut his bleating mouth for him. He's a nice one to laugh at other people – he's just a runaway, a fly-by-night, not worth his own piddle. You know what? I could piss all round him and he wouldn't know which way to turn. It takes a lot to make me lose my bleeding rag, but... rotten meat's riddled with worms. Look at him laughing. What's he got to laugh about? Did his father pay good gold for the little brat? A Roman *eques*,* are you? What a coincidence: I'm the son of a king. 'So why were you a slave?' you ask. 'Cos that's what I wanted to be, a slave, OK? I preferred being a Roman citizen to being a provincial tax-payer.* And the lifestyle I can afford now ain't nothing for nobody else to make fun of, I very much hope! *Homo sum*, you know, a *mensch*, 'a man among men' and all that. I can walk round with my head held high. I don't owe a brass farthing to nobody. I've never had to go to court. Nobody's ever had to buttonhole me in the market and said: 'Pay up!' I've bought a few bits and pieces of land; I've got a copper or two to my name. I feed twenty bellies and a dog, too. I bought my partner* out of slavery, so nobody would try to wipe his hands on her luscious glory. I paid one thousand denarii for my own freedom. They made me a *sevir* and I didn't even have to pay. When I die, I hope I won't have anything to blush for. Anyway, what about you? So busy judging others you don't get to take a look at yourself? You can see the little louse on the other guy, but you can't see the way your own big bum sticks out. Nobody else seems to find us amusing except you. Look at your Prof. He's older and wiser than you. *He* likes us. You're still a milksop, a squealer that don't know *mama* from *baba*, a flowerpot man... No, a damp douche bag, that's you: soppier, not better. Got more money to throw around than everyone else? Treat yourself to two lunches and two dinners a day, then! I've got a reputation for decency, and that's worth more than loadsamoney. You know what? Has anyone ever had to ask me twice for anything? Forty years I was a slave, but nobody could tell whether I was slave or free. I was a boy with long hair when I came to this town; the town hall hadn't even been built. I did my level best to make sure my master was satisfied with me. A fine man he was, a real gent. The whole of your body ain't worth a single fingernail of his. True, there were people in the household, left and right, who kept trying to trip me up. But – thanks to my master's guardian spirit! – I didn't go under. It was a real struggle, but I made it. Compared to that, being born free is as easy as 'Help yourself!' But what you staring at me for, like a goat in a field of vetch?"

58. Giton, standing at my feet as my waiter, had been desperately trying not to laugh, but finally gave a derisive great snort. The guy who'd been laying into Ascyltos spun round at the noise and turned his fire on the boy.

"You too, eh? You having a laugh? You curly-headed little onion! Oh, Happy Saturnalia* to you too! December already, is it? When did you pay off your 5% freedom tax?...* Just look at him. He don't know where to put himself. Deserves crucifixion. Let the crows peck at him. I'll make sure Jupiter gives you what for. Same goes for him there who can't even keep you in order. Sure as I've eaten my bellyful of bread, you'd get what's coming to you from me this very minute, only I have a bit of respect for my fellow freedman.* We're all having a really nice time, but those dumb buggers who can't keep you under their thumbs... I see what's what: like master, like slave. I can barely stop myself from... I don't fly off the handle easily, but get me going and I wouldn't give tuppence for my own mother. You can count on it: you'll be seeing more of me. Out on the streets – you little rat, you toadstool! I'm not going to grow taller or shorter by a day till I shove your master's head in the nettle patch, and I won't forget you neither, you can scream all you like to Jupiter on Olympus, by god. I'll see to it that those dinky long curls of yours and that tuppeny-ha'penny master of yours are of no use to you at all. I'm going to eat you for breakfast, you see if I don't. Either I don't know myself, or you'll be laughing on the other side of your face – even if you grow a golden beard. Athena's going to give you what for, I'll take care of that, and the same goes for him, the one who first trained you to lick his *derrière*. Never knew much about geometry, me, nor your literary appreciation and all that crap. *Sing of the wrath...* no blind sense in that. But I can do BLOCK CAPITALS, and I know my weights and measures, I can do percentages, I know the meaning of hard cash. Tell you what. Let's have a little bet, you and me. Come on: here's my money. You'll soon see your father's chucked his money away on your education, even if you do know your classics. How about this one:

I am part of us, I come far, I come wide. Who am I? *Solve me.*

Here's another one:

It runs and runs and never changes place.

And:

It grows and grows and smaller grows apace.*

Ah, that's got *you* on the run! Can't do it, eh? You look shit-scared, like a mouse in a piss pot. So you keep your freaking mouth shut, or don't go round bothering your betters. They were unaware you even existed. Think I'm taken in by those boxwood rings? You nicked 'em off your girl. Occupo* will bring me luck... Let's pop over to the marketplace and see who's got the most credit. You'll soon see people trust the seal on my iron ring. You'd look like a drowned fox. A real sight for sore eyes. I hope to make a fortune and die a good death so that people will swear by my demise, but before that, I'm going to hunt you down wherever you go. And when I catch you, I'll be wearing my toga back to front.* Fine bloke he is as taught you to behave like that. A twerp, not a teacher. Now in my day we was educated proper. Our teacher used to say to us, 'Got all your things safe? Straight home you go. Don't gawp. Don't cheek your elders.' And now? Total anarchy.* When the kids leave school they ain't worth tuppence. But *I* thank the gods I got a decent training. Made me the man I am."

59. Ascyltos was about to retort to this hectoring when Trimalchio broke in. He'd enjoyed his fellow freedman's tirade, but now he said:

"Let's keep the bickering out of this. Mind your language: we're having good clean fun. And Hermeros, don't be so hard on the kid. He's got a temper, but you shouldn't stoop to his level. When people squabble like that, the only way to win is to back down. When you were a young cock you used to crow too: cock-a-doodle-do! – not an ounce of sense in you. Let's pretend all this hasn't happened and just enjoy the fun. Look: here come the Homeristas!"*

Straight away in marched the troupe, banging their spears on their shields. Trimalchio himself sat up on his cushion, and while the Homeristas spouted Greek verse at each other, in their usual show-off way, he read the Latin translation aloud from a book, in a sing-song drone.

Then he called for silence.

"Do you know," he asked, "what story they're telling? There were two brothers, Diomedes and Ganymede. They had a sister called Helen. Agamemnon ran off with her and replaced her with a deer for Diana. So the bit we're at is where Homer describes the war between Troy and Tarentum. 'Course he won, Agamemnon that is, and married off Iphigenia, his daughter, to Achilles. This drove Ajax mad* and… well, let's see how it all ended!"

When Trimalchio had finished, the Homeristas all gave a great whoop and the slaves started running every which way and a boiled calf was brought in on a silver plate – 200 lbs it weighed. It was wearing a helmet. It was closely followed by Ajax, pretending to be mad and slashing at it with his sword; he used his weapon to slice it lengthways and breadthways and distributed kebabbed slices of the meat to the guests on the point of his sword. Pretty amazing.

60. But we didn't have much time to admire this surprising show of skill and taste. A violent din suddenly came from the ceiling panels and the whole dining room shook. I jumped up, terror-stricken, afraid that an acrobat was going to come down through the roof. All the other guests were just as mystified and all stared up, waiting to see what fresh marvel was being announced by the heavens. And lo and behold, the ceiling panels were pulled apart and all at once a huge hoop, apparently knocked out of a gigantic barrel, was let down. From all round its rim there dangled golden crowns and alabaster jars full of perfume. We were told to take these for our party bags. Then I looked back at the table [...]

a tray with several cakes on it had been placed there, and the pastry-maker had baked a statue of Priapus in the middle. The god was holding out his apron, filled with every kind of fruits and grapes, as per usual. Our mouths watered as we greedily grabbed at this pile of offerings, only to witness yet another *coup de théâtre* that had us in stitches all over again. We only had to touch the cakes and the fruit, and each piece started to squirt out saffron: but the stinking juice spurted right into our faces. We assumed this dish must have some religious significance, as it came perfumed by this ritual liquid,* and so we all rose in our couches and chanted, "Hail Augustus, Father of the Fatherland!" But even after this acclamation, there were some people reaching out for the fruit – so we too filled our table napkins with them, especially me. After all, I could never pour too much largesse into Giton's lap...

Meanwhile in came three boys, with their white tunics all tucked up. Two of them put Lares figures decorated with amulets on the table; the third brought round a bowl of wine, intoning, "May the gods bless us" [...]

He was saying that one of the images was called Hireling, the second Luck and the third Lucre. And there was the exact likeness of Trimalchio too: as everyone else was kissing it, we thought we'd better do the same.*

61. So when everyone had wished for good health and wisdom, Trimalchio glanced over at Niceros and said:

"You used to be more fun at parties; can't get a peep out of you now, dunno why. Please, if you want to put a smile on my face, tell us what happened."

Niceros was delighted by his friend's affable words. "May I go bust if I'm lying, but for ages now I've been trying not to explode with pleasure at seeing you in such great shape! Anyway, let's treat this as just a bit of fun, OK? I'm afraid those bright lads here are going to laugh at me. But let 'em laugh; I'm going to tell my story; what have I got to lose if someone laughs at me? It's better to have 'em laugh with you than at you."

Thus spake our hero and forthwith embarked upon his tale.

"Once upon a time, when I was still a slave, we used to live in Narrow Alley – in what's now Gavilla's house. There, as the gods decreed, I fell in love with the wife of Terentius, who managed the tavern; you'll remember her – Melissa, from Tarentum, a pretty little thing, plump and peachy. But I swear I wasn't just after her body. No, I didn't just want a screw; she had a lovely nature, that's what really attracted me. I'd only have to ask her for something, and she never said no; if I had a bob or two, I poured it into her lap and she never cheated me of a thing. One day, out on the estate, her husband passed away. I was ready to go through hell and high water to have her. As the proverb says, a friend in need... **62.** As luck would have it, my master had gone off to Capua to sort out something or other, so I seized this opportunity and persuaded a guest staying at ours to come out with me as far as the fifth milestone. A soldier he was, as strong as the devil. So we got our arses into gear about cockcrow, when the moon did shine as bright as day. We came to a place where there were tombs alongside the road: my friend needed to go and do his business at one of the gravestones, so I sat down, humming away to myself, and counted the tombs. Then I glanced round at my travelling companion; he was stripping himself bare and laying all his clothes by the side of the road. My soul was in my nose; I was already choked half dead with fear. Then he laid a trail of piss all round his clothes and, lo and behold – he turned into a wolf. I'm not kidding; I wouldn't lie for all the money in the world. Anyway, as I was saying, no sooner had he turned into a wolf than he started to howl, and ran off into the woods. At first I hardly knew where I was, then I went over to pick up his clothes – but they had turned to stone. Guess who nearly fainted away with dread? Yep: *moi*. But then I drew my sword and ran all along the road slaying shadows, till I reached my lady love's farmhouse. In I went, looking like a ghost, the soul almost bubbling out of my lips, sweat running down my crotch, my eyes glazed, barely alive. Dear Melissa asked in astonishment what I was doing gallivanting about at this time of the night.

"'If you'd turned up earlier,' she said, 'you could at least have given us a hand. This wolf got into the farm and mauled all the sheep [...]

Bled them like a butcher he did. He got away, but I'm not sure he'll have the last laugh; one of our slaves lunged at him with a lance, and holed him in the neck.' Once I'd heard that, I didn't sleep a wink. Soon as it was daylight, I ran back home like an innkeeper chasing a guest doing a runner, and when I came to the place where the clothes had been turned to stone, all I found was a pool of blood. But when I reached home, there was my soldier boy, lying in bed like a great ox, with a doctor bandaging up his neck. Then I realized he was a werewolf, and I could never sit down to break bread with him after that, not even if you'd killed me first. Other people are welcome to their own little opinions about all this, but if I'm lying, may your guardian spirits punish me."

63. Everyone was staring at him, dumbstruck. Trimalchio said:

"Sounds perfectly likely to me. You know, you've made every hair on my head stand up!* You see, I know that Niceros never talks crap: totally reliable, never talks through his backside. I too can a tale unfold, ah, horrible, most horrible – but I'm a donkey on roof tiles in comparison. Here's my story. I was still a long-haired youth, as I'd lived a life of Chian ease* ever since childhood, when my master's darling died. A bloody pearl of a bum boy he was, one in a million. So his poor old mum was weeping and wailing, and most of the rest of us were sharing her grief, when all of a sudden these witches started to screech. You'd have thought there was a dog chasing after a hare. At the time, we had a bloke from Cappadocia on our staff, tall chap, real beanpole, didn't fear a thing, and strong with it; he could lift a raging bull off the ground. He boldly whipped out his sword and, dashing outside – he'd carefully wrapped his left hand up – thrust it right into the belly of one of the women: look, right here (fingers crossed nothing ever happens to this part of *me*!). We heard a groan, but, to be perfectly frank, we didn't actually see the witches. Meanwhile old beanpole staggered back in and threw himself down on the bed; his whole body was black and blue, as if he'd been flogged. No doubt about it: the Evil Hand had touched him. We locked and bolted the door and went back to watch over the corpse, but when the mother came to embrace her son's body, she stretched out her hand and saw that it was a straw manikin. No heart, no innards, no nothing inside. It was obvious that the witches had swooped on the boy and replaced him with a little baby straw man. Please, you've got to believe me; there are wise women and night-riders who turn everything topsy-turvy. As for old beanpole, the colour never came back to his cheeks after that. He died a few days later, stark staring mad."

64. We were horrified. We all believed his story and kissed the table, begging the night-riders to stay indoors when we went home after dinner [...]

Actually, to tell you the truth, I was starting to see double: the lamps were swimming in front of me and the whole dining room looked kind of weird. Then Trimalchio shouted, "Hey, Plocamus, don't you have a story for us? Nothing to entertain us with, eh? You used to be so much better company. You could spout lovely blank verse, and spice it up with some nice songs. Alas, alack, oh deary dear, where are the sweet green figs of yesteryear?"

"I'm afraid," replied Plocamus, "that my days gadding about in the two-horse chariot of verse are over and done. Gout, you know. Otherwise, when I was a young lad, I used to sing so much I almost did my lungs in. I was an all-singing, all-dancing, one-man barber-shop quartet! Could anyone hold a candle to me? (Well, apart from Apelles?)"*

And he put his hand to his mouth and whistled out some hideous sounds. Greek it was, or so he claimed afterwards.

Trimalchio wasn't going to let himself be outdone. He did a pretty good imitation of a trumpet, and then started looking round for his darling boy, the one he called Croesus. A bleary-eyed kid he was, with a mouthful of rotting teeth. He had this puppy, a black bitch, an obscenely bloated thing that he was tying up in a green hanky. He put a half-pound loaf on the couch and then proceeded to cram it down the reluctant mutt's mouth until she puked it up again. This reminded Trimalchio of his own duties. He ordered them to bring in Scylax, "the guardian of the house and all the dwellers therein". No sooner said than done: a huge great dog on the end of a chain was brought in and given a good kick by the porter to make him lie down, so he curled up in front of the table. Trimalchio chucked him a hunk of white bread. "Nobody in my house," he said, "loves me more than Scylax." His lover boy was miffed at the way Scylax's praises were being sung so effusively; he placed his own puppy on the ground and prodded her to launch an attack. As you might expect, Scylax, a canine to his back teeth, filled the dining room with the most godawful barking and almost tore Croesus's little Pearl limb from limb. All hell was let loose

– and the dogfight was just the start of it, as a candelabrum fell onto the table and smashed all the crystalware to pieces, and spattered some of the guests with hot oil. Trimalchio didn't want to appear in the least bothered by the breakages, so he gave his lover boy a kiss and told him to hop up onto his back. Without a moment's hesitation, Croesus clambered onto his steed and started heartily slapping Trimalchio on the shoulders, and as everyone roared with laughter he shouted, "Guess how many, win a penny!" Trimalchio put up with this for a while and then ordered a big bowl of wine to be mixed... and drinks to be poured for all the slaves sitting at our feet. He added this proviso: "If anyone won't take his medicine, pour it over his head. Daytime is for work, now it's time to partayyy!"

65. Ah, such largesse... Just then they brought in some savouries and I only have to think about them and, well, take my word for it, it makes me shudder. Instead of thrushes, fattened chickens were brought round to each of us, and goose eggs with their hats on, and Trimalchio started egging us on to eat, saying they were boneless chickens. Then a lictor* came knocking on the dining-room door, and a night-reveller in a white robe came in with a whole throng of others. He looked like an official; he made me feel pretty nervous – I thought the praetor* had turned up. So I tried to get up off the couch and plant my bare feet on the ground. Agamemnon saw how scared I was and snickered.

"Pull yourself together, you great twit! It's Habinnas, the *sevir*. He's a mason. Dead good at carving tombstones, they say."

I breathed a sigh of relief and fell back onto my couch, watching wide-eyed as Habinnas made his grand entrance. He was already pissed, and was having to lean with both hands on his wife's shoulder; there were several wreaths piled onto his head, and scented oil was trickling down his forehead into his eyes. He plopped himself down in the place of honour* and immediately called for wine and hot water. Trimalchio was really pleased to see the newcomer looking so merry; he called for a bigger cup for himself, and asked about the party Habinnas had been to.

"We had all we could possibly have wanted," came the reply, "except that *you* were not there! My bestest mate was *here*. But oh my god, it was some party. Scissa, you know, was holding a ninth-day funeral feast for his poor little slave. As soon as the slave was at death's door, he set him free. But I reckon he'll still have to pay the 5% tax-collectors quite a pile. Fifty grand the dead man was worth, they reckon.* Anyway, it was a lovely occasion, even if we did have to pour half our drinks out over the dead bugger's bones."

66. "Yes yes," said Trimalchio, "but – what did you have to eat?"

"Er... I'll tell you if I can remember. My wonderful memory, you know: I even keep forgetting my own name. Oh yes: the first course was a pig crowned with sausages, garnished with black pudding and giblets done to a turn, and beetroot, of course, and home-made wholemeal bread; I prefer it to white bread personally, it's good for me, and it makes having a crap a pure pleasure (it usually brings the tears to my eyes). The next course was a cold tart with a drizzle of warm honey doused in a very fine Spanish wine. Well, I only had to have a nibble at that tart and I practically drowned myself in the honey. Apart from that, there were chickpeas and lupines, and a choice of nuts and an apple each. Actually, I took two; look, here they are, tied up in my napkin; I have to bring back a little something for my pet slave boy, else there's trouble. Oh, yes, my better half here has just reminded me. There in front of us was this joint of bear meat. Scintilla was rash enough to try some. Nearly puked her guts out, she did. But I ate over a pound of it. Tasted like wild boar. Actually, if you ask me, a bear can gobble up a poor chap, so surely a poor chap's got even more right to gobble up a bear? To round off the meal we had soft cheese mellowed in new wine, and a snail apiece for everyone, and slices of tripe and liver in little dishes and eggs with their hoods on and turnips with mustard and some nasty little dish that tasted like shit, *pax Palamedes*.* And they brought round pickled olives in a dish, too, and some greedy bastards helped themselves to three fistfuls. We passed when it came to the ham. **67.** Anyway, dear Gaius, tell me, why isn't Fortunata eating with us?"

"Oh," said Trimalchio, "you know her better than that, don't you? Until she's tidied the silverware away, and divided up the leftovers between the slave boys, she won't touch so much as a drop of water."

"Oh," said Habinnas. "Well, if she ain't here, I'll bugger off."

He'd just started to haul himself up when a signal was given, and all the slaves yelled, "Fortunata!" four times and more. And in she came, with her yellow waistband hoicked up so high that it revealed her cherry-red slip below. She was wearing criss-crossed anklets and dainty white slippers with gold embroidery. She wiped her hands on her neckerchief and settled down on the couch where Habinnas's wife Scintilla was draped, clapping her hands at Fortunata's appearance.

Fortunata kissed her.

"My dear," she said, "fancy seeing you here!"

Fortunata then proceeded to pull the bracelets off her chubby arms and dangle them in front of Scintilla's admiring eyes. She didn't stop there; she eventually slipped off her anklets and her gold hairnet – twenty-four carat, she said. Trimalchio glanced over at her and ordered the whole lot to be brought over to him.

"The proverbial ball and chain," he said. "You can see how stupid sods like us are robbed blind. Six and a half pounds of gold she must be wearing. Actually, I've got a bracelet thing myself, not an ounce under ten pounds it weighs. Had it made out of the 0.1% I owe Mercury."* And just so nobody would think he was just bullshitting, he ordered the scales to be brought in and the weight carried round and verified. Scintilla was no better. Round her neck she was wearing a little gold casket; her Lucky Box, she called it. She took two jingling earrings out of it and handed them over for Fortunata to inspect.

"A gift from hubby," she purred. "The best you can get."

"Eh?" interrupted Habinnas. "You damn well cleaned me out, just so I could buy you a glass bean or two? Know what? If I had a daughter, I'd bloody well cut her ears off. If it wasn't for women, life would be dirt cheap. That's how it is: piss hot and drink cold."

By now the women were all pickled, shrieking with tipsy laughter and plastering kisses on each other's lips. One boasted of what a good housewife she was; another said her hubby was useless and he had too many lover boys. They were chattering away together when Habinnas quietly got up off the couch, grabbed Fortunata by her ankles and flung her up arse over tip on the couch.

"Ow! Ow!" she yelled, as her skirt flew up past her knees. She huddled up in Scintilla's arms and hid her burning red face in her napkin.

68. After a pause, Trimalchio ordered the second courses* to be brought in; the slaves took away all the tables and carried in new ones. They scattered sawdust sprinkled with saffron and vermilion, and – something I'd never seen before – powdered mica.

"I might even leave the meal at that," he mused. "After all, you're all on your seconds. But you there, if you've got anything particularly nice, let's have it."

There was a lad from Alexandria serving the hot water. All of a sudden, he piped up like an imitation nightingale.

"Oy, change your tune!" Trimalchio kept shouting.

We had another good laugh when the slave sitting at Habinnas's feet – I imagine his master had asked him to – launched into a sing-song rendition of:

Meanwhile Aeneas steered his fleet to sea.*

I'd never heard such a cacophonous assault on my eardrums. Apart from the fact that, like some ignorant barbarian, he sometimes bawled the verses out and sometimes just muttered them, he mixed in some Atellanic verses too. Result: for the first time in my life I found I couldn't stand the great Virgil. Anyway, when he eventually stopped, exhausted, Habinnas applauded and said:

"The lad never went to school. I personally took his education in hand – made him listen to all the pedlars in the marketplace. So nobody can touch him when it comes to doing an impression of mule-drivers or pedlars. Bloody wicked, he is – he's a cobbler too, and a cook, and a confectioner: talk about talent! Actually, he does have two failings – if he didn't, he'd be *numero uno*. (1): he's had his tip snipped. And (2): he snores. OK, so he's cross-eyed too. Am I bothered? No: he looks like Venus. So he never pipes down, and hardly takes a moment's shut-eye. Three hundred denarii I paid for him."

69. At this point Scintilla broke in.

"You're obviously forgetting some of the tricks that slave gets up to. He's a pimp. But I'll make sure he's branded."

Trimalchio laughed.

"Yes, I'll admit he's a Cappadocian: he doesn't let himself go short.* And I bloody well admire him for it, I really do. Can't take it with you. And listen, Scintilla, just turn off the jealousy. Believe you me; we know your type. To tell you god's honest truth, I used to bang my own master's wife a bit, till even he started to think something was up. So he packed me away to manage one of his farms. But soft, my tongue, and I shall give you bread."

The lousy slave seemed to take this as a compliment; he pulled a clay lamp out of his tunic and for more than half an hour made imitation trumpeting noises while Habinnas pulled his lower lip down and howled along with him. Finally the lad came right into the middle of the room, shook a bundle of reeds and imitated a band of pipe players, and then he wrapped a cloak round himself, cracked a whip and acted out the life of a mule-driver. Eventually Habinnas called him over, planted a kiss on him, offered him a drink and remarked, "Your best performance yet, Massa. You've earned yourself a pair of boots."

The whole wretched business would never have come to an end if one last course hadn't been brought in: thrushes made of fine pastry, stuffed with raisins and nuts. These were followed by quinces, with thorns stuck all over them so they looked like sea urchins. We might have coped with this, just about – but an even more bizarre dish made us feel that we'd far rather starve than eat it. It was set down in front of us and we thought it was a nice fat goose garnished with fish and all kinds of birds, till Trimalchio said:

"Friends! What you see placed before you here is made out of *one* body."

I wasn't born yesterday. I knew immediately what it was. I looked at Agamemnon and murmured:

"I'd be very surprised if it isn't all made out of wax. Or clay, of course. I've seen artificial dinners like this in Rome, at Saturnalia."

70. I hadn't even finished speaking when Trimalchio continued:

"May my property grow more than my belly, but it was all made by my chef, out of one pig. You won't find a smarter bloke. You only have to ask, and he'll make you a fish out of a sow's womb, a wood pigeon out of bacon, a turtle dove out of a haunch of ham or a chicken out of a knuckle of pork. This gave me the bright idea of giving him a name that fits him to a tee: Daedalus.* And as he's such a clever chap, I brought him a present back from Rome: some knives of Noricum* steel."

He immediately ordered them to be brought in, and looked them over admiringly. He even gave us a chance to test the temper of their edges on our cheeks.

Suddenly in came two slaves; they looked like they'd been brawling at a well, or at any rate they were still carrying amphorae on their shoulders. So Trimalchio sat as judge on the case, but they both refused to accept his verdict – in fact, they each smashed the other's amphora with a cudgel. They were clearly off their faces with drink, and we watched open-mouthed and helpless as they traded blows – until we saw oysters and scallops sliding out of the bellies of the pots. A slave boy went round picking them up and brought them round on a dish. It was quite a display of culinary finesse: but the clever chef was equal to the challenge, and offered us snails on a silver griddle, singing in his horrid quavering voice.

I blush to say what happened next. I'd never seen anything like it in my life. Some long-haired slave boys brought in aromatic oil in a silver basin, and anointed the feet of all the guests as they reclined – after they had first strung little garlands round our feet and ankles. A quantity of the same oil was then poured out into the mixing bowl and the lamp.

Fortunata had been itching to dance for quite a while, and Scintilla was clapping her hands faster than she could speak.* Trimalchio called out:

"You have my permission, Philargyrus – even though you *are* a notorious supporter of the bloody greens* – to tell Menophila, your lady friend, that she can take her place next to you."

As you can guess, we were almost pushed off our places as the slaves barged in and filled the whole couch. At all events, I saw the chef plumped down in the place above mine, the one who'd made a goose out of a pig – and he stank of salt pickle and sauces. Not satisfied with having a seat, he immediately began taking off Ephesus the tragedian;* then he insistently started egging on his own master to make a bet. "Green to win first prize at the next games!" he said.

71. Trimalchio was beside himself with pleasure at this little contest.

"My friends!" he declared. "Even slaves are men, and have drunk the same milk as us, even if a cruel fate has trodden them down. If I live, they shall soon taste the water of freedom! No – more than that – I propose to set them free in my will, every last one of them! I'm even bequeathing a farm to Philargyrus; he can have his lady friend too. And I'm giving a block of tenements to Cario, plus his 5% manumission fees, and a bed (plus bedding). I'm making Fortunata my heir, you see, and I commend her to all my friends. And I am making all this public so that my slaves will love me right now every bit as much as if I were dead."

Everyone had started to voice their thanks for their master's kindness, when he suddenly turned serious and ordered a copy of his will to be brought in, and then proceeded to read it aloud from beginning to end while the slaves all sobbed. Then he looked at Habinnas and said:

"What have you got to say to that, my old friend? You're building my funeral monument as I ordered you to? Please, if you will, put a figurine of my little dog at the feet of my statue, and some wreaths, and bottles of ointment, and all the fights that Petraites took part in, so that, thanks to your friendly offices, I'll live on after death. Oh, and I want the monument to be a hundred feet long at the front, and two hundred feet back into the field. I want all kinds of fruit trees to grow around my ashes, you see, and a really nice display of vines. You know, it's just not on for a man to keep his house in fine repair while he's alive, and not care a hoot about the place where everyone will need to stay for rather longer. So, first and foremost, I want these words added to the inscription: THIS MONUMENT IS NOT TO BE PASSED ON TO MY HEIR.* What's more, I'll take good care that my will ensures no injury is done me once I'm dead; I'm appointing one of my freedmen to act as guardian of my tomb so that none of the plebs comes running up to have a crap right next to it. And if you will, put some ships too... on my monument, breasting the waves with sails stretched full, and place me there sitting on my official seat in my official purple-striped toga, with my gold rings, all five of them, pouring out coins to all and sundry from my purse; after all, as you know, I did lay on a big public feast – it cost two denarii a head.* Include a picture of the dining couches too, if you like. And the whole of the town should be depicted, partying as if their lives depended on it. At my right hand place a statue of my darling Fortunata holding a dove, and she must be leading her little doggy leashed to her girdle, and my darling boy, and big-bellied amphorae nicely sealed with gypsum – don't want the wine spilling out! And you must have a broken urn carved, and above it a wee boy, weeping. A sundial in the middle, so whoever looks to see what time it is will read my name, whether he wants to or not. The inscription – well, have a good think and see if this doesn't seem suitable:

"CAIUS POMPEIUS TRIMALCHIO
FREEDMAN OF MAECENAS
R.I.P.
APPOINTED SEVIR IN ABSENTIA

ELIGIBLE FOR ALL GUILDS IN ROME
TURNED THEM ALL DOWN*
PIOUS, UPRIGHT, TRUE
STARTED WITH ZILCH
WORKED HIS WAY UP
LEFT 30 MILLION SESTERCES
NEVER LISTENED TO A PHILOSOPHER
ADIEU TRIMALCHIO
AND ADIEU TO YOU TOO"

72. So spake Trimalchio, and forthwith started to weep bucketfuls of tears. And Fortunata wept, and Habinnas wept, and then the whole household of slaves wept, as if they'd come along as guests to his funeral, and filled the dining room with their weeping and wailing. Even I had started to sob, when Trimalchio said, "And so – since we know we're all going to die, why don't we enjoy life? I want you to have fun: so let's all hop into the bath. I say it as shouldn't, but you won't regret it. It's as hot as a furnace."

"You're *so* right," replied Habinnas. "Packing two days into one: can't beat it, in my view."

He rose to his bare feet and started to pad along after Trimalchio, who had now brightened up.

I looked at Ascyltos.

"What do you reckon?" I said. "Personally, if I see a bath, I'll expire *super spottum*."

"Let's go along with them," he whispered, "and then, when they're all heading for the bath, we can slip away in the crowd."

It seemed like a good idea, and Giton led us through the colonnade to the front door, where the dog on the chain began barking his head off, and freaked us out so much that Ascyltos actually fell plop into the fish pond. I was one over the eight too – and I'd even been scared by the painted dog – and now, trying to pull him out as he thrashed about, I was dragged down into the watery depths too. But we were rescued by the porter; he quieted the dog down and hauled us, shivering, out onto dry land. Actually, Giton had already cunningly bought off the dog; as it barked, he chucked all the leftovers from dinner we'd given him* at the enraged mutt, and thus distracted the creature by filling him with food. But we were frozen, and when we asked the porter to let us out at the door, he replied, "You're mistaken if you think you can get out the same way you came in. No guest has ever left by the same door; they come in through one and out another."*

73. We despondently wondered what on earth to do. Here we were, trapped in a new labyrinth: the idea of having a bath had suddenly started to seem attractive in comparison. So, instead, we asked him to lead the way to the bath, where we stripped off (Giton started to dry our clothes in the anteroom); we went into the pool – a narrow little place it was, rather like a cold-water cistern, and Trimalchio was already standing erect in it. And even here we couldn't escape his filthy boasting; he kept going on about how there was nothing better than having a wash when it wasn't crowded, and how a bakery had once stood on this very spot. Then, as if tired, he sat down and – encouraged by the echo from the vault – he lifted his tipsy snout up to the ceiling and started to murder the songs of Menecrates* (or so the people who could understand his words told me). The other guests all joined hands and were jog-trotting round the edge of the bath, rattling the door hinges as they hooted with laughter. There were some whose hands were tied up; they were trying to pick up rings off the floor, or else they got down on their knees and tried to bend their heads backwards to touch the tips of their big toes. But while the others played about, we went down into the steam tub that was being heated up for Trimalchio.

By this time we were starting to sober up. We were led into another dining room, where Fortunata had laid out her treasures [...] we saw lamps with little bronze fishermen, and solid silver tables, and clay goblets with gold inlay, and wine being filtered through a cloth right in front of our eyes.

"My friends!" Trimalchio then said. "Today a slave of mine has celebrated his first shave – a decent cheese-paring chap, touch wood. So – down the hatch, cheers, chin chin! And let's keep dining until breakfast time."

74. At his words, a cock crew.

Trimalchio started at the noise, and ordered wine to be poured under the table and the lamp to be sprinkled with undiluted wine.* He even changed a ring onto his right hand, saying, "There must be some reason why that trumpeter blew a warning signal. There must be a fire. Or someone in the neighbourhood is just about to pop his clogs. Not our problem hopefully?... A handsome reward for anyone who catches that bringer of bad tidings!" Hardly had he finished speaking when a cock was brought in from nearby, and Trimalchio ordered it to be killed and cooked in a bronze saucepan. So the star chef who, not long before, had made birds and fishes out of a pig proceeded to chop it up and throw the pieces into the cooking pot. Meanwhile Daedalus drew off the seething brew, and Fortunata ground up pepper in a boxwood pepper-grinder.

These titbits went down a treat. Trimalchio then turned to his slaves and said, "So why haven't you lot had dinner yet? Off you trot; it's time for the next shift." So the next lot hove into sight. Those leaving said, "Bye, Caius!" those arriving said, "Hi, Caius!"

But at this juncture something really did put a damper on the proceedings; a slave boy came in, not bad-looking either, one of the new shift of waiters; Trimalchio was soon all over him and starting to smother him with kisses. Whereupon Fortunata decided to insist on her rights; sauce for the gander and all that. She started bad-mouthing Trimalchio and calling him a filthy this and a randy old that, and a man who just couldn't keep his hands to himself. Finally she flung in his face: "Dirty dog!"

This rattled Trimalchio so much that he flung a wine cup at her face. She shrieked as much as if he'd bashed her eye in, and put her trembling hands up to her face. Scintilla was alarmed too, and took her quivering friend into her protective arms to shield her. A slave boy even dutifully applied a cool little jar to her cheek, and Fortunata leant her face against it and started to groan and weep. But Trimalchio retorted, "Excuse me, but has this Syrian flute-player completely forgotten that she started out on the sales platform? That's where I plucked her from, and made an honest woman out of her. But she goes puffing herself up like a frog, and doesn't spit in her own bosom;* she's a wooden top, not a woman. But if you're born in an attic then even in your dreams you can't have the faintest idea about what life in a real house is like. So I'll be damned if I don't bring that smarty-boots Cassandra to heel. I'm a tuppeny-ha'penny fool – to think I could have married ten million sesterces. You know I'm not lying. Agatho – he runs the perfume shop – took me to one side only recently. 'I beg you,' he says, 'don't let your family line die out.' But I'm a good-natured bloke, I don't want people to think I play around. So I've stuck the axe into my own leg. OK: I'll make sure... with your claws you'll want to dig me up again. But you've really dropped yourself in it this time. So, Habinnas, I absolutely forbid you from placing any statue of her on my tomb, otherwise she'll be trouble and strife even when I'm dead and gone. *And*, so she feels the edge of my anger, I forbid her to kiss me even when I'm lying there dead."

75. After this explosion of wrath, Habinnas started asking him to calm down a bit.

"*Humanum est errare*," he said. "We're men, not gods."

Scintilla burst into tears and said the same and appealed to Trimalchio's better nature and begged him not to be so stern. Trimalchio couldn't hold back his tears.

"Let me ask you, Habinnas," he sobbed, "if you want to enjoy your wealth, then tell me: if I've done anything wrong, just spit into my face. I kissed that fine upstanding boy not because he's a handsome lad but because he's so hard-working. He knows his ten times table, he can read a book just by looking at it, he's bought a suit of Thracian armour out of his own pocket and he's bought a round-backed chair with his own cash, and a couple of ladles too. Isn't he worth more than a passing glance from me? But oh no, Fortunata won't have it. Standing on our dignity, dear, are we, my little goose? Don't bite off more than you can chew, you vulture, but don't make me show my teeth, my love, or I'll give you the sharp edge of my tongue. You know me: once I've made my mind up, it's written on tablets of stone. Anyway, time to think of the living. My friends! Do make yourselves comfortable! You know, I used to be where you are now. But thanks to my sterling qualities, look what I've achieved! A bit of common sense, that's all a man needs; the rest's all rubbish. I buy cheap and sell dear, no matter what anyone else says. I'm positively bursting with happiness. Hey, my old snoreress, still snivelling? I'll give you something to snivel about. Anyway, as I was just saying, if I've reached these giddy heights, it's thanks to my frugal living. When I came over from Asia, I was no taller than this candlestick. Actually, I used to measure myself by it every day, and smear grease from the lamp onto my lips, to grow a beard quicker. By fourteen I was my master's darling boy. And there's no disgrace in doing what the master orders. The master's wife used to enjoy my company too, know what I mean? Say no more, eh? But I'm not the sort to boast. **76.** Then, as the gods willed, I became master of the house, and lo and behold I was the brains, and the boss was soon dancing to my tune. Not much more to say, really: he made me a joint heir with Caesar,* and I came into an estate that would do a senator proud. But nobody's ever satisfied. I got the business bug. I won't bore you with the details, but I built five ships, loaded 'em up with wine (worth its weight in gold back then) and sent the freight off to Rome. You'd think it was a put-up job: every single ship got wrecked. No, you couldn't make it up. Neptune swallowed thirty million in one day. Think I lost heart? No, damn it! Bitter, me? Just pretended it never happened. I built new ships: bigger, better, luckier. Nobody was going to say *I* was lacking in balls. You know, a big ship's actually a big brave gutsy thing. I loaded 'em up with more wine, bacon, beans, perfume, slaves. That was when Fortunata 'gave to the poor', bless her. All her jewellery she sold, her whole wardrobe too, and pressed over a hundred gold coins into my hand. They were the leaven that made my fortunes rise. When the gods decree, there's no delay. In one single voyage I made a nice round sum: ten million. I immediately bought back the estates that had belonged to my late master. All of 'em. I build myself a house, I buy slaves, pack mules; whatever I touched just grew and grew like a honeycomb. When I was starting to own more than the whole town put together, I threw up the game; I retired from business and started to use freedmen as agents. I was already starting to get bored with business when this astrologer who'd turned up in our town, a little Greek chap called Serapa – had the ear of the gods – bucked up my ideas. He even told me things I'd already forgotten; he explained everything to me – needle, thread, the lot; he could see right into my guts; he almost knew what I'd had for dinner the day before. You'd have thought he'd lived with me since for ever. 77. Go on, Habinnas – you were there, I think, at the time? 'This is how you won your lady wife. You don't have much luck with your friends – people never thank you as much as you deserve. You possess some huge estates. You're nourishing a viper in your bosom.' Etc. And – though I shouldn't really say this to you – he told me I've got thirty years, four months and two days left to live. What's more, I'm going to inherit any day now. So says my oracle. If I can extend my estates just as far as Apulia, I'll have done enough for one life. In the meantime I built this house, while Mercury watched over me. As you know, it used to be a tumbledown old place; now it's a temple. It has four dining rooms, twenty bedrooms, marble colonnades (two), a suite of rooms upstairs, the master's bedroom (where I sleep), a nest for this little viper here, a bloody lovely room for the porter... and the guest wing can sleep a hundred. Any old how, when Scaurus* came, he wouldn't stay anywhere else – and *he* has a house he inherited from his father, down on the seafront. There are plenty of other things for you to see. I'll show you in a jiffy. Believe you me; if you've got a penny, you're worth a penny; if you've got it, flaunt it. So your friend was once a frog and is now a prince. Meanwhile, Stichus, bring in the shroud I want to be carried off in. Bring aromatic oil too, and a taste of what's in that jar; I want my bones to be washed in it."

78. Stichus jumped to it and brought a white winding sheet and a purple-edged ceremonial toga into the dining room [...]

We were requested to feel the quality of the wool. Then he gave a little laugh and said, "See to it, Stichus, that neither mice nor moths corrupt them, else I'll burn you alive. I want to go out in a blaze of glory, so that the whole neighbourhood will pray for me." He straight away opened a little bottle of spikenard, and anointed us all, saying, "I hope this will refresh me as much when I'm dead as now that I am alive." And he ordered a little wine to be poured out into a wine bowl and gravely said, "Consider yourselves invited to my memorial service."

It was really getting too vomit-inducing. But then Trimalchio, quite disgustingly drunk, ordered the next act – a group of trumpeters – to be brought into the dining room, and propped himself up on his pile of pillows and stretched out full-length on his deathbed and said: "Now I want you all to pretend that I'm dead. Play something nice."

The trumpeters started blaring out a noisy funeral march. One of them in particular, a slave of that undertaker who was about the most decent man among them, blew such a loud blast that he woke up the whole neighbourhood. So the nightwatchmen on duty in the area thought Trimalchio's house had caught fire. They smashed the front door in and started to spread chaos, as per usual, with water and axes. This was our chance. We muttered some excuse to Agamemnon and legged it as fast as if there really had been a fire [...]

79. There was no torch to guide us on our way as we stumbled along, and it was midnight. There was silence everywhere, and not much chance of meeting anyone with a light. On top of that, we were still drunk, and we didn't know the area at all, so even in the daytime we'd have felt lost. And so, for nearly a whole hour, we dragged our torn and bleeding feet over the sharp flints and broken pots that dotted the road, until finally Giton's bright idea put us straight. The clever lad had marked all the posts and pillars with chalk, as he'd been afraid of getting lost even in broad daylight; we could see them even through the pitch-black darkness, and they shone bright enough to show us wanderers our way. But our troubles weren't over even when we did find our way back to our lodgings. The old gal there had been swilling the booze with her lodgers all night long, and now you could have set fire to her and she wouldn't have felt a thing. And we might even have had to spend the night on the doorstep if a messenger hadn't turned up.* He raised a bit of a racket, but not for long: soon he broke down the door and let us into our lodgings.

*

Oh what a night that was, gods and goddesses!
How soft our bed! How hot our clinging bodies,
Our straying mouths panting such deep dark kisses,
Our souls melting and drifting here and there.
Farewell, all mortal care!
So I began to perish.

I spoke too soon. I was completely sozzled and my hands trembled and fell, and Ascyltos, the inventor of every crime in the book, stole away my boy from me in the darkness of the night and bundled him into his own bed, and took every liberty you can imagine – with somebody else's bro, a lad who either didn't realize what he was doing wrong or else hid his feelings... So Ascyltos dozed off in the arms of another man's lover, oblivious of every human law. So when I woke up and groped round my bed I found it empty, my sweat cheat gone [...]

If there is any faith in lovers... I didn't know whether I ought to run my sword through them and push them over the edge from sleep to death. Then I decided on a more sensible plan of action, and started pummelling Giton until he woke up, and I glared at Ascyltos and hissed, "You bastard! So much for our so-called friendship! It's over. Just get your things and go. Move it. Find somewhere else to do your dirty business."

He didn't put up a fight. We divided our proceeds fair and square, but then he said, "Right! So now we divide the boy up too." **80.** I thought this was just a glib parting shot. But he wasn't joking; he drew his sword, murder in his eyes. "Think you're going to dote on this prize all by yourself? No way. I need my share; if I don't get it, I'll just carve myself out a portion with my sword."

I followed his example; I wrapped my cloak round my arm and stood there ready to fight. We measured each other up like pathetic lunatics; the boy felt wretched, and kept clasping our knees crying and begging us to stop. He didn't want an ordinary lodging house to be the scene of a Theban tragedy,* and he didn't want us to stain such a beautiful, holy friendship with each other's blood.

"Listen!" he yelled. "If you really must fight, here's my bare throat. Bring it on! Stick your swords in! I'm the one that should die – I've totally ruined a sacred friendship!"

We were touched, and dropped our swords. Ascyltos broke the silence.

"We need to sort this out. Listen. The boy can decide who he wants to go with. It's up to him who he wants as a bro. His call."

Well, Giton and I went back for ever. We were practically blood brothers. I wasn't worried. I rashly accepted the conditions, and placed my fate in the judge's hands. He didn't even pause to think it over; didn't even pretend to hesitate – I'd no sooner voiced my agreement than he jumped to his feet and announced that he wanted to go with Ascyltos. I felt as if a thunderbolt had struck me; there and then I flopped down on the bed. My death sentence had been pronounced and I'd have killed myself there and then – but I didn't want my enemy to gloat over his triumph. Ascyltos swanned off with his prize and abandoned me. I'd been his dearest comrade-in-arms just moments before; we'd gone through thick and thin together, and here I was, left in a strange place, alone and rejected.

> When a friend needs me, he calls me "loyal friend".
> but it's really just a game of snakes and ladders.
> When Lady Luck smiles on me, friends, you smile;
> and when she frowns, then you run off a mile.

The players come to act their farce onstage;*
"Father", or "Son", or "Rich Man" are their names.
But soon they're all rolled back into the scroll:
we see reality behind the role.

----

81. I didn't waste much time on tears. I was worried that Menelaus the assistant tutor might find me alone in my lodgings; that would have been the last straw. I gathered up my things and rented a remote little place down by the beach. Here I glumly shut myself away for three days. The thought kept coming back to me of how alone and rejected I was; I beat myself up over my fate, I fell positively ill, I moaned and groaned aloud. "If only the earth would open up and swallow me! Or the sea – its storms don't even spare the innocent! I fled from justice, I cheated the arena, I killed my host – oh yes, so many badges of bravery... and now I'm a beggar, an outcast, stuck in lodgings in some little Greek town, alone. And whose fault is it that I've been abandoned like this? Some horny teenage boy just itching for it – even *he* freely admitted he deserved to be packed away for good. He won his freedom by offering up his arse... selling his good looks like that... people could screw him for the price of an admission ticket... using him like a girl even though they knew he was a boy... And the other one? The day he was supposed to wear a man's toga he wore a dress instead; his mother persuaded him never to grow up to man's estate; in the slaves' prison he played the tart; then he went bankrupt and started swinging the other way, broke up an old-established friendship and, like some come-with-me-sweetie girl, sold it all for a one-night stand. Bugger him! And now they're lovers and lie in each other's arms all night long. I bet they have a real laugh at me, all here on my ownsome – once they've screwed each other senseless. But they're not going to get away with it. Call me a woman and a slave if I don't pay them back in their own stinking blood."

82. I belted my sword round my waist and sat down to a square meal: I needed to shape up for the forthcoming fight. Then I dashed outside and started combing the colonnades like a madman. I looked like some thuggish desperado, intent on nothing but slaughter and bloodshed, and I kept clutching at the hilt of my death-devoted sword – when a soldier spotted me. He was just dossing around, maybe, or maybe he was a midnight mugger.

"Hey there, comrade," he said, "what's your legion? Who's your centurion?"

Lying through my teeth, I invented a legion and century for myself.

"Pull the other one," he replied. "Soldiers in your army ponce around in pansy slipslops like that then, do they?"

My face fell and I started to tremble; it was obvious to him I'd been lying, and he ordered me to hand over my weapons, or else. So I was robbed – and worse, my revenge was nipped in the bud. I made my way back to my lodgings and, as I gradually calmed down, started to thank my lucky stars that I'd been robbed

*

Water water everywhere
but not a drop to drink:
fruits hang above your head
but from your hands they shrink.
Tantalus, so tantalized,
like all men of wealth:
nothing spread before your eyes
is good for your health.
Empty gapes your mouth:
eat hunger, drink drought.

*

There's little point in trying to plan things out in advance: Fortune has designs of her own

*

83. I entered the picture gallery, which contained a superb and varied collection. The work of Zeuxis's own hands was on show, not yet faded or damaged by time, and I found Protegenes's rough sketches quite awesome – so realistic that they rivalled nature: they were spine-tingling. But Apelles's painting – the one the Greeks call μονόκνημον* – well, I positively worshipped it. The figures were outlined with such subtlety and precision that you'd have thought he'd actually captured

their souls in paint. You could see the eagle soaring through the sky as he carried the boy from Ida* up to heaven, and you could see the innocent Hylas repelling the advances of a Naiad hot for him.* Apollo was cursing his own bloodstained hands, and with a fresh-budded flower he adorned his unstrung lyre.*

Among the faces of all these lovers, even if they were just painted, I felt utterly alone.

"So," I exclaimed, "even the gods are prey to passion. Jupiter could find no one to love in his heavenly home, but, although he came down to earth inflamed by lust, he harmed nobody. The nymph who forced herself on Hylas would have restrained her feelings if she'd only thought that Hercules would come to dispute her claim. Apollo summoned his boy's shade back into a living flower; in all the myths, people enjoy love's embraces without a rival. But look at me: *I* took under my wing a comrade who turned out to be crueller even than Lycurgus."*

But then, lo and behold, as I lashed out with my tongue at the empty air, a white-haired old man* suddenly entered the gallery. He had a worried expression on his face – and yet there was a certain air of distinction about him that seemed to promise greatness. He was, however, pretty poorly dressed – and so it was quite obvious he was a writer, the kind that wealthy people just can't stand. Anyway, he came over and stood by my side

*

"I," said he, "am a poet, one – I hope – of no tame imaginings, to judge (if one may) from laurel crowns which – admittedly – are sometimes granted to rank amateurs. 'So why,' I hear you say, 'are you so shabbily attired?' For that very reason. Never has the love of things of the mind made a man wealthy.

"Trust to the sea: it's worth it.
The soldier makes a rich profit
and brings home spoils from the war.
The gigolo sprawls on a carpet
of purple, and tries not to vomit:
he's bladdered, but *just one more...*

It's a sin to go after young brides –
yet after the chase, what a prize!
But don't even think about art:
nobody gives a fart.
You'll just shiver in rags,
mocked by the wags,
filling the air with your sighs.

84. "There's no doubt about it; that's how it is. If a man sets his face against every vice, and proceeds to stride down the straight and narrow path of life, he is immediately hated, just because he is different – after all, nobody can tolerate difference, can they? And then, people who are interested only in making a fortune refuse to accept that anything might be considered more valuable than their own possessions. And so they furiously attack the lovers of literature every way they can, hoping to make them too seem of less importance than money

*

"I cannot explain why, but poverty is the sister of integrity"

*

"If only the man who hates me for my modest condition were decent enough to be mollified. But he's a battle-scarred old thief, and craftier than any pimp"

*

85. "Once I'd been taken to Asia in the retinue of a quaestor;* I was invited to stay at a place in Pergamum. I was more than happy to live there: not only was it a pleasant, cultivated home, but my host's son was a real cutey. So I thought up a good way of having him without the father suspecting me. Whenever we were all having dinner together, and mention was made of men who had affairs with pretty boys, I flared up and closed my ears to such obscene gossip; I looked so offended that the boy's mother in particular took me for a high-minded philosopher. Soon I was accompanying the handsome lad to the gymnasium in person; I supervised his studies, I was the one who acted as his teacher and warned him that nobody should be let into the house who might try to prey on his young flesh

*

"One evening we were resting on the couches in the dining room, because it was a holiday and lessons had finished early – and we'd stayed up so late having fun that we were now too tired to go to bed. It must have been about midnight; I noticed the boy was still awake. So I timidly murmured a little prayer. 'My lady Venus,' I said, 'if I can get to kiss this boy without him noticing, I'll give him a brace of doves tomorrow!' The boy heard what his reward for my pleasure would be: he immediately started to snore. So I sneaked up to the young impostor and planted a series of little kisses on him. I was very pleased things had started so well; the next morning, I got up early and chose a fine brace of doves and gave them to the boy, who was waiting impatiently. Thus I fulfilled my vow. **86.** The following night provided me with another opportunity: I raised the stakes and said, 'If I can get my dirty hands on him without his noticing or saying anything, I'll give him a brace of cocks, real fighting cocks.' The boy overheard my prayer and wriggled into position – actually, I think he even started to feel afraid that *I* might go to sleep. I removed any anxieties on that score; I snuggled up to him, full length, exploring his whole body... but I didn't go all the way. Then, the following day, I gave him everything I'd promised, much to his delight. When the third night gave me yet another chance, I got up and whispered into his ear (he wasn't really asleep): 'Immortal gods! If I can get what I desire from this sleeper, and enjoy a slow comfortable screw* with him, I'll be so happy that tomorrow I'll give him the best thoroughbred horse from Macedonia – so long, of course, as he doesn't notice.' The handsome boy had never slept more soundly. So I first cupped his milk-white tits in my hands, and then breathed a long deep kiss into his lips, and finally obtained all that I desired in a single spasm.

"The next morning he was sitting in his little bedroom waiting for me to fulfil my promise, as usual. You know how much easier it is to buy doves and cocks than a thoroughbred horse from Macedonia, and in any case, I was afraid such an ostentatious gift might make it seem that my kindliness had ulterior motives. So I went out for a stroll and returned to my lodgings a few hours later, and simply gave the boy a kiss, no more. But he looked all round and then flung his arms about my neck.

"'Please, sir,' he said, 'where's my fine horsey?'"

*

87. "Since I'd broken my promise, he wouldn't allow me to make any more overtures to him. But I soon resorted to bold measures. Just a few days later, another stroke of luck meant that we found ourselves in the same fortunate situation, and when I heard the father snoring, I begged the boy to make up, i.e. to quietly let me have my way with him – all the things you invent when it has been so long and hard for you to wait. But he was obviously annoyed and just kept hissing, 'You go to sleep, or I'm telling Father this minute.'

"But when you are bent on having your wicked way, nothing is too arduous.

"He kept saying, 'I'm going to wake Father up!' but I coiled my way up to him, and conquered (not that he put up much of a fight), and came. Anyway, he wasn't all that annoyed at my naughtiness, though he did whine that he was being taken advantage of and nobody respected him and his school friends all made fun of him because he kept boasting about the things I'd bought him... and then he said, 'Anyway, I'm not going to be like you. You'll see. If you want to, do it again.' So we kissed and made up, and I was in the scamp's good books again, and I took advantage of his willingness and then slipped off into a doze. But he wasn't satisfied with the same old thing; he was a handsome lad, fully mature, old enough to take it like a man. So he shook me awake.

"'Is there anything you'd like?' he asked. Obviously, at this stage it wasn't exactly an onerous task. Anyway, with a great deal of panting and sweating, I rubbed and pounded, and he obtained what he'd wanted all that time, and I again dozed off, tired but happy – but in less than an hour he started poking me and prodding me and saying, 'Why aren't we doing it?' He'd woken me once too often: I lost my temper and flared up and mimicked his own words, saying, 'You go to sleep, or I'm telling Father this minute!'"

*

88. I was all agog to pick his brains [...] about how old the pictures were and about some of the stories depicted that were unfamiliar to me, and at the same time to discuss our present decadence, since the fine arts had died out, and painting, for example, had vanished into thin air.

"It's money," he said. "Greed. That's what's led to the general debacle. In the good old days, virtue didn't need any finery; she was loved for her naked self. The noble arts were thriving, and everyone competed to discover whatever might be of benefit to future generations. So Democritus extracted the juice of every plant and herb, and devoted his whole life to experiments that would reveal the virtues of stones and twigs. Eudoxus passed his later years on the peak of a lofty mountain, tracing the courses of the sky and the stars, and Chrysippus purged his mind with three doses of hellebore to stimulate his powers of invention. Then there are the sculptors: Lysippus starved to death trying to perfect the outline of one single statue, and Myron, who almost captured the souls of human beings and wild animals in bronze, was the last of his line.* But we are besotted by wine and women and don't even try to understand the arts we have inherited: no, we criticize the old traditions, and whatever we learn and teach is depraved. What's become of dialectic? What's become of astronomy? What's become of the royal road to wisdom? Who has ever been into a temple and vowed a sacrifice in return for eloquence? Or prayed to drink from the fountain of philosophy? Men don't even ask for intelligence or health; they haven't even set foot on the threshold of the Capitol and they're already promising a sacrifice if only they can bury a rich relative, or dig up some hidden treasure, or make thirty million sesterces without busting a gut (or getting busted). Even the Senate, that guardian of law and morality, often promises a thousand pounds of gold to the Capitol, and provides Jupiter with a mass of clinking coins. So obviously, it's perfectly all right to have an itch for money. You can hardly be surprised that painting has declined, when an ingot of gold glitters more in the eyes of all, gods and men together, than everything ever created by those eccentric little Greeks, Apelles and Phidias.

89. "Anyway, I can see that you're absorbed in that picture showing the Sack of Troy. So I'll try and explain it to you. In verse.*

"Already the tenth harvest of siege had come;
the Phrygians were shaking their heads in doubt and dread.
Calchas's* reputation
was hanging in the balance. Darkness. Fear.
But then, as the Delian ordered,
the woody peaks of Ida were chopped down,
dragged and then sawn till the planks fell into a heap.
The plan was to turn them into a scary horse.
Inside it a huge cave is hewn,
a great grot of a hidey-hole
for a whole army of soldiers.
Brave spirits embittered by the decade-long war
creep in, the solemn Danaans crowd in,
they pack themselves in, and there in the swaggering trophy
they lie in wait.
O *patria mia!* We thought they'd sailed away
beaten, the thousand ships,
leaving our land at peace.
On that wild beast an inscription had been carved;
this, and Sinon's* brazen lies
overcame our hesitations. He had a mind
intent and most ingenious to deceive.

"Already the crowd is rushing out of the gate
to pray at this shrine. They are free; it's all over, the war.
Their eyes and cheeks run with tears,
the joy of a tremulous mind weeps where before
terror had left them dry-eyed. But the priest
of Neptune, his hair unbound,
Laocoön his name,
made the whole mob indignantly yell as he drew his spear
back and prodded the horse's womb...
But Fate stopped his hand short.
The blow rebounded. Our faith in the fake was confirmed.
But he finally steels his doddery hand again,
and sounds out the horse's high flanks with an axe. They shudder! –
the young men pent up there inside. They murmur!
And the wooden mass echoes

and echoes
   and echoes
    with fear,
foreign,
   strange...
The warriors in their prison, there to prise Troy
from the Trojans. What a surprise, for what a prize!
More tricks, total war.

"Behold!
New monster-portents soon surge into view.
Tenedos blocks the sea with its rocky ridge,
and there the sea rises, swelling,
and the wave hitherandthithering quieter than calm,
as when in the silence of night the plashing of oars
carries far, and when fleets plough the sea
and its marbled surface is beaten and groans
under the weight of the fir wood.
We spin round.
Snakes! Two of them, coiling shorewards
borne on the swell to the rocks,
their swelling breasts like tall ships
churning the sea against the coast.
Their tails slap the waves, their crests
Rise through the waves as blood-red as their eyes [...]
gleam, a flash as of lightning
makes the sea one red,
steaming,
and the waves hiss around.
Our minds misgave.
The priests were standing there, wearing white woollen fillets,
the two dear sons of Laocoön
dressed in the Phrygian ritual robes
often used in this kind of sacrifice, and
suddenly
suddenly
suddenly
the glistening snakes are coiling themselves around them!

The two little boys
clap their hands to their mouths
and each helped, not himself,
but his brother first: behold such brotherly love!
Dire destiny doomed both unselfish dreads
to dual death. And see, ah see,
their father laid down his body on that of his boys,
in vain, and the snakes, gorged on death,
seize him by his arms and legs
and drag him down.
The priest lies there
a sacrificial victim between the altars,
thrashing on the ground. The sacred rites
have been profaned and Troy is doomed,
her gods are lost.

"Now full-faced Phoebe had risen with her white gleam,
leading the smaller stars by her torch's bright light,
and, among the Priamids buried in night and wine,
the Danaans unbolt the gates and pour out the soldiers.
Their leaders test the strength of their steel in combat –
like a four-footed stallion untied from the knot
of a Thessalian chariot
who stretches his neck and shakes his thick mane and – *charges!*
They draw their swords;
they shake their shields;
they thrust and parry.
One truncates the lives of wine-dozy Trojans
and prolongs their sleep into the last sleep of death;
another lights torches from the altar flames
And 'gainst the Trojans summons the Trojan fanes..."

90. There were people walking through the colonnades: some of them
heard Eumolpus's recitation and started hurling stones at him. He
accepted this as the usual applause awarded to his genius; he threw
his cloak over his head, and dashed out of the temple complex. I was
afraid they might take me for a poet too. So I ran after him as far as the
beach and, as soon as we were out of range and could pause for breath,

I said, "Listen. *What* is your *problem*? Are you mad or something? You've been with me for less than two hours, and the way you talk is more like a poet than a real man. So I can't say I'm surprised that ordinary people start stoning you. I'm going to fill my pockets up with stones too, and whenever you start ranting and raving, I'll draw blood from that head of yours."

He pulled a face.

"My dear young chap," he said, "today wasn't the first time I've made an appearance and been greeted like this. You know, every time I go into a theatre to recite something, this is the warm welcome I regularly meet with. But I don't want to pick a quarrel with you too. So, reluctantly, I'll keep my mouth shut for the rest of the day."

"OK," I agreed. "In fact, no more crazy talk from you today – and then we can have dinner together"

*

I gave the innkeeper orders about a bite for supper

*

91. Who did I see but Giton, clasping towels and skin-scrapers, leaning against the wall, looking glum and perplexed. It was easy to see he wasn't enjoying his job. I wanted to see what was what with my own eyes [...]

He turned round and his face broke into a smile.

"Sweetie," he said, "I'm sorry. No weapons to worry about here: I can speak my mind. Get me out of the clutches of this bloody robber, and punish me however you want. I'm so sorry. Be really hard on me. I pronounced judgement on you: now it's my turn. I feel so wretched that I'll be totally happy if you order me to die."

I told him to stop whining: somebody might overhear and guess what we were up to. We left Eumolpus to his own devices – he'd launched into a poetry recitation in the bathhouse – and I dragged Giton out through a dark, dank passage, and ran all the way back to my lodgings with him in tow. I slammed the door shut behind us, pulled him to me and hugged him tight, rubbing his tear-drenched face against my cheek. For a long while neither of us could speak; the boy's sweet chest was heaving with sobs.

"It's a downright scandal," I muttered. "You dumped me and I still love you. You broke my heart, but it didn't even leave a scar. What have you got to say for yourself, Mr Little-Bit-On-The-Side? What did I do to deserve all this?"

Once he realized he was still loved, he stopped hanging his head in shame [...]

"I didn't want anyone else to decide between us. But no complaints – just so long as you'll say sorry and mean it," I sobbed, tears streaming down my face. But he wiped his face on his cloak and said:

"Listen, Encolpius, just think back carefully. Did I really dump you – or did *you* drop *me* in it? OK, I'll admit it, I won't deny it: I saw two armed men in front of me, I had to make my mind up quick, I chose the stronger bloke."

I kissed him on his chest, over and over, that clever, big-hearted boy, and flung my arms round him. I wanted to make it clear that I'd let bygones be bygones, and that we were the best of buddies again, and I hugged him tight to me.

92. By now it was the middle of the night and the woman had brought the supper we'd ordered. Suddenly Eumolpus banged on the door.

"How many of you are out there?" I asked, peering intently through a crack in the door to see whether Ascyltos had come along too. When I saw that he was the only visitor, I let him in straight away. He flung himself down on a bed – and then spotted Giton, laying the table.

He nodded approvingly.

"Full marks for your Ganymede," he said. "Looks as if it's going to be a really nice day."

I wasn't exactly pleased at this strange opening gambit, and I was already worried that I'd allowed another Ascyltos into our relationship. Eumolpus was persistent, and when the boy passed him his drink, he leered, "I would rather have you than a whole bathhouse full of the rest of 'em."

He greedily knocked back his drink and started moaning that he'd never had such a rough time of it.

"Do you know what?" he said. "I was nearly thrashed while I was in the bath, simply because I began to recite some poetry to the men sitting round the pool, and I was chucked out, and started looking in every corner and shouting for Encolpius at the top of my voice. A little further off there was a young lad, naked – he'd lost all his clothes

– and angrily yelling out, just as loud, for Giton. So the boys started taking me off, chortling at me as if I were some idiot, laughing themselves silly; they were extremely rude, but a huge crowd started to gather round the young man, clapping their hands and gazing at him, overawed. He was so well-endowed, you see, that he looked like a mere appendage to his own great weapon. Strapping young chap! He'd never get worn out: oh no, I bet he could start yesterday and still be hard at it tomorrow. So he soon found a helping hand – somebody, I don't know who, an *eques* from Rome (something of a louche character, or so they were saying), stopped him as he wandered round, wrapped his own clothes round him and took him home. If you ask me, he just wanted to enjoy his windfall all alone. As for me, I'd never even have got my own clothes back from that attendant if I hadn't produced someone who could vouch for me. It just goes to show: it's better to rub your prick than try to be a clever dick."

Listening to Eumolpus, my face kept changing its expression – naturally I revelled in my enemy's failures, and begrudged his successes. Anyway, I kept shtum as if I didn't realize where this story was leading, and told him what we'd ordered for dinner

*

93. "If it's allowed, we don't want it; our minds are easily misled and choose what's bad for us.* So:

> "The pheasants obtained from Colchis
> near where there flows the Phasis*
> are tasty meat, so fresh and sweet,
> like African fowls, so hard to get,
> which is why they're all such a treat.
> But a good white goose or a pretty duck
> seem dull because they cost just one buck,
> while a wrasse from afar is wonderful fare,
> ploughed up from Syrtis,* where *mal de mer*,
> and even shipwreck await you.
> Mullet's a bore, just like the missus:
> life is short – have an affair!

The rose reveres the cinnamon,
there's nothing new under the sun
except the recherché and the rare."

"So is this what you'd promised?" I said. "No more poetry today? For god's sake spare us this, at least! *We've* never stoned you. If anyone drinking in the same tavern so much as sniffs the name of a poet, he'll rouse the whole neighbourhood and we'll all be tarred with the same brush. Leave us out of it: don't forget what happened in the picture gallery and the bathhouse."

Giton took exception to me talking like this. He's a gentle lad at heart: he didn't think it was right for me to slag off an older man, and said I'd forgotten my manners – after all, I'd been kind enough to order dinner, and now I was spoiling it all by being plain rude. And he added some sound advice, in his even-tempered and modest way. His words just made him seem even prettier

*

94. "Blessed be the womb that bare thee!" he exclaimed.* "And jolly well said! Beauty allied to wisdom: a rare combination. So don't go thinking you've been wasting your breath. No, you've found a man who loves you. I will sing your praises in my poems. I will be your teacher and guardian. I will follow you, even if you do not ask me. Encolpius won't mind; he's smitten with another man."

Eumolpus was lucky that the soldier I'd met had taken my sword off me, otherwise I'd have quenched the anger I felt against Ascyltos in the blood of Eumolpus. Giton noticed as much. So he left the room on the pretext of going to fetch some water, and he calmed my anger by this timely absence. So, as I started to cool down a bit, I said, "Eumolpus, I'd rather listen to you spout poetry than utter prayers of that kind. I get angry easily; you get horny easily: we'd never get on. OK, I'm a madman, if you say so. Look out, there's a loony about! Just piss off out of here this minute."

Eumolpus was gobsmacked at this outburst; he didn't pause to find out why I was so angry, but made a hurried exit, slamming and locking the door behind him and – to my dismay – taking the key with him. Then he ran off after Giton.

Trapped! I'd had enough. I decided to hang myself there and then! I'd just tied my belt to the frame of the bed (I'd pushed it upright against the wall), and was just slipping my head into the noose when the door was unlocked and in dashed Eumolpus and Giton, calling me back to the light, just as I was about to reach that bourn from which... Giton was grief-stricken and then furious; he started yelling, and pushed me with both hands down onto the bed, shouting:

"Encolpius, you've got it all wrong if you think you can die before me. *I* thought of it first! I looked everywhere for a sword when I was at Ascyltos's. If I hadn't found you in time, I'd have jumped off a cliff. I'll show you that death isn't far away if you look for it – now it's your turn to gaze at the sight you wanted *me* to see!"

He grabbed a razor from Eumolpus's hired servant, slashed at his throat with it, once, twice, and slid down to our feet. I screamed, dropped to the floor with him and tried to follow him into death with the same weapon – but Giton didn't have the trace of a wound, and I didn't feel the slightest pain. The razor wasn't sharp; in fact it was a specially blunt one designed to give apprentice barbers confidence as they practised their art, and it was still in its sheath. That explained why the servant hadn't turned a hair when the razor was snatched off him, and why Eumolpus hadn't interfered in this fake death scene.

95. This lovers' tiff was still being played out when the landlord came in with the next course of the modest dinner I'd ordered. He stared at us as we rolled round on the floor with a complete absence of dignity, and then said:

"Pardon me for asking, gents – but you been drinking? Or runaway slaves? Or both? Who upended the bed? You up to something you shouldn't be? Damn me if you ain't planning to do a runner without paying the bill for your room. Real fly-by-nights, eh? I'll see about that. Let me tell you something: this block of apartments doesn't belong to some poor widow. No, it belongs to Marcus Mannicius!"

"What? Are you threatening us?" shouted Eumolpus; he took a swing and slapped the man full on his face. The landlord had been boozing with his guests, and was feeling reckless; he grabbed a little earthenware jug and hurled it at Eumolpus's head; the old man gave a bellow as the vessel smashed into his forehead, and the landlord scarpered off out of the room. Eumolpus wasn't one to stand for such an insult; he grabbed hold of a wooden candlestick, chased after the fugitive and avenged his bleeding forehead with a hail of blows. All the household slaves rushed in to watch, and a crowd of drunken lodgers pushed their way in. Here was my chance to get my own back on Eumolpus. I slammed the door on him: that way I was shot of the old brawler and had no rival to worry about: I was in possession of the room, and the night was mine.

Now that he found himself locked out, the cooks and the locals were giving him a good thrashing. One mighty warrior jabbed a spit full of hissing innards at his eye, while another seized a fork from the meat cupboard and thrust it at him, like a true soldier. A bleary-eyed old hag wrapped in filthy rags led the assault: hobbling along on an uneven pair of wooden clogs, she brought in a dog of mighty stature on a chain and set him onto Eumolpus. But lo, our hero, doughtily swinging his candlestick, warded off every peril.

96. We watched the whole thing through the chink in the door left by the broken lock. I didn't begrudge seeing Eumolpus taking his medicine. Giton lived up to his reputation for kindness – he kept insisting we ought to open the door and go to Eumolpus's help. But my wrath was not yet assuaged, nor did I restrain my mighty hand: no, I gave the soft-hearted little wimp a smart thwack on the head with my bare knuckles. Whereupon he burst into tears and sat down on the bed. I then applied each of my eyes in turn to the chink in the door, and hungrily watched as Eumolpus suffered: it was meat and drink to me, and I urged his attackers to take their time. By this point the manager in charge of the block of flats, Bargates by name, had been roused from his dinner, and was carried by two porters on a litter into the midst of the brawl – seems he had gouty feet. He then with raging and barbarian voice against the drunks and runaway slaves declaimed: but when his eyes upon Eumolpus settled, he quoth:

"O of poets the most eloquent – was it you? And will those most vile slaves not depart more hastily, or withhold their hands from all this argy-bargy?"

*

"My girl goes all snooty on me.* So, do me a favour if you will, slag her off in verse, bring her down a peg or two"

*

97. While Eumolpus was conversing with Bargates at the door apart, into the inn came a town crier with an official and a ragtag and bobtail of other people. Waving a torch that gave out more smoke than light, he read out the following description:

"Hear ye! Hear ye! Slave boy recently gone missing in bathhouse, aged about sixteen, curly hair, nice figure, pretty lad, name of Giton. Reward: one thousand sesterces to anyone willing to bring him in or indicate his whereabouts."

Ascyltos was standing by the crier dressed in a coat of many colours, holding out the description and the reward in a silver platter. I ordered Giton to slip under the bed sharpish and hook his feet and hands into the straps holding the mattress in place and make like Ulysses, hanging upside down from the bed (instead of from the Cyclops's ram) to avoid detection.* Giton didn't need asking twice; in a second, even wilier than Ulysses, he'd slipped his hands into the strap. I didn't want to leave any room for suspicion, and stuffed the bed with clothes arranged in the shape of a man about my own height.

Meanwhile Ascyltos was searching all the rooms with the official. He came to mine, and when he found the door carefully bolted, his hope swelled within him. The official inserted an axe into the joints and prised the bolts loose. I fell at Ascyltos's feet and begged him to remember our friendship and what we'd been through together, and to let me at least see my little bro. I was faking it, of course, but to add a touch of plausibility to my request, I added, "I know you've come here to kill me, Ascyltos. Why else bring axes? Fine: take your revenge! Look, here's my neck, shed my blood, that's what you're after: the search warrant is just a front."

Ascyltos said this wasn't what he wanted, he really was only after his runaway slave, and didn't want anyone at all to die, especially not anyone begging for mercy, and certainly not a boy whom – even after their fateful quarrel – he still loved dearly. **98.** But the official was made of sterner stuff. He grabbed a rod from the innkeeper and lunged under the bed with it, and poked it everywhere, even into the cracks in the walls. Giton twisted his body out of reach, hardly daring to breathe, and even pressing his face against the bedbugs in the bedding [...]

Now that the door was smashed, it couldn't keep anyone out of the room; in stormed Eumolpus in a violent rage, yelling, "The thousand sesterces are mine! I'm off after the town crier, and I'm going to tell him. It's what you so richly deserve for shielding Giton."

As he continued yelling, I flung my arms round his knees and begged him not to kill those who were already at death's door.

"You'd be right to flare up," I said, "if you could actually produce the boy you're after. But he ran off into the crowd; where he's gone I haven't the foggiest. For god's sake, Eumolpus, bring the boy back. Give him to Ascyltos, even."

He was just starting to believe me – but Giton couldn't hold his breath any longer. He'd have burst. He sneezed three times in succession, so hard he made the bed shake. The noise made Eumolpus turn round: why, *bless you*, he said to Giton. He yanked away the mattress and saw there a Ulysses that even a starving Cyclops might well have spared. He spun round to me.

"So, you young thief? Caught in the act! You didn't have the guts to tell me the truth. So there *is* a god who judges human affairs – if he hadn't forced the boy hanging there to betray his whereabouts, I'd still be traipsing round the taverns like a complete and utter fool"

*

Giton was much better at smooth talk than me. First he stanched the wound on Eumolpus's forehead with spider's webs soaked in oil. Then he gave Eumolpus his own little cloak in exchange for the torn tunic, and – now that the older man was calming down – covered him with a soothing balm of kisses and said, "On you, Father dearest, on you our fate depends. If you love your little Giton, it's up to you to save him right now. If only a raging fire would engulf me, me alone, or the winter sea swallow me up! For I am the sole motive of all these misdeeds – I the sole cause! With me gone, enemies would be best of friends"

*

99. "I have always lived my life, wherever I have found myself, so as to enjoy the light of each day as if it would never return"*

*

The tears were streaming down my face. I begged him and implored him to make up with me: lovers couldn't help going berserk with jealousy. But I'd make sure I never said or did anything else that might offend him. Still, he must scrape away all irritation from his heart like a real master of kindly arts, leaving not even a scar. "On untilled fields the snow does linger on, but when the earth shines bright under the plough, the light frost thaws before you can say 'now'. Thus anger does lay siege to savage minds, but slips from learned men like melting rinds."

"That is so true," said Eumolpus, "and here is a kiss to prove it. I am not angry any more. Good luck to us! Now get your stuff together and follow me – or lead the way, if you'd rather."

He was still talking when there was a loud knock at the bedroom door, and it creaked open. A sailor with a straggly beard was standing just outside. "You're standing there like lah-mana, Eumolpus, you bloody disgrace. Get a move on!"

We didn't hang about; we all rose to our feet and Eumolpus ordered his servant (who'd been asleep for ages) to set off with the bags. Giton and I gathered all we needed for the journey. I sent up a prayer to the stars, and went on board

*

100. "It really bugs me, this bloke fancying my boy.* But so what? Don't nature's masterpieces belong to everyone for free? The sun shines on everyone. The moon, with countless stars in attendance, even shows wild beasts the way to their food. Can anything be considered more beautiful than water? And yet it flows for everybody. So shall love alone be something to be stolen rather than openly prized? The truth is that I don't consider any possessions to be mine unless ordinary people envy me for them. One man – an old man at that – won't be much of a nuisance; if he tries to get his hands on my goods, he'll start puffing and panting with exertion and give the game away."

I ran through these arguments in my mind without really believing in them, and tried to quiet my uneasy suspicions; wrapping my cloak round my head, I pretended to be asleep.

But all of a sudden, as if Fate was testing my resolve, a voice on the ship's afterdeck started groaning aloud like this: "So, he's cheated me!" It was a man's voice and seemed somehow familiar to my ears; I shuddered, and my heart started thudding. But then a woman, equally vexed and angry, broke out even louder and shouted, "If any god would only deliver Giton into my hands, what a gracious welcome I'd give the runaway!"

This completely unexpected sound came as a shock; the blood drained from both of us. Me in particular: I felt as if I were being shaken to and fro by some dreadful nightmare. It took me a while to find my voice; then, with my trembling hands, I tugged at the hem of Eumolpus's cloak (he was already drifting off to sleep).

"For god's sake," I whispered, "Father, whose ship is this? Who's on board? Any idea?"

He was cross at being woken up.

"Is this why you had the idea of choosing an out-of-the-way corner on deck – so we wouldn't get any sleep? What on earth does it matter if I tell you that the ship's master is Lichas from Tarentum? He's taking Tryphaena there; she's forever roaming the world."

I trembled from head to toe, thunderstruck. I bared my throat and moaned, "OK, Fortune. You win."

Giton flung himself on my breast; he'd already practically fainted away. Then we both broke out in a cold sweat, which brought us back to life. I flung my arms round Eumolpus's knees.

"Help us!" I cried. "We're dead men! Give us a helping hand – we're fellow scholars! Death is here, and he's welcome if you deny us your aid."

Eumolpus, taken aback by our panicky demands, swore by the gods and goddesses that he had no idea what had happened. No, he hadn't any sinister designs in mind, but in complete innocence and good faith had brought us along on board with him, on this journey that he'd long been planning.

"What danger lies in wait for us here, then?" he asked. "Is there some Hannibal sailing with us? Lichas of Tarentum is a most respectable gentleman – not only is he master and captain of this ship, but the owner of several estates and a trading company; he's transporting a cargo to market. So he is the 'Cyclops', the 'dread pirate' to whom we owe this journey, and then there's Tryphaena, the most beautiful woman in the world – she cruises around from place to place. A pleasure-seeker."

"They're exactly the people we're running away from," retorted Giton, and proceeded to explain why they had reason to hate us, and the danger now menacing us. Eumolpus started to tremble. He lost all his composure. Unable to make up his mind what to do, he asked each of us to think of something quick.

"Just imagine we *have* entered the Cyclops's cave," he said. "We need to find some way out, unless we're shipwrecked (though at least that way we won't have any more to worry about)."

"No," said Giton, "persuade the helmsman to sail the ship into some harbour – you'll need to bribe him, of course – and tell him your bro's feeling seasick and is at death's door. Your worried expression and the tears in your eyes will conceal the true state of affairs. That way the helmsman will feel sorry for you and listen to your request."

Eumolpus said this just wouldn't work.

"Big ships like this cannot sail into small harbours," he pointed out. "And it is hardly likely that my bro would have started feeling sick so suddenly. Add to which, Lichas might want to have a look at the sick lad, just out of duty. You can see what a fine mess we'd be in if we ourselves led the master to the runaways. And even if we divert the ship from her long-distance route, and Lichas doesn't decide to go round the sickbeds; how will we manage to sneak off the ship without being seen by everyone? Heads covered or uncovered? Covered, and everyone will want to give a helping hand to the sick. Uncovered, and we might as well put 'wanted' signs round our necks."

102. "I've got a better idea," I said. "Why not cut to the chase and escape down a rope into the little boat? Then we cut off the tow rope and trust our lucky stars. I don't want to drag Eumolpus into this – too risky. It's not fair to saddle an innocent bloke with somebody else's troubles. I'll just be happy if we manage to abseil down safely."

"Hm," said Eumolpus, "not a bad plan... if only if it had the slightest chance of succeeding. But won't everyone spot you making your getaway? The helmsman will, at least – he's on watch all night and even keeps an eye on the movements of the stars. Say you want to slip off without his unsleeping eyes seeing you – you could try to escape from another part of the ship: but as it is, you want to slip down the stern right near the helm. And another thing: I am amazed that it hasn't occurred to you, Encolpius, that there's always one sailor lying on duty in that boat, night and day, and you're not going to dislodge him unless you kill him or shove him overboard. Do you think you lot can do that? Are you really men enough? Just look at yourselves. And as for wanting me in on the plot, I'll take any risk if it has a chance of success. But as for squandering your lives as if they were worthless – well, I guess even *you* don't want that. Look, see what you think of this idea: I'll roll you up in two blankets, tie you up and put you in with my clothes in the luggage hold – I'll make sure I leave a few openings so you can breathe and eat. Then, in the middle of the night, I'll start yelling that my slaves became worried they were going to be even more severely punished, and jumped into the sea. Then once we've arrived in harbour, I'll carry you out as luggage. No one will suspect a thing."

"I see," I retorted. "You're going to tie us up like bags and baggage? Or have you forgotten we're a trifle prone to stomachs that might just turn nasty on us? Like we never sneeze or snore? Or is it because a trick like this just happened to work out on one occasion?* OK, imagine we can last out just one day tied up: but what if the ship's held up by a lull in the breeze, or by a storm? What are we supposed to do then? Tie up clothes for too long and they get all wrinkled; bundle papers together and they get creased. We're young chaps, not used to living rough, and now we're supposed to be roped up in rags and chains like statues for export?"

*

"No: we need to find some other way of escape.* Look, I've come up with an idea. Eumolpus is a writer: he's bound to have some ink. Let's use that to dye ourselves from our hair to our toenails. Then we'll look like Ethiopian slaves in your retinue. No torture for us, hurray! Once we've blacked up, we'll fool our enemies."

"Oh yeah…" sneered Giton. "Like and why don't you snip our tips too, so we look like Jews, and pierce our ears so we pass for Arabs, and chalk our faces so Gaul will greet us as her own sons: as if just colour could disguise our faces! You need all sorts of factors to combine if a trick like that is going to take people in. So even if you imagine the dye on our faces lasts long enough, and even if a trickle of water doesn't leave telltale marks on our bodies, and even if our clothes don't stick to the ink (as so often happens, even without added glue) – all right, but can we make our lips swell up in that revolting pouty way? Can we curl our hair with a curling iron? Can we dig scars into our foreheads? Can we strut around bandy-legged? Can we drag our feet along the ground? Can we trim our beards foreign-style? An artificial colorant just makes your body dirty, it doesn't really change it. Listen, let's take the coward's way out: tie our clothes round our heads and dive into the depths."

103. "May gods and men," exclaimed Eumolpus, "prevent you from ever putting such a vile end to your lives! No, do as I say instead. As you'll have noticed from his razor, my servant's a barber: he can shave off not only your hair but your eyebrows too, right this minute. Then I'll come and mark your foreheads with a realistic inscription that will make you look like slaves punished by branding. So the words will divert any inquisitive suspicions, and your faces will be half-hidden by the branding."

We tried the trick straight away, slipping across to the side of the ship and offering our heads and eyebrows to the barber for shaving. Eumolpus filled both our foreheads with enormous letters and daubed our faces liberally with the inscription denoting runaway slaves. But as luck would have it, one of the seasick passengers was clutching the side of the vessel puking his guts out, and by the light of the moon happened to notice the barber busy at work. Odd time to do something like that! The passenger cursed the sight as a bad omen – it looked like the last sacrifices of men about to go down with their ship* – and flung himself back down on his bunk. We pretended not to hear him chundering and cursing, and returned to our glum task, and then lay down in silence and spent the remaining hours of the night in uneasy sleep

*

104. "In my sleep, it seemed that Priapus was telling me, 'You ask of Encolpius: know then that he has been led by me aboard your ship'."*

Tryphaena shuddered.

"You'd think we'd been sleeping in unison," she said. "In my dream too, it seemed that Neptune's statue, the one I saw in the four-columned temple at Baiae, was addressing me and saying, 'You shall find Giton on Lichas's ship'."

"This just shows," rejoined Eumolpus, "that Epicurus was a simply divine man – he is so witty, so scathing about ridiculous nonsense like that" [...]

Still, Lichas prayed to avert the ill omen in Tryphaena's dream.

"Who's stopping us from checking out the ship, just to show we're not actually treating the works of the divine mind with contempt?" [...]

The man, Hesios by name, who'd unfortunately caught us up to our tricks the night before, suddenly yelled, "So who are these blokes as was being shaved by moonlight last night? Not setting much of an example, damn it! I've heard that no mortal should cut a single hair or fingernail while on board, unless the wind's whipping up the sea."

105. Lichas flared up in alarm when he heard this.

"So," he roared, "somebody's had a haircut on board, eh? And in the middle of the night, what's worse! Bring the bastards out here this minute. I want to see who's for the high jump if we're to end our journey safely. They're bleeding well going to pay!"

"*I* ordered it," said Eumolpus. "But I didn't have anything unlucky in mind, especially as I'm sailing on this same ship – it was because those thugs had long straggly hair and I didn't want to look as if I was turning the ship into a prison hulk, so I ordered the dirty fellows to be given a good clean-up. Plus, the branding inscription was all covered over by their hair; we can't have that – it should be visible for anyone to read. Among other things they'd squandered *my* money on a shared lady friend – I'd dragged them away from her only the night before, reeking of booze and perfume. In fact they still stink of my inheritance, or what's left of it" [...]

And so, to appease the ship's guardian spirit, it was decided to inflict forty lashes on both of us.* They didn't hang about; the sailors were furious and came at us with ropes and tried to appease their guardian spirit with our poor blood. *I* managed to stomach three blows with Spartan stoicism. But Giton only had to feel the lash just once, and he screamed so loud his familiar voice reached Tryphaena's ears. The mistress was thoroughly alarmed – and all her servant women, drawn by those familiar tones, came running up to see him being whipped. But Giton was such a pretty boy that he'd already disarmed the sailors and, even without speaking, had started to plead his cause to that savage crowd – and now all the servants started wailing together, "It's Giton! Giton! Leave him alone, you vicious brutes! It's Giton, miss! Help!"

Tryphaena was already inclined to lend an ear to their plea; convinced by their words, she positively flew over to the boy. Lichas knew me well; as if he'd heard my voice, he bustled over. He didn't even glance at my hands or face, but looked down and reached out for my privates, which he proceeded to caress with an officious hand.

"Well *hello*," he said. "Encolpius!"

Nobody should be surprised that Ulysses's nurse* discovered the scar which proved his identity after twenty full years, when a clever bloke like this, presented with a runaway whose every bodily and facial feature was disguised, unerringly hit on the one thing that would betray me! Tryphaena burst into tears when she saw us being punished – she thought the marks on our foreheads were real prisoners' brands – and she started to ask plaintively what jail had interrupted our wanderings, and whose hands had been so cruel as to inflict this pain on us. But then, she added, slaves who've run away just because they get tired of their comforts *do* deserve some punishment […]

106. Lichas was stung at these words and leapt forwards. "You stupid bitch," he roared. "Do you think a branding iron made the wounds for the ink to sink in? I wish their foreheads really *had* been branded – it would have been some last consolation to us. But as it is, we've been taken in by a ham performance and fooled by a fake inscription."

Tryphaena was inclined to take pity on us, since she still had feelings… but Lichas hadn't forgotten the way his wife had been seduced and he himself slandered and mocked in the Porch of Hercules,* and his face darkened even more.

"The immortal gods *do* intervene in human affairs, Tryphaena: I suppose you know that. They brought these sinners on board my boat without them realizing, and informed us what they had done by sending similar dreams to both of us. So ask yourself whether we can pardon men when a god himself has handed them over to us for punishment. As far as I'm concerned, I'm not a cruel bloke, but I'm scared that, if I let them off, it's me that'll be for it."

Tryphaena completely changed her tune when she heard words of such supernatural significance, and decided not to interfere in the punishment – in fact she agreed that it was exactly what we deserved. She'd been just as wronged as Lichas – after all, her reputation as a clean-leaving woman had been questioned in public [...]

*

107. "I believe I am a man of some repute, and my clients have chosen me to perform this duty and to reconcile them with men who were once their closest friends.* Do you really think that these young men fell into this snare by chance? But all travellers first ascertain whether they can trust the man conveying them. You feel you have already gained partial satisfaction; be merciful, and let these men go to reach their destination. Even savage, merciless masters rein in their cruelty once their runaway slaves have penitently come back home – we spare the conquered, and the proud in battle tame. What more do you want? What more can you desire? There, in front of you, you see them, lying prostrate: young men who are freeborn, decent and (this must weigh more than either argument) former close friends of yours. By god, if they *had* stolen money of yours, if they *had* betrayed your confidence and damaged your reputation, even then the punishment you've witnessed would be satisfaction enough. Look: you can see slavery written all over their foreheads, and their freeborn faces disfigured by a self-imposed sentence."

This plea for mercy was interrupted by Lichas.

"Stop confusing the issue," he retorted, "and just deal with one thing at a time. Point number one: if they came back of their own accord, why did they shave all the hair off their heads? A man who disguises his face isn't trying to say sorry, he's plotting some new crime. Point number two: if they really wanted to make amends, with you as an intermediary, why did you do everything you could to hide your protégés away? From all of this it's obvious that these buggers fell into the trap by accident and that you desperately started looking round for some way of evading our anger. When you try to make us out to be the villains of the piece by calling them 'freeborn' and 'decent', just make sure you don't spoil your case by sounding smug. What's an injured party supposed to do when the guilty men fly slap-bang into their punishment? So what if they *were* our friends once? That just means they deserve even harsher punishment. A man who just hurts strangers is called a thief, but if it's his own friends, well, that's just inhuman."

Eumolpus interrupted this most unfair litany of complaints.

"I know it is looking bad for these poor young chaps," he said, "especially because of that haircut in the middle of the night: this makes it seem that they came on board accidentally rather than on purpose. But I want you to hear the plain and simple truth of the matter, just as it happened. The fact is, even before they came on board, they wanted to shed that bothersome and superfluous weight off their heads, but a favourable wind suddenly rose and they had to postpone their planned haircut. And they reckoned it was quite irrelevant *where* they actually started on the task, once decided – they were ignorant of the law and lore of sailors."

"But why shave their hair off, given the mess they found themselves in?" persisted Lichas. "Unless of course bald men generally attract more sympathy... Anyway, what's the point of trying to get at the truth through an intermediary? What have you got to say, thief? What salamander has singed off your eyebrows? What god have you sacrificed your hair to? Just tell me that, you poisonous bastard."*

108. I was dumbstruck at the prospect of being punished, and too confused to think of anything to say, since the case was all too clear. My head was completely shaven and I looked a fright [...] I had no eyebrows, my whole forehead was bald, I was in no position to say or do anything at all. But when a soaked sponge was wiped over my tearful face and the black ink had run all down my cheeks and dissolved all the distinguishing marks into a sooty cloud, they weren't just mad at me, but filled with loathing [...]

Eumolpus yelled that he wouldn't stand for it. Nobody was going to harm young freemen: it was wrong, and illegal. And these weren't just empty words: as the men moved in, threatening and shouting, he stood his ground. His slave joined him in his protest, as did one or two of the passengers – but they were pretty feeble, and their support was moral rather than physical. I didn't stand idly by, but shook my fist right in Tryphaena's face and declared, loud and clear, that I'd resort to violence if she didn't stop mistreating Giton. She was a real bitch, I shouted – the only one on the whole ship who deserved a thrashing. This display of aggression on my part made Lichas even angrier, and he jeered at me, saying I'd given up my own case as a bad job and was now shooting my mouth off on someone else's behalf. Tryphaena was just as blazing mad, and divided everyone on board into two rival camps. On our side, the freelance barber, already armed, handed out his trusty blades to us; on the other side, Tryphaena's slaves were air-boxing with bare fists: nor did the field of battle fail to resound to the shrill cries of the slave women. The helmsman alone swore that he'd leave the ship to drift if we didn't put an end to this stupid nonsense – we were a pack of frigging fools, he yelled. But it was too late to stop the brawl: our enemies were fighting for vengeance; we were fighting for our lives. Many fell, on both sides, though none were actually killed; even more were wounded and, drenched in blood, retired from the field: but we were too angry to let up. Then the mighty hero Giton turned a razor against his own damn prick and threatened to cut it off, since it had done quite enough damage already – but Tryphaena stepped in, sincerely anxious to prevent such a horrible crime. I kept raising a barber's razor to my throat, though I had no more intention of killing myself than Giton had of carrying out his threat. But he played his tragic part with more assurance; he knew that he was holding the same razor that he'd already made a pretend cut in his throat with.

The battle lines thus being drawn up on each side, and this clearly threatening to be no ordinary skirmish, the helmsman not without difficulty induced Tryphaena to conclude a truce, like a herald with a caduceus. Oaths were uttered and accepted, according to the custom of our forefathers; she brandished an olive branch which she had seized from the ship's figurehead, and strode boldly towards us, shouting:

> "What madness changes now peace into strife?
> Have we deserved this fate? No Trojan hero
> abducts aboard this ship an Atreid's wife!
> No mad Medea takes her brother's life
> to fight her foes!* Yes – despised love is strong,
> but why resort to arms to right that wrong
> amid the waves? Won't one death do for you,
> without the need to fill the sea with blood,
> or with a sword provoke the enchafed flood?"

109. So, in a loud, impetuous voice, the woman poured out her words; the line of battle wavered for a while; hands were recalled to the ways of

peace; arms did cease their warfare. Taking advantage of this change of heart, Eumolpus our leader gave Lichas the rough edge of his tongue, but then signed the peace treaty. It read: "You, Tryphaena, do hereby solemnly promise not to lay any complaint *re* any wrong done to you by Giton, nor, if any such has been perpetrated prior to this day, will you bring a case or in any other manner whatsoever pursue an action against him; nor will you order the boy to do anything against his will, neither a hug, nor a kiss, nor indeed a nice long shag, without forking out for the said privilege the sum of one hundred denarii up front. Furthermore, you, Lichas, do hereby solemnly promise not to pursue Encolpius with your slanderous insults, nor to pull horrid faces at him, nor to enquire where he sleeps at night, and if you do so enquire, for each individual injurious act committed against him you shall pay two hundred denarii up front."

So, the truce with these words having been sealed, we laid down our arms, and – lest any anger be left in our minds after the oath thus sworn – we decided it would be a jolly good idea to kiss and make up. Cheers and applause on every side; hostilities subsided; we now tucked cheerfully into the picnic that was spread out on the battlefield. The whole ship thereupon echoed to our songs, and as a sudden lull had slowed down our course, some men aimed their spears at the leaping fish, while others hauled in the wriggling prey on freshly baited hooks. Various sea birds even settled down on one of the yardarms, and an experienced hunter threw a woven web of reeds over them; they became entangled in the limed twigs and were let down into our hands. The breeze stripped their feathers off while they were still mid-air, and the plashing foam sent the feathers fluttering and skimming over the waves.

Lichas had just started to cosy up to me again, and Tryphaena was just sprinkling the dregs of a drink over Giton, when Eumolpus, who himself was pretty pickled by now, decided to start taking the piss out of bald men and branded criminals. He soon exhausted his frigid wit and returned to his poems, proceeding to declaim a funny little elegy on the subject of hair:

> "The only real emblem of beauty is hair,
> and lo and behold, it's no longer there:
> it's all fallen out like leaves from the trees
> in the chill blast of winter's breeze.

The brow is bereft of its curly roof,
and the naked scalp is no longer sun-proof.
O shifty gods! The first gift you give,
the joy of our youth, you swiftly remove."

*

"Poor guy, your hair had *such* a sheen,
more lovely than Phoebus and Lady Di,
but now your coiffure's a pure has-been,
your scalp is a mushroom worn smooth by the rain,
you run away from the mocking crowd,
in front of the girls you feel quite cowed,
decrepitude fills you with feelings of dread,
for part of your head
is already dead."

110. He had more of the same in store, I believe, even more inept than
this attempt, but at that point one of Tryphaena's maids led Giton below
decks and sexed up the boy's head with one of her mistress's curly wigs.
Then she took some eyebrows out of a casket and, skilfully following
the outlines where he'd been defaced, restored all his beauty. Tryphaena
recognized the one and only Giton; she sobbed with relief before giving
the boy a true-love kiss. I was naturally glad to see the lad looking as
handsome as before, but I kept hiding my own face away, and realized
that I looked pig ugly – after all, not even Lichas deigned to speak to
me. But as I waited there glumly, the same servant girl came over to help;
she summoned me to one side and gave me an equally lovely set of curls.
Actually, I was even more radiant: *my* wig was *blond*!

*

Then Eumolpus, our staunch supporter in times of peril and the man
responsible for peace now breaking out all over, realized that our spirits
might flag without a story or two, and started to slag off women:
fickle, they were, he said, always falling in love, soon even forgetting
their children – and no woman was so well behaved that she couldn't
be led from the straight and narrow by some dalliance with a stranger

that turned into a mad passion. It wasn't old tragedies he had in mind, or famous figures from history, but something that had happened in his own lifetime: he'd tell us, if we wanted to hear it. So, all ears, we turned to listen, and he began his story.

111. "There was a married lady from Ephesus,* and she had such a reputation for never straying that even the women from the surrounding areas were impelled to come and gaze at her in wonder. So when she lost her husband, she wasn't content just to follow the funeral procession with her hair down, beating her naked breast in front of all the bystanders as custom dictated. No, she even followed the dead man into his tomb, and settled down to keep watch over the body – it was laid out in an underground vault, Greek-style – and proceeded to weep for him day after day and night after night. She tormented herself in this way, as if bent on death by starvation. Neither her parents nor her relatives could dissuade her; she sent the magistrates packing and they eventually abandoned her; everyone mourned her as a unique and exemplary woman, since it was already her fifth day without food. As she faded away, her faithful servant woman sat with her, shedding tears in sympathy with the mourning woman and rekindling the lamp in the tomb every time its light started to fade. In the whole town, they talked of nothing but her; people of every class agreed unanimously that they'd never seen such an example of fidelity and love.

"Just then, the provincial governor gave orders for some robbers to be crucified near the little building in which this woman was weeping over her recently deceased husband. So, on the following night, when the soldier guarding the crosses to prevent anyone taking a body down for burial spotted a light shining brightly between the tombs and heard the lamenting voice of a mourner, he was – as is only human – very curious to know who it was and what they were up to. So he went down into the vault, where he saw this beautiful woman – and at first stopped in his tracks in fright, as if he'd seen some apparition, or a ghostly figure from the underworld. But then he noticed the dead man lying there, and observed the woman's tears and her nail-scratched cheeks, and deduced the fact of the matter: she was racked by intolerable grief at the death of her loved one. Whereupon he brought his supper into the tomb and tried to cheer the mourner up. She shouldn't take on so, he said, there wasn't any point; she shouldn't go breaking her heart like this; we all had to go some day, to the same resting place, etc., etc.

– in short, he said all the things people say to heal minds smarting with pain. But she turned a deaf ear to his soothing words; she beat and scratched her breast even more vehemently, and tore out her hair and laid it on the dead body lying there. The soldier wouldn't give up; he kept on talking to her soothingly, and offered her a bite to eat, but then the maid, who I imagine found a whiff of his wine more than she could resist, yielded to temptation, accepted his invitation, reached out and helped herself to food and drink – and then started laying into her mistress for being so obstinate.

"'What use will it be to you if you faint away with hunger? Or bury yourself alive? Or breathe out your last for no reason at all, before the Fates have called your number?

"'*Dost think that buried shades or ashes feel?**

"'Why won't you come back to life? Why won't you stop behaving in this stupid womanish way, and instead enjoy all the gifts of daylight while you can? This body lying here ought to be enough to persuade you to live.'

"Nobody can ignore an invitation to life. So the woman, who was parched and starving after several days of abstinence, allowed them to overcome her stubborn refusal and filled herself with food just as greedily as the servant girl who had been the first to yield.

112. "Anyway, you know what usually tempts a person when his stomach's full. The soldier had smooth-talked this modest lady out of dying; now he used the same words to seduce her. Modest she may have been, but he seemed a nice young man; he wasn't bad-looking; he had a way with words. The servant urged her mistress to give him a friendly hearing, and repeated the words:

"'*Would'st fight against a love that pleaseth thee?**

"Enough said. She'd gone for too long without food and drink – and other things too. So: hail the conquering hero. They spent their honeymoon night together, and the night after that, and a third night too; they shut the doors of the vault, of course, so that anyone, friend or stranger, who came along to the tomb would think that this most virtuous of wives had expired on her husband's body.

"Anyway, the soldier was delighted with this beautiful woman and his secret adventure; he brought along all the good things he could afford, and at nightfall hurried along to the tomb with his provisions.

"Meanwhile the parents of one of the men who'd been crucified saw that the guard wasn't on duty. During the night, they took their son down from the cross and performed the last ceremonies over him. That way they evaded the soldier's notice while he was taking time off – and when, the next day, he saw that one of the crosses was empty, he was terrified that he'd be for it now, and explained to the lady what had happened. He wasn't going to wait for the court martial to pronounce sentence, he said; he'd punish his own negligence with a thrust of his sword. So she'd better prepare a place for him to end it all; the gloomy vault would now do for both her husband and her lover.

"The lady was as tender-hearted as she was virtuous.

"'The gods forbid,' she retorted, 'that, at one and the same time, I should look at the bodies of the two men I love most. Better put a dead man to good use than kill a man still alive.'

"Whereupon she ordered him to take her husband's body out of its coffin and fix it to the empty cross. The soldier took advantage of this clever woman's ruse – and the next day, people wondered how the dead man had climbed onto the cross."

113. This story made the sailors roar with laughter; Tryphaena blushed all over, and nuzzled Giton's neck affectionately. But Lichas wasn't laughing. He shook his head angrily.

"If the governor of that province had done the right thing, he'd have put the dead husband back in his tomb and crucified the woman."

He was probably thinking about Hedyle, and the way his ship had been pillaged when she eloped.* But we'd agreed on a truce, and it was time for him to move on – and we were now all feeling so cheerful that anger was out of the question. Anyway, Tryphaena was now sprawled across Giton's lap, covering his chest with kisses one minute, smoothing the curls on his shaven head the next. I was feeling depressed and not best pleased by the terms of this new treaty, and didn't touch any of the food or drink, but cast resentful sidelong glances at each of them in turn. Every kiss of theirs pierced me, every sweet little nothing that horny bitch uttered. I couldn't decide whether I was angrier with the boy for pinching my mistress, or with my mistress for leading the boy astray: I hated the situation for both reasons, it all hurt me more than the captivity I'd just escaped from. Add to which, Tryphaena didn't talk to me the way you'd expect of an ex you were still on friendly terms with, and Giton wasn't keen to drink my health in the usual way, nor – and this was the least he could have done – did he include me in the general conversation; he was afraid, I suppose, that he'd open an old wound, just as we were all making up. I was in despair; tears choked my chest; I just stifled a sob, but the effort almost killed me

*

He* tried to inveigle his way into the general merrymaking, dropping his snooty look and pleading as if with a friend

*

"If you've got one drop of decent blood in you, you won't rate him as any better than a common tart.* If you're a man, you won't go with that bum boy"

*

Nothing made me feel more ashamed than the fact that Eumolpus might realize what had been going on. I reckoned he might get his own back by lampooning me in verse. Him and his sharp tongue. Bastard!

*

Eumolpus swore a solemn oath

*

114. So we chattered away, but meanwhile the waves rose, clouds gathered on every side, and the light of day was blotted out. The sailors rushed to their posts, terror-stricken, and furled the sails before the storm. But the wind drove the waves every which way; the helmsman was at a loss which course to steer. One minute the wind was driving us towards Sicily; more often, the north wind, a frequent menace over the coasts of Italy, made it zigzag helplessly. More dangerous than any squall was the really thick darkness that, all of a sudden, had blacked out the daylight, so that the helmsman couldn't even see the prow distinctly. Then, damn me, Lichas saw that the angry waves were still rising and started to tremble; he threw himself at my feet and stretched his hands out to me.

"We've had it! Encolpius, you've got to help us! Give the ship back the goddess's robe and the *sistrum*!* Take pity, *please*! You're usually so kind!"

But even as he yelled, the wind tossed him overboard into the sea; a current undersea swept him round and round as he entered the whirlpool, and he was swallowed up in its voracious maw. Tryphaena was practically dragged away from the scene by her faithful slaves; they placed her in the little boat with most of her luggage, and in this way rescued her from certain death [...]

I hugged Giton tight, weeping and wailing.

"Is this what we've deserved from the gods? Are we to be together at last only in death? No: Fortune is too cruel even to grant us this. Look! The waves will capsize the boat. Look! The angry sea will tear us out of each other's arms. So, if you ever loved Encolpius, give him a kiss while you can, and seize this last joy from the Fates as they strike."

As I spoke, Giton pulled off his clothes; I wrapped my shirt round him and he lifted up his face for a kiss. And, to prevent any baleful wave sweeping us apart as we clung together, he tied his belt tightly round both of us.

"Whatever happens," he said, "at least death will take us off together, or the sea may have pity and throw our bodies both up onshore, and either some passer-by will cover us with stones out of ordinary kindness, or the waves, even if still raging, will perform their last task, and the unthinking sand will bury us." So I accepted this, the last of my chains, and waited like a man laid out on his deathbed, expecting an end I no longer even feared. Meanwhile, at the behest of the fates, the storm was at its height and flung itself on what was left of the ship. Not a single mast was left, not a helm, not a rope or an oar; like a rough, ill-shapen lump of wood, she drifted along with the tide

*

The fishermen quickly put out in their light little boats and rushed to seize their booty. But when they saw men prepared to fight for their belongings, they changed their minds; instead of attacking, they rescued us

*

115. We heard a strange low noise and a stifled roar, like a wild animal trying to escape, from under the master's cabin. We followed the sound – and found Eumolpus sitting there, filling a huge piece of parchment with line after line of poetry. So, amazed to see him able to find time to compose poetry with death so close, we dragged him off, in spite of his vehement protests, and begged him to be a sensible chap. But he flew into a rage at being interrupted.

"Let me finish my piece!" he shouted. "I'm having a bit of trouble with the last lines!"

What a maniac! I grabbed hold of him and told Giton to help me drag the petulant poet ashore

*

When we'd finished this job, we sadly made our way to a fisherman's cottage, ate and drank as well as we could (the good stuff had all got spoilt during the shipwreck) and passed the most dismal night imaginable. The next day, as we were discussing what direction to head off in, all of a sudden I caught sight of a man's body, floating along on a gentle eddy, being brought to shore. I glumly halted and, teary-eyed, started to inveigh against the sea's treachery.

"Here, perhaps, is a man," I declaimed, "whose wife blithely awaits him in some faraway country, or else his son, unaware of the storm, or his father – someone, at all events, on whom he bestowed one final parting kiss before departing. So this is all that remains of mortal plans! This is where the prayers uttered by lofty ambition all lead! See how man drifts along!"

I was still shedding tears over him, thinking that he was a complete stranger, when a current underseas rolled him over and his unblemished face turned to face shorewards – and I recognized Lichas, once so fearsome and unyielding, now practically flung at my feet. I did not even try to hold back my tears; I beat my breast again and again.

"Where now," cried I, "is your temper, where your outbursts of anger? Ah, look at you – a prey for fish and wild beasts, when not long ago you were boasting of your power and might! And the great ship you commanded has left not even a single plank for you to cling to. Go then, you mortals, and fill your hearts with proud imaginings! Go then, lay your cunning plans for the next thousand years, and invest your ill-gotten gains! Ah yes, it was but yesterday that this man was inspecting the accounts of his family property; ah yes, he had even fixed on the day he planned to return. Gods and goddesses, how far away he lies from his planned destination! But it is not only the sea that keeps its promises to mortal men in this way. One man will be fighting and his weapons fail him; another is praying to heaven when his house collapses all around him, burying him and his household deities; another man falls from his carriage, and his overhasty soul is smashed from his body. The greedy man chokes on his food, the frugal man dies of starvation. If you reckon it up properly, you will find shipwreck everywhere. Yes, I know: anyone swallowed by the waves has no burial place. As if it were of any importance whether our bodies are consumed by fire, or water, or the passing of time: to this favour they must come. Whatever you do, it all ends the same way. True enough, wild beasts will tear his corpse to pieces – but is fire any more agreeable? After all, we believe that punishment by fire is the worst we can inflict when angry with our slaves. What madness, then, to take such pains to ensure that the grave will leave nothing of us behind"

*

So it was Lichas who was burnt, on a pyre built by the hands of his enemies. Eumolpus duly composed an epitaph for the dead man, gazing towards the far horizons for inspiration

*

116. We gladly performed this last duty, and then headed off in the direction we had chosen, and before long had sweated our way up a mountain from which we could see, not very far away, a town on the top of a high hill. We didn't know what town it was, being strangers here – but then a farm bailiff told us it was Croton,* a very ancient settlement, once the first town in Italy. We eagerly asked him what kind of men lived on this noble soil, and what kind of business they engaged in most readily, now that so many wars had depleted their wealth.

"My friends," he replied, "if you are businessmen, think again, and look for some safer way of life. But if you think you're rather more sophisticated chaps, and brazen liars into the bargain, you've chosen the right road to a fast buck. In this town, you see, education isn't prized; there's no place for eloquence; a frugal lifestyle and a high level of morality reap no reward – no, I can tell you this much: the people you'll see in this town are divided into two categories. Either they're fortune hunters, or someone else is after *their* fortunes. In this town, nobody raises children, as whoever has heirs of his own is never given a dinner invitation or a ticket to the shows. Instead, he's barred from all pleasures, and skulks among the dregs of humanity. But those who've never married, and have no close relatives, attain the highest honours; they alone are considered as the 'most valiant' and the 'most decent' of folk. You will soon," he continued, "be in a town that looks like a plain ravaged by plague, where there's nothing but corpses being pecked to pieces, and crows to do the pecking"

*

117. Eumolpus was more cautious. He pondered the novelty of the case before admitting that this kind of hunting – for fortunes – rather appealed to him. I thought the old fellow was joking, in his whimsical poetical way – but then he added: "I only wish I could make more of a theatrical impression – I mean with a more suitable outfit and more fashionable accoutrements... now that would take people in pretty effectively! Heavens above, I wouldn't hesitate: I'd make you rich in the twinkling of an eye. Anyway, I promise" [...]

given the right outfit, to do whatever his partner in crime wanted, and to give him whatever had been found in Lycurgus's villa during the burglary. As for the money for immediate needs, he was sure the mother of the gods* would provide, with her usual generosity...

"So," said Eumolpus, "there is nothing to stop us performing our little comedy then, is there? If the business meets with your approval, I will run the show. Agreed?"

Nobody felt like rejecting such a harmless plan. So that our secret would remain safe with us, we swore on oath that we would do as he said: we'd be burnt, chained, flogged and put to the sword, and whatever else Eumolpus might order. Just like real gladiators we devoutly pledged our bodies and souls to our master. So we took the oath and then disguised ourselves as slaves, bowing before our lord Eumolpus, who thereupon gave us our lines. The story was that the poor old fellow had lost his son, a young man of enormous eloquence and promise, and then left his country to avoid having to see his son's dependants and friends and the tomb that made him shed tears every day. To add to his woes, he'd recently suffered shipwreck, and lost over twenty million sesterces. Actually, it wasn't the money that bothered him, but now that he had no attendants, he couldn't pull rank. Besides, in Africa he had thirty million sesterces, in land and bonds, and he had such a huge number of slaves in every corner of his possessions in Numidia that he could even capture Carthage.

To make this all seem more plausible, we ordered Eumolpus to keep going into fits of coughing, and to complain of loose bowels, loudly finding fault with all his food; he needed to keep mentioning gold and silver and his disappointing farms and the way his lands were always barren; every day he must sit down and do his accounts, and alter his will every month. To make the comedy complete, whenever he tried to call one of us, he'd muddle our names, so as to give the impression that he was thinking of yet other slaves who weren't present.

So it was all arranged; we prayed to the gods that all would turn out happily and well, and set off. But Giton soon wilted under the heavy load he wasn't used to, and the hired servant Corax, a grumbling lazybones, kept putting down his bundle and swearing at us for going too fast. He'd either chuck his bundle away, he threatened, or run off with it.

"Take me for some beast of burden, do you?" he growled. "Or a barge, ferrying stones? You hired a man, not a bloody horse. I'm just as free as what you are, even if my dad did leave me in the lurch, money-wise." Not content with cussing blind, he kept lifting his leg and filling the road with a disgusting noise and vile smell. Insolent bugger! Giton just laughed, and matched him fart for fart [...]

*

118. "My young friends," said Eumolpus, "poetry has caused a great deal of frustration. A man gives his lines the right metre, and weaves some subtle meaning into his period – and, lo and behold, he thinks he's already on Helicon's height. So people who are tired of the rhetoric of the law courts often take refuge in the peace and quiet of poetry, thinking it a haven of tranquillity in comparison – they imagine that a poem is easier to piece together than a polemical sally with its vivid, catchy, ahem, 'sound bites'. But a nobler spirit loves more wholesome fare, and the mind cannot conceive or bring to birth anything at all unless it be steeped in the mighty flood of literature. Eschew at all costs what might be called vulgar diction, and espouse words that are too *recherché* for the riff-raff. 'I hate the common crowd and send them hence'* – amen to that! Furthermore, let me add, care must be taken that the bright ideas do not stand out from the body of the speech; their gleam must be fully woven into the 'text-ure', as they say, of the piece. Witness Homer, and the lyric poets, and our Roman Virgil, and Horace's ingenious inventions. The others, you know, either did not see the right path to poetry, or saw it and were too afraid to walk along it. Take the Civil War: a huge theme – and anyone who tackles it needs to be a real man of letters if he is not to sink under the burden. It is not a matter of making poetry out of real events: the historians can write about those far better. No: allusions, and divine interventions, and episodes inspired by the high sentences of myth and fable – this is the route down which a free spirit must plunge headlong, creating the impression more of a revelation uttered by some divinely mad prophet than an accurate statement made on oath before witnesses.

"If you like, here is an example: a little sally of mine, even if I have yet to provide it with a final polish"*

*

119. "VICTOR, THE ROMAN triumphed on all fronts:
by land, by sea, by air, by moon, by sun...
but still he wanted more.
The prows of heavy-laden ships
whipped up the foaming waves, and if
a secret bay lay hidden beyond, or if
some land held out of the promise of brown gold,

it was potential prey; grim wars of plunder
brewed, *as the Fates decreed it thus*.
The ordinary joys of life
were now deemed dull, and pleasure stale,
rubbed worn by common use. The wave-tossed soldier
sea-shantied songs of praise to Ephyran bronze;
earth was prodded and probed for her glittering treasures
brighter than purple. Here, Numidians...
and there the Chinese had sleek silks despoiled,
and Arabs had stripped bare their very own fields.
CRASH!
Oh no, more violence...
Now look – peace torn and rent!
They hunt wild beasts through the forests of the Taurus Mountains.
Ammon, far off in Africa, is frisked
for his tribute of monster tusks (so many lives lost).
Weird-hungered creatures freight the fleets,
the padding tiger in his golden cage
is trundled in to gorge on human blood.
'Yeehah!' 'Howza!' 'Go get 'em!' (shouts the crowd).
Oh god... what fate will bring is barely...
it's shameful, it's...
    total ruin...
They mimic Persian rites and snip
the foreskin of boys scarce in their teens
and ruin their tools of love.
The best years of their lives are pent and blocked [...]
Where's nature now? She looks to see. She's gone.
He-whores mince by, togged up, limp-wristed, very
alluring, as on a catwalk, hair let down... but
they are no-men with, no, nothing there.
Look!
Torn from the soil of Africa, a table
of citrus wood, its polished gleam reflects
those hordes of slaves, those lovely purple gowns;
its maculations mimic vulgar gold.
Eye-catching... but it's sterile, common wood,
and round it gathers a crowd of wine-soused yobs;

the soldier with an appetite for pillage
grabs for his sword, and heads off after plunder.
The palate too is dainty:
a wrasse is brought from Sicily to table
still swimming in sea water, and the sea foods
dredged from the banks of the Lucrine Lake* will sell
a meal, they're so *de luxe*, and thus delicious...
The waters of Phasis are orphaned of their birds;*
silent now lie its shores; a lonely breeze
breathes on the leaves in lonely solitude.
Madness afflicts the Field of Mars as much;
the freeborn Roman sells his vote for gain.
The people are for sale, a Senator's seat –
yours at a price! Old men have lost their virtue,
their freedom; all their ex-power now bows down
to money; their ex-majesty
grovels for gold.
Even Cato loses power and is pushed out
by the mob; the man he loses to
wishes he hadn't won, and rues the day he tore
the rods of office from Cato:*

It wasn't a man who got pushed out, it was,
in this one man, Rome's power and decency.
Rome was shafted.
She took it like a woman, she let them screw her,
and not one solid man stood up for her.
Populus Romanus just went down the plughole:
Glug! High interest rates.
Glug! Mounting debts.
'Safe as houses'? No: repossessions rising.
Mortgaged up to the hilt is every body.
Like the virus seeding in the silent marrow
the illness ravages from head to foot,
baying and yelping.
The last resort for desperate men is violence,
they hack their way back to commodities squandered by wealth.
For the destitute, attack is best defence.

So there she lies, ROMA,
wallowing in an aroma of shit,
   snoring her head off.
Could the arts of reason stir her back to health?
Or only madness, war and iron bloodlust?
120. Fortune produced three generals; all three
ended up buried beneath a pile of weapons,
killed off by Enyo* in a mighty gorefest.
Parthia holds Crassus;
The Great lies by the waters of Libya;
   Julius* infused treacherous Rome with his own blood;
and, as if earth could not take such a weight of graves,
She scattered their ashes. *Sic transit gloria mundi.*
Between Parthenope*
and the fields of the thriving city of Dicarchis*
there lies a chasm cut deep down through the earth,
perfused with the waters of black Cocytus.
This sinister phenomenon
is due to the wind spirit,
effusing furious foam.
This land in autumn is not green;
neither does the flourishing field nourish the grass
on its turf, nor do the leafy thickets ring
or echo to the songs of rival birds
in spring,
but chaos, and tumble-jagged rocks of black
pumice stone grin in the grim
   gloom of the cypress grove.
In this abode Father Dis* lifted his head,
lit by the flames of pyres,
flecked by the whitened ash,
and yelled out against winged Fortune:
'O ruler of the fates of men and gods,
Chance, enemy of all hubristic rulers,
lover of change, and restless mover-on,
Ah! Can't you feel the weight of Rome now pressing
down on you, can't you prop that doomed mass up?
The youths of Rome hate their remaining strength,

and can barely handle their crushing wealth. Just look!
They waste their piles of pillage and spoils on raves.
They build houses of gold and palaces high as the stars.
Waters are expelled with stones,
the sea is born in the fields,
and, the-fixed-order-of-things having-been-overturned,
they rebel.
Ach! Even MY kingdom they're after now.
Earth is torn open for them to lay their foundations
– the fools! – and gapes in dismay: the caves
hollowed in the hillsides dismally echo, as men
invent useless uses for stones, and the shades of hell
whisper about their hopes of winning heaven.
So, Chance, to work! Change your looks from peace to war!
Stir the Romans up! My kingdom needs more corpses!
My long-dry lips thirst for a new perfusion of blood!
My gal Tisiphone* hasn't washed her bloodthirsty arms
in blood since Sulla's sword supped full,* and earth
bristled with corn and pushed up into light
grain that had grown thick and fat on blood.'
121. Thus Dis, and heaved to take her hand in his,
strained till the earth cracked wide. Then Fortune poured
words from her fickle heart and thus she did reply:
'O my begetter,
the darkest deeps of Cocytus obey you;
if I may tell the truth without fear or favour,
your wish will be granted; my anger's as great as yours;
deep in my breast the flame burns my bones as deep.
All I have bestowed upon towering Rome I hate;
all the gifts I have given I rue. The god
who raised those lofty towers will topple them now.
I cannot wait to cremate those men and glut
myself on their blood. I see it, I see it already!
The field of Philippi filled with the fallen, twice!
The pyres of Thessaly and tombs of Iberia too.
In Libya I see, o Nile! your barriers burst;
the bay of Actium; everyone falls back
in terror of

the army of

APOLLO

– so open wide the thirsty realms of your kingdom
and beckon fresh-dead souls to enter in!*
Porthmeus* the boatman
will struggle to ferry the ghosts of the men in his skiff;
he'll need a whole navy… And you, Tisiphone,
pale girl, fatten yourself up a bit – eat, eat!
Slurp at the bleeding wounds. Down to the Styx
and its shades the whole wide mangled world is led.'

122. Fortune had spoken, and straight away
a cloud quivered and was shivered by a bursting flash
of flickering lightning. The father of shadows subsided,
closed the gap in the earth,
trembled all over, white with fear.
Lo, his brother* had thundered!
Omens from heaven revealed
the disasters of war and the travails to come: for behold,
the Titan's* face was twisted and bolted with blood,
and he turned back to the dark to hide, as if
already he'd seen the throes of civil war.
Over there Cynthia* hid away her full round face
and withheld her light from the crime. The mountain tops
came clattering down and the peaks echoed and boomed;
the doomed rivers no longer wound their way
between familiar banks, but mazed and failed.
The sky resounds to the sound of the shock of steel;
the quavering trumpet blares up Mars to the stars;
Etna at once is licked by weird new fires,
and shoots her lightning bolts into the sky.
Look…
Over there…
Between the tombs and the piles of unburied bones,
the faces of ghosts, all shrieking and gibbering. The horror!
A blazing flame surrounded by unknown stars
sucks new blazes after it. And Jupiter

descends afresh in a rain of blood.
These riddles were soon made plain by the god. For Caesar
stripped off his lazy cloak and thought, 'Revenge!'
He threw down his *De Bello Gallico* weapons.
He seized his weapons instead for *De Bello Civili.**
Up in the airy Alps
a Greek god once bestrode cliffs that tumble down
and allow men to clamber up, and so there is
a place sacred to the altars of Hercules.
A wall of snow seals off this place in winter,
and lifts its white summit right up to the stars.
The sky seems to have fallen away here.
The snow never thaws in the sun's full radiant heat,
it never melts in the breezes of the spring;
it spikes erect in the ice and frost of winter.
On its louring shoulders it could hoist up the whole round earth.
Over these peaks marched Caesar,
his army shouting, 'Hoo-rah!' He chose a place
and from the mountain top surveyed the fields
of fair Hesperia,* far and wide, and raised
both hands to the stars, and said with his voice, he said:
'Jupiter, You-Who-Can-Do-All-Things!
And you, Saturn-Land!
Land that once thrilled to the sound of my steel,
land over which my triumphs tramped and tramped,
hear me!
I am reluctant to launch Mars against the enemy lines;
my hands do not want to strike.
But I must – insulted and injured,
exiled from my city, though I stain the Rhine with blood,
though I cut off the Gauls when they march yet again on our Capitol,
victory makes exile even more inevitable for me.
I have slaughtered the Krauts;
I have been granted sixty triumphs;
I am clearly starting to get a bit too big for my boots.
But who exactly are those men that fear my fame?
And who are the ones that stop me from waging war?
Traitors and mercenaries! Rome, my mother, will

stepmother them... You want my opinion? No
vile coward will keep my right hand from its strength,
Not without a fight – it's time to kick ass. So – *Soldats!*
¡Hasta la victoria siempre!
Vorwärts – marsch!
Forwards, *compañeros*, forwards!
Make eloquent tongues of your swords!
All of us stand accused of the one crime, all
face wipe-out if we fail. *Merci, mes braves*!
I wasn't alone when I *veni vidi vici.*
Since reprisals threaten our every triumph,
and our victories have been rewarded with a hail of shit,
let Fortune judge: *alea iacta, un coup
de dés*, et cetera. Cry *havoc* and do
Your damnedest. Well, that's all I have to say:
armed here I stand:

                  with such warriors how fail?'

So he proclaimed; from the sky the Delphic bird
flew, a good omen, and beat the air as it moved.
From the left side of the bristling grove, strange voices
were heard, and a fiery flame flashed fiercely forth.
Even Phoebus streamed with a brighter gleam than usual,
and a golden glow haloed his beaming face.
123. Caesar, emboldened by these encouraging omens,
advanced the standards of Mars and made the first move
in this quite new-fangled tale of derring-do.
At first
the ice and the ground bound in white frost did not
put up a struggle but lay low in the kindly cold.
Then
the regiments broke through the fettered clouds,
the four-footed skittish steeds
smashed the bonds of the waves,
I.e., in short, the snows melted. Soon rivers from the peaks
were gushing newborn down, but then these too –
it seemed like someone had ordered them to... – stood still
and the waves stammered themselves static. Ruin? Frost?

The running sore of waters now lay hard
enough to cut. It had played them up before
and let them down again; feet slithered and slid;
all in a clatter the men the horses the weapons:
A congestion, a heap.
It never rains but it pours, and now it hailed
on Caesar's men, the clouds were concussed by a gale
of solid ice and shook their burdens loose;
winds torn apart by the blast,
the sky broken apart by lumps of hail.
Now the clouds broke too and clattered down on the swords,
and congealed ice showered them like a wave of the sea.
Earth was overwhelmed by the weight of snow;
overwhelmed were the stars above in the sky;
the rivers were glued to their banks, quite overwhelmed.
But Caesar was not (overwhelmed, that is); he leant
on his mighty spear! He crushed the frost-stiff fields
under his fearless foot! He strode on down
that mountain like Amphitryon's fierce son*
clomping down from Caucasus's lofty heights,
or Jupiter when he put his grim face on,
and lowered himself down from the pinnacles of
towering Olympus, dashing aside the spears
of the Giants-about-to-die.
Meanwhile,
as Caesar storms down the lofty mountain ramparts,
Rumour in terror, beating her fluttering wings,
flies to the towering top of the Palatine Hill
and ominously bangs into all the statues of the gods
with this Roman thunder. 'Fleets are out at sea!
Through every Alpine pass they come, the troops
dripping with German gore!'
Swords blood slaughter fires,
all the *desastros della guerra*
flit to and fro before their eyes.
Thud!
Thud!
Thud!

The hearts of terrified men,
this way and that dividing their swift minds.
One thinks *I'll head inland without delay.*
Another *I'll put out to sea; safer for me*
than staying at home. Another doughtily
thinks *I will stand and fight. Fate orders so; let's see…*
[…]
Uproar.
The people
– unedifying sight – desert the city, and headlong rush
where panic leads them. *Rome n'est plus dans Rome!*
Her once-proud citizens are shit-scared by war,
at Rumour's cue they leave their homes in grief.
One clings to his children with trembling hands;
one hides his Penates under his shirt and quits
his sorrowing threshold and slaughters the enemy,
from a safe distance…

in his dreams…
Some hug their wives, their breasts heaving with sobs,
young men stagger under their geriatric fathers' weight […]
Unused to carrying anything, they choose
to take what they're most anxious to save. One man
drags all he owns along with him
And heads unerringly towards the battle
where all his stuff will soon be captured. Dumb klutz!
Imagine a strong south wind up in the sky
rushing and swooping down upon the waves,
driving them white and black; the sailors see
rigging and rudder fail. Then one
lashes together the heavy planks of pine, while one
decides to steer for shore, an inlet, safety:
he spreads his sails for flight;
he trusts his luck to Fortune.
These are piffling complaints, no?
Take Mr Big* –
He was an earthquake for Pontus;*
He added savage Hydaspes to the Roman repertoire;*
He was the rock that wrecked the pirates, *he*

116

– not long ago – held three victory parades
and even made Jupiter jumpy.
To him the anfractuous coasts of Pontus bowed;
to him the submissive waves of Bosphorus sank.
BUT – the shame of it! – with the brace of consuls he legged it;
shucking off the title of *imperium*,
so that Fortune might see the runaway back of
mighty Mr Big himself.
(*Ain't* she just fickle?...)
124. This virus spread everywhere,
even among the gods, whose power it sapped.
Helter-skelter they scarpered: rout in heaven!
The kindly hosts of deities were repelled
by the waves of anger and fear sweeping the earth.
They forsook them, and turned their faces from
the battalions of men to swift destruction doomed.
The snow-white arms of Peace are black and blue
with bruises; she hides her face, defeated, in
Her helmet, shuns the world, seeks shelter where
inexorable Dis holds gloomy sway.
She's not alone: with her come humble Trust,
and Justice (her hair all loose), and Concord too
in floods of tears, her cloak all torn and rent.
But over there,
the palace of Erebus* yawns open wide,
and out there pour the dancers of grim Dis,
spooky-shaggy Erinys,* Bellona* frowning sombre,
and Megaera* juggling her burning torches,
and Havoc
and Treachery
and the lurid Imago of Death;
item Raving Madness,
like a creature plunging for freedom when its reins snap,
tossing her bloodstained head,
her face nothing but a goulash of gaping gashes,
which she veils with her blood-boltered helmet;
her dented Martian shield,
hedgehogged by a hundred spears,

sags, and clings to her left hand, while her right
shakes a blazing brand
and sets the world on fire.
Earth registered the seismic shock of gods;
the stars wobbled and tried to regain their poise,
and all the palaces of the sky
cracked and collapsed with a crash. And Dione* first
leads on the forces of her favourite, Caesar,
and Pallas joins her too, and the Martian man
waving his huge spear about. Mr Big
On his side has Phoebus-and-sister, and the Cyllene kid,*
and the hero of Tiryns,*
his equal in *faits et gestes*.
A quavering blare of trumpets.
Discord (also having a bad-hair day) lifted
Her Stygian head to the upper atmosphere.
The blood on her face had congealed;
her poached-egg eyes ran with tears;
her bronze-capped teeth were scabbed with rusty scurf,
her tongue flowed with gunge and pus,
her face was a nest of hissing dragons;
her tits were mangled and torn
beneath her shredded shift;
and her wavering right hand shook a blood-glowing lamp.
She – having left the gloom of Cocytus
And Tartarus behind – strides up the steep
slopes of the proud Apennines, and from their peak
could every land and every strand survey
and, streaming over the whole planet,
bodies of irregular and foreign soldiers.
And from her maddened heart she erupted these voices:
'Your hearts are fighting mad!
Now is the time: *aux armes!*
Aux armes! and torch the cities.
Whoever hides has had it.
All women now – up and at 'em!;
all lads, and all doddery old-timers too;
let the earth tremble

and the ripped-open rooftops rebel.
Marcellus!* Defend the law!
Curio!* Kick the plebs in the pants!
Lentulus!* Don't hold brave Mars down!
And you, hero-from-heaven,*
draw that shilly-shallying sword of yours,
smash down the gates,
bash in the city walls,
grab what booty you can – OK?
And you, Mr Big, can't you hold
the citadels of Rome?
Move then against the walls of Epidamnus!*
The multitudinous seas incarnadine
of Thessaly, and make it thine!'

   AS Discord decreed,
     THUS was it done upon earth."

So Eumolpus poured out his unstoppable torrent of words, and we finally reached Croton. We found lodgings in a small inn, but next day we went out to look for somewhere a bit classier, and found ourselves among a gaggle of legacy-hunters, who started asking us who exactly we were and where we hailed from. As pre-arranged, we too poured out an unstoppable torrent of high-flown words, telling them who we were and where we were from: and they easily believed us. They immediately started quarrelling over who should offer Eumolpus their financial services [...]

The fortune-hunters all vied with one another to see who would win Eumolpus's favour

*

125. This state of affairs lasted quite a while, in Croton [...] and Eumolpus, flushed with success, soon forgot how badly off he'd been before, and started bragging that nobody here could cross his path, and that his protégés would get off scot-free if they committed any crime in this town: he had friends in high places. Personally speaking, though day after day I'd been stuffing my already well-upholstered body with more and more of the good things flowing in, and though I thought that Fortune had stopped frowning on me, all the same, I couldn't help thinking that it all too good to be true, and I kept saying to myself, "What if some clever-clever fortune-hunter sends a spy over to Africa to suss out our lies? What if Eumolpus's hired servant gets tired of his present good fortune, tips off his pals and betrays our plot out of sheer spite? Oh yes: we'll have to do a runner yet again; back to the begging game, reduced to the poverty we thought we'd seen the last of. Gods and goddesses! It's a tough life for outlaws, knowing that any second they might meet with the punishment they deserve"

*

126. "Just because you know you're a handsome lad, you ponce around with your mind intent on filthy lucre; your body isn't up for a cuddle, but after cash.* What's the point of your nicely combed hair, your face thick with beauty cream, and those lingering, come-hitherish glances? What's the point of that way you mince along, so calculated that your feet measure out each step to the inch? Answer: you're showing off the fact that you're touting for trade. Just look at me: don't know much about astrology, ain't much bothered about omens, but I can see a man's character in his face, and when I see the way he walks, I can read his mind. So go on then, you sell us what we're after, there's a buyer waiting – or, if you're feeling more generous, just do it as a favour: we'll owe you one. You've said you're a slave, a nobody – but that's just what turns *her* on. She's got the hots for you. There's some women as letch after your lower classes, and nothing gets 'em going but slaves or servants showing a nice bit of leg. Some find their juices flow for a gladiator. Or a mule-driver covered in dust. Or an actor strutting his stuff on stage. My mistress falls into this last category. She jumps over the first fourteen rows in the theatre* and looks for something to love among the lowest of the low."

She certainly knew how to flatter a guy. I turned on the charm.

"So... this woman who's fallen for me... not you, by any chance, is it?"

The servant chortled at such a lack of imagination.

"In your dreams, mate! I ain't never opened my knees for no slave before, and the gods forbid that I throw my arms round someone who might well end up crucified! More the scene of married women, that:

they like kissing the scars left by a flogging, they do. OK, so I may be just a servant girl – but I'm not getting on anybody's lap unless he's a real gent."

This really made me think: two women with such opposite tastes! Kind of pervy, somehow: a servant as proud as a married lady, a married lady slumming it like a servant!

We carried on joshing each other and then I asked the servant girl to bring her mistress into the grove of plane trees. Good idea, she said. So she hised up her petticoats and turned off into the laurel grove that ran along the path. It wasn't long before she brought her mistress out of her hiding place and led her to my side. She was prettier than any picture.* Words fail me when I try to describe her beauty. She was just so... like... Her hair was naturally wavy and flowed down over her shoulders, she had a neat little forehead, with the roots of her hair swept tight back, and her eyebrows curved from the top of her cheekbones almost to between her eyes, which shone brighter than the stars in a moonless sky, and her nostrils were nicely flared, and her lips were like those imagined for Diana by Praxiteles. And as for

- her chin
- her neck
- her hands
- her white feet shod in delicate gold sandals...

well, she would have outshone the marble of Paros! So now at last I could draw a line under my old passion for Doris:

---

*

Whatever's happened, Jupiter?
You've dropped your weapons and just lie there,
among the heaven-dwellers, a silent fable?
Now, now is the hour
to sprout horns on your lowering brow,
now to hide in feathers your white hair.
This is a real Danaë.
I dare you: just touch her body:
your limbs will flow with flame and fuse with fire.

127. She found this charming, and laughed. She looked so sweet – like the moon emerging from behind a cloud and showing her full face. Before long her words expressed what her wandering fingers were already demonstrating.

"If you're not averse," she said, "to a rather distinguished lady who's only been going with men for less than a year, then I've got just the sis* for you, my love. Oh, I know all about your bro. I made so bold as to make enquiries. But what's stopping you having a lady friend too? *Me*, that is. I can kiss nicely too, you know. You only have to try me, whenever you like."

"Ah," I replied, "you're just so totally gorgeous: *I* should be asking *you* not to turn away a wanderer who wishes to be admitted among your worshippers! I'll be a faithful follower if you just allow me to adore you! And don't think I'm trying to get into this Temple of Love for free. No: I'm making a sacrifice for you. My bro."

"What?" she exclaimed. "You're sacrificing him to me? But you can't live without him! You hang on his lips, you love him as much as I want you to love me."

As she was speaking, her voice sounded so lovely, and such melodious music caressed the listening air, that it seemed as if the Sirens were singing harmoniously in the breeze. I was wonderstruck, and the sky seemed somehow to shine more brightly; so I decided to ask my goddess for her name.

"Oh," she said, "didn't my maid tell you? Circe. Not Circe as in the-daughter-of-the-sun Circe* (of course) – and *my* mother, if you please, has never stopped the world from moving. But I'll have heaven to thank if the Fates bring us together. You know, some god is already hatching a secret plot. There's a good reason for Circe to love Polyaenus:* put these names together and – what a blaze! So go on, please, put your arms round me. Don't worry about anyone spying on us: your bro's miles away."

So saying, Circe enfolded me in arms softer than the wing of a bird and pulled me down to her amid the green grass with its earthy smell.

Just as Mother Earth
once did shower

many a flower
from Ida's peak
when Jupiter
took her in his arms
in lawful love*
and the flames did quiver
in his great heart;
roses sparkled,
violets too
and soft rushes, oh;
white among green,
laughed lilies from the field:
so the soil
called Venus down
amid the soft grass;
brighter the white day,
protecting hidden love.

There we lay, side by side in the grass, kissing and kissing playfully, yes, till our pleasures became more urgent

*

128. "What's wrong?" she said. "Don't you like the way I kiss? Have I got bad breath? I haven't been eating much, you know. Am I a bit sweaty under the armpits? Or is it something else?... Are you... scared of Giton?..."

I blushed crimson, and my already flagging virility completely failed. It was as if my whole body had let me down.

"Please, princess," I said, "don't laugh. I feel wretched. I've been poisoned"

*

"Tell me, Chrysis – the truth, now!* Am I so very ugly? Is my hair a mess? Is there some defect I was born with that's ruined my looks? I'm your mistress: no fibbing. I've done something wrong. But what?"

Then she snatched the mirror from the silent girl's hand, and tried out every expression that usually brings a smile to lovers' lips; she shook out the soil-stained cloak, and hurried off into the Temple of Venus. But I felt guilty as hell and as horrified as if I'd seen something terrible, and started to wonder whether I'd been deprived of real pleasure.

Night brings sleep
and dreams deceive
a wandering eye,
and the fresh-dug soil
brings gold to the light of day:
so too our greedy hands
finger their spoil [...]
and our minds are gripped
by a terrible fear
that someone will find
our secret gold
and shake it out
of our shirt where it's hid:
then, when these pleasures have fled
from the mind they mocked, and the true
shape of things returns –
why then, the spirit yearns
for what it has lost for good
and desperately gropes
among the images of the past

*

"Well, thank you.* You love me with a true Socratic love. Alcibiades didn't lie so safe, untouched in his master's bed"

*

129. "You've got to believe me, bro: I don't think I'm a man.* I don't feel a thing. That part of my body where I was once an Achilles is now dead and buried"

*

The boy was afraid there might be gossip if he was caught with me; he tore himself away and ran off into the inner rooms

*

Then Chrysis came into my bedroom and handed me a letter from her mistress. It read:

Dear Polyaenus,
If I were a woman always up for it, I'd complain about how disappointed I was, but now I can actually thank you for your flabby performance. I've toyed with the shadow of pleasure for quite a while now. But I'm really writing to find out how you are, and whether your feet even managed to carry you home. Doctors, you know, say men just can't walk without stiff sinews... I'll tell you one thing, my young friend: beware of paralysis. I've never seen a sick man in such great danger; you're half dead already. And if the same chill spreads to your knees and hands, you might as well send for the funeral trumpeters. Anyway, where does this leave us? Well, even if I do feel deeply offended, I won't begrudge such a poor chappy as you his medicine. If you want to get better, dump Giton. You'll get some lead back in your pencil, I reckon, if you sleep for three days without your bro. As far as I'm concerned, I'm not worried: any future lovers of mine will be rather more responsive. My mirror doesn't lie, nor my reputation. Get well soon – if you can.
Circe x

Chrysis watched me read through this petulant missive and then said:

"It happens, this kind of thing – especially in this town. The women here can drag the moon down from the sky...* I'm sure this can all be sorted out too. Just write back to my mistress, a nice letter, polite and heartfelt: it'll make her feel better. There's one thing I really must tell you: ever since you hurt her, she's not been herself."

130. I was happy to obey the servant girl and wrote a letter as follows:

Dear Circe,
I admit, my princess, that I've often done wrong; I'm only human, and still young. But I've never done anything quite so bad as this before today. It's all my fault; I confess: there you have it. Whatever sentence you impose, I'll have deserved it. I've betrayed people, I've killed a man, I've profaned a temple: just demand that I be punished for these crimes. If it's my death you want, I'll bring along my sword; if you're content with giving me a flogging, I will run naked to you, my princess. Remember just this one little thing: it wasn't me who failed, but the tool of my trade. I was a soldier ready for battle, but I had no weapons. Who put a spanner in the works? I don't know. Perhaps the spirit was willing but the flesh was weak; perhaps I wanted you too much, and left it too late. I can't work out what I did wrong. Anyway, you're telling me to beware of paralysis: as if it could get any worse, now that it's deprived me of the means of having you, yes, you! Anyway, my apology in a nutshell: give me one more chance before you give up on my love. I'll make it worth your while.

Polyaenus x

*

I sent Chrysis off with this promise, and then put in some quality time with my body, the source of all my troubles. I went without a bath, and rubbed ointment over myself in moderation; then I ate some nourishing food – onions, snails' heads (no seasoning) and just a drop of wine. I took a gentle stroll before bed to calm myself down, and then went into my room – without Giton. I was so concerned to satisfy her that I was afraid my bro might drain me dry. **131.** Next day, feeling altogether sound in body and mind, I got up and went down to the same grove of plane trees, even if this inauspicious place did make me feel a little nervous, and settled down among the trees to wait for Chrysis, who would take me to the right place.

I walked up and down for a while, then sat down where I'd been the day before, and then along came Chrysis, bringing with her an old woman.* She said hello and then:

"Well now, you picky lover: have you decided to be sensible?" [...]

She took a twist of threads, all different colours, from out of her dress and tied it round my neck. Then she made a little mixture of spittle and dust, dipped her middle finger into it, and made a mark on my forehead. I wasn't too keen on this [...]

She chanted her incantation and then ordered me to spit three times, and then, again three times, to drop some pebbles onto my lap; she'd said a spell over them before wrapping them in purple. Then she held out her hands and started to feel around my tackle. Before you could say "hey presto", the sinews in my prick obeyed her command and filled the old woman's hands with a wacking great hard-on. She was pretty pleased.

"You see, my dear Chrysis?" she said. "You see what I've done? Got the little rabbit out of his hole for someone else to catch!"

*

The noble plane tree had diffused a summer shade
and Daphne* berry-crowned
and tremulous cypresses
and the shorn pine trees with their swaying tops.
Among them, with wandering waters, the foaming river
played, and vexed the pebbles with its querulous water.
This was the place for love: witness the wood nightingale
and town-dwelling Procne* – they darted between the grass holms
and the tender violets,
chasing their stolen *amours* with song [...]

She was lying there, her marble neck sunk into a golden bed, fanning the quiet air with a spray of blossoming myrtle. So when she saw me, she blushed a little, since she naturally remembered the little unpleasantness of the day before. Then, when everyone had left us, I sat down at her invitation and she laid the myrtle spray over my eyes. Now that there was, so to speak, a wall between us, she lost her shyness.

"So, how's things, you poor paralytic? Are you all man today?"

"Why ask?" I replied. "Why not find out?"

I lay on top of her, taking her in my arms, and kissed her. No black magic at work here: I kissed her again and again until I was sated

*

132. What a beautiful body;* it called out to me, a clamorous invitation to love. Mouth to mouth we kissed, great wet smackers; our fingers met and folded and wandered into every nook and cranny of love; body to body we held each other tight, one body, souls mingling

*

The lady was exasperated by my open insult, and finally decided to take her revenge.* She ran off to summon her chamber grooms, and ordered them to give me a good whipping. This was humiliating treatment enough, but she wanted more. She called in all her seamstresses, and the meanest and lowest of her slaves, and ordered them to spit at me. I covered my eyes with my hands, and uttered not a single plea for mercy: I knew what I deserved, and so I was beaten and spat on and flung out of doors. Proselenos was ejected too; Chrysis was flogged, and all the slaves were downcast and muttered to each other, asking who could have upset their mistress when she'd been in such high spirits [...]

I weighed up this change of circumstances and started to perk up. I carefully hid the scars left by my whipping: I didn't want Eumolpus to jeer at my disgrace, or Giton to be put out. I did the only thing I could to hide my shame, and pretended I was feeling ill all over; I clambered into bed and turned my blazing anger entirely against the thing that had been the cause of all my misfortunes.

> Three times I took my axe in hand,
> three times I wilted away from the deed,
> like a cabbage going to seed.
> I shied away from the steel, in dread.
> I knew what to do: I was just too scared.
> I couldn't do it.
> I wanted to, but now
> I couldn't do it.
> My todger, more frozen with fear
> than frosty midwinter solstice
> had hidden away in my belly,
> quivering like a jelly,
> so I couldn't uncover its head and put it to death,

but, anxious about the response of that old drooper,
I resorted to words to awaken it from its stupor.

Then, propped erect on my elbow, I harangued the stubborn little thing. It went a bit like this:

"What have you got to say for yourself? You're a disgrace to all men and gods! Even to call you by your proper name would be treating you with too much respect! Have I deserved this from you – being dragged down to hell when I was in heaven? Or being betrayed by you in the flower of my age, young and vigorous, and reduced to being a doddery old-timer with one foot in the grave? If you please, show your true mettle, and this time *keep it up*!"

But my angry outburst had no effect:

It looked away, its eyes fixed on the ground,
It did not bat an eyelid at the sound
Of my voice coaxing. Eloquence can talk,
But not arouse the willow from its swound
Nor raise the poppy on its drooping stalk.*

But after bad-mouthing it so nastily, I started to feel sorry for losing my temper, and secretly blushed, reflecting that I'd forgotten all sense of shame by bandying words with a part of the body that more serious-minded men don't even spare a thought for.

I rubbed my forehead for quite a while. Then I continued:

"But what was so wrong about my venting my annoyance by speaking my mind? It's only natural. And then, don't we often have harsh words for other parts of our body – our bellies, our throats, even our heads – when they keep hurting? Well? Doesn't Ulysses quarrel with his own heart, and some tragic characters lay into their own eyes, as if they could hear? Sufferers from gout damn their feet; sufferers from arthritis damn their hands, those with cataracts their eyes, and those who have often stubbed their toes blame all their pains on their feet!

Hah! Catonians!
Why do you stare at me
with furrowed brows?
Why do you condemn a work

of freshness and simplicity?
My words are pure! A life-affirming grace
laughs in them,
    and my innocent tongue reports just what folk do.
Who is ignorant of sex?
Who is ignorant of the joys of sex?
Who forbids us to warm our limbs in a hot bed?
Nay, nay, thrice nay!
The father of the truth, Epicurus
said *all you need is love*,
    for love is the τέλος* of life"

*

"There's nothing falser than people's stupid pompous opinions,
nothing sillier than their fake morality"

*

133. After my speech, I called Giton over and said, "Tell me, bro, and no lying now: that night when Ascyltos poached you from me, did he stay awake long enough to do it, or was he happy to spend the night alone, with no funny business?"

The boy touched his eyes and swore black was blue that Ascyltos hadn't forced him to do the dirty

*

I knelt down on the threshold* and prayed to the god who had turned away from me:

    "Companion of the Nymphs and friend of Bacchus,
    lovely Dione* gave you supernal power
    over the leafy woods,
    glorious Lesbos
    and green Thasos
      obey you,
    the Lydian worships you

in *adoration perpétuelle*
and has built a temple for you
in his own city of Hypaepa:*
be with me, o guardian of Bacchus,
delight of dryads,
    hear my humble prayers.
I come to you
not stained with enemy blood, I have not raised
my right hand against
your temples like an enemy: I was poor
and in want, worn out, I sinned...
but not with my whole body did I sin.
A poor man's sin is less. And so I pray:
take the burden from my mind,
    pardon this slight offence,
and whenever the time comes
for Fortune to smile on me,
    I will not leave your glory unacknowledged.
A goat will trot to your altars, Holy One,
yea, even a hornèd goat,
    father of his flock,
        trotting to your altars,
    and the young of a squealing sow,
    a sacrifice still suckling.
The *nouveau cru* of the year
will bubble in the wine bowls;
the young men
will merrily walk round your shrine three times
                    (feeling rather tipsy)"

*

During my prayer, as I was keeping a close eye on my offering, into
the sanctuary came an old woman, with her hair all torn and straggly,
dressed in shapeless black clothes; she grabbed hold of me and dragged
me out through the porch

*

134. "What nightbird hags have eaten your sinews away?* What pile of shit did you tread on, in the middle of the night, at a crossroads? Or was it a corpse? You couldn't even get away from that boy – you're a wimp, a wuss, worn-out like a horse going uphill, all that effort and sweat for nothing. And it wasn't enough for you to do wrong yourself; no, you had to make the gods angry with *me*" […]

*

And she pulled me along back into the priestess's room – I didn't put up a struggle – and pushed me over the bed; then she grabbed a cane hanging by the door and – when I didn't even respond – gave me a thwack. And if the cane hadn't snapped at the first thwack, thus lessening the force of the blow, she might well have broken my arms and fractured my skull. She made me yell with pain, and I wept bucketfuls of tears, shielded my head with my right arm and buried it in the pillow. She was quite put out, and started crying too; she sat down on the other side of the bed and, in a quavering voice, cursed the way old age slows you down. At that point the priestess* came in […]

"What's all this?" she exclaimed. "You've come into my room as if you were mourning at a freshly dug grave. On a holiday, too, when even mourners are allowed a laugh" […]

"Oh, Oenothea," she said.* "See this boy here? He was born under a bad star. Fact is, he can't sell his goods to boys or girls. You've never set eyes on such an unhappy bloke: he's a douche bag with no balls. In a nutshell: what do you think of a man who clambers off Circe's bed without even having a good old shag?"

Oenothea listened; she sat down between us and slowly shook her head.

"I know that illness," she said. "And nobody but me can cure it. And don't think I'm having you on: I just ask our young man to spend a night with me […] if I don't make that thing of his stiffer than a horn:

> "Everything in the world you can see
> is in thrall to me.
> The flowering earth,
> when I decree,

faints and languishes
when her juices run dry;
when I decree, she pours out her wealth,
and boulders and rugged rocks
spurt out waters like the Nile.
The ocean submits its inert waves to me
and the zephyrs lay their silent blasts
before my feet.
The rivers obey me,
and all the Hyrcanian tigers,
and I commanded the snakes, saying *go upright.*
But these are mere trifles...
even the image of the moon
is drawn down by my spells;
Phoebus is filled with fear
and is forced to revoke his fiery steeds
at my bidding."

135. I shuddered in horror at the miracle cure she was promising – surely some scam? I stared more closely at the old woman.

"OK," exclaimed Oenothea, "just do as I say!" [...]

She carefully wiped her hands clean, leant over the bed and gave me a kiss, and then another [...]

Oenothea placed an old table in the middle of the altar, covered it with live coals, and used warm pitch to repair a wine cup that had cracked with age. A nail had come away from the smoky wall when she took the wooden wine cup down: she now hammered the nail back in. She quickly wrapped a square cloak round her shoulders, and put a huge pot on the fire in the hearth, at the same time using a fork to take from off the meat hooks a bag with a store of beans in it, and some mouldering scraps of a pig's head that had been chopped into a thousand little pieces. She unfastened the string of the bag, she poured some of the beans out onto the table, and told me to shell them carefully. I did as I was told, and with careful fingers prised the beans out of their filthy pods. But she gave me a real bitching for being useless at it, snatched them away from me, tore off the pods with her teeth, just like that, and spat them out onto the ground like so many shrivelled dead flies

*

I was greatly impressed: necessity is the mother of invention – and here, each detail had been artfully arranged:

> No Indic ivory tricked out with gold shone here,
> and the earth did not gleam with marble trodden underfoot,
> sneered at for her gifts – no, the grove of Ceres on her holy day
> was adorned with willow hurdles and new clay [...]
> Cups, shaped by the swift rotations of the humble potter's wheel.
> Here there was a cistern made of soft lime wood,
> and wicker-work platters made of slow-moving bark,
> and a jar dyed with the juice of Lyaeus.*
> And the wall was filled with hollow chaff and pliable clay,
> with slim stalks of green rushes and rows of rough nails.
> The little cottage with its roof of smoky beams
> also preserved its wealth – the mellow sorb apples
> hung entwined in sweet-smelling wreaths [...]
> and dried savouries and bunches of grapes:
> as once in Attica
> the earth welcomed guests:
> Hecale,* the divine, worshipped from ages unto ages,
> as spake by the Muse,
> son of Battus's city,* in the years...
>   when...
> the poet...

*

136. She* nibbled at a hunk of meat as well [...]
and then with the fork replaced the pig's head (the old pig must have been born the same day as she was...) on the meat hook: but just then, the rotten wood of the stool she'd been using in order to look taller snapped, and toppled her right onto the fire in the hearth. So the neck of the pot broke and extinguished the fire that had hardly got going. A burning brand grazed her elbow, and a cloud of ashes flew up and completely covered her face. I jumped up in surprise and pulled the old woman out. I couldn't help laughing [...]

She* didn't want the sacrificial ritual to be held up by anything, so she dashed off to her neighbours' to ask them to get the fire going again [...]

So I went back to the narrow door of the house [...]

when lo and behold, three sacred geese (I imagine they came every noontime for their daily feed from the old woman) made a sudden rush at me. They had me surrounded, cackling like crazy things. They made a hideous racket; I was terrified. And one tore at my shirt, and another untied my sandal strings and tugged them right off, and one, the ringleader and chief of this savage attack, didn't think twice about pecking fiercely at my leg with his jagged bill. I forgot all my other worries – they seemed trivial: I wrenched off a leg of the little table and, using it as a weapon, started laying into the aggressive creature. Nor was I satisfied by one blow alone; I took my vengeance, and slew that goose:

> I guess it was the same when the birds of the Stymphalian lake fled
> off into the sky
> when the might of Hercules threatened them,* and the Harpies
> dripping with pus, when
> Phineus's tantalizing banquet
> was soaked in poison.* The air above shuddered with terror
> and new lamentations, and heaven's palace
> were in uproar

*

The remaining geese had already pecked up the beans that lay scattered all over the floor, and I guess that, now they'd lost their leader, they'd returned to the temple; so I, elated at my prize and my victory, chucked the dead goose behind the bed, and bathed my leg wound (it wasn't deep) with vinegar. But then, as I didn't want a bollocking, I decided that discretion – i.e. scarpering – was the better part of valour: I gathered my belongings and started to leave the house. But I hadn't even crossed the doorway of the room when who should I spot but Oenothea, coming across with a jar full of live coals. So I stepped back and tore off my jacket and, as if I was patiently waiting for her, stood at the entrance. With some broken reeds she made up the fire, and piled wood on top; then she apologized for being a bit late – her excuse being that she'd popped in to see a woman, a friend of hers, who'd refused to let her go back home until the usual three glasses had been drained.

"Anyway," she asked, "what have you been getting up to while I was away? And where are the beans?"

Personally, I'd been thinking that I'd done something really rather praiseworthy, and so I described the whole battle to her, detail by detail, and tried to cheer her up by producing the goose: it would compensate for her losses.

When the old woman saw the goose, she raised such an almighty shriek you'd have thought the geese had come waddling back into the room. I was taken aback and pretty flabbergasted that she thought I'd done something so wrong, and started to ask why she'd flared up and why she felt sorrier for the goose than she did for me. 137. But she wrung her hands again and again and spat out:

"You stupid bastard! How can you even say such a thing? You don't know what a terrible crime you've committed: you've killed Priapus's favourite, the goose that's every married woman's pride and joy. Don't even imagine you've done nothing wrong: if the magistrates find out, they'll crucify you. Literally. You've defiled my house with blood, and it was pure as pure till today, and thanks to you, anyone who's got it in for me can have me expelled from the priesthood"

*

"Please, please, pipe down!" I pleaded. "I'll replace your goose! Instead, I'll get you – an ostrich!"

*

I watched dumbstruck as the old woman sat on the bed and shed bitter tears over the death of the goose. Then Proselenos came in with the equipment for the sacrifice, and when she realized the goose had been killed she asked how it happened; then she too started sobbing, and told me how very sorry she was for me. You'd have thought I'd killed my own father, not just a common-or-garden goose.

I'd just about had enough of this nonsense.

"Please," I begged, "let me wash my hands of it all. I'll pay [...]

if I'd insulted you or murdered someone. Look, I'm putting down two gold pieces, so you can bribe the gods and buy some geese."

Oenothea stared at the money.

"I'm really sorry, young man," she said, "but I'm worried about you. I'm saying all this to you out of real affection, not ill will. So we'll take good care nobody finds out. But – you need to pray to the gods to forgive what you've done."

Got money?
The wind will blow your way.
You can safely steer your fortune wherever you want.
Marry Danaë! Go on!
Tell Acrisius to believe what he told Danaë!*
Write poems!
Speechify!
Tell the whole world to go and screw itself!
Win your cases!
Out-Cato Cato!
Proceed to the bar and have your "Proven", "Not proven"…
The equal of Servius and Labeo* (remember *them*?).
I've had my say.
Make a wish; if you've got money, it's granted.
You've got Jupiter locked up in that safe of yours

*

Under my hands she placed the jug of wine, made me stretch out all my fingers and rubbed them with leeks and celery; then, saying a prayer, she dropped filberts into the wine. And, depending on whether they rose back to the top, or sank to the bottom, she foretold the future. It didn't escape my attention that the empty nuts, the ones without a kernel but filled with air, floated on the wine, while the heavy ones, full and ripe, sank to the bottom

*

She cut the goose open, pulled out its very fat liver and from it foretold my future.

What's more, to remove any trace of the crime, she ran the goose through with a spit, and made a real feast for me – even though, as she pointed out, I'd been at death's door just a moment ago [...]

Cups of neat wine flew round too

*

138. Oenothea pulled out a leather dildo, dipped it in a mixture of oil, finely ground pepper and crushed nettle seed, and slowly started to insert it in my anus [...]

The old woman* sprinkled my thighs with the mixture... Ouch! *Bitch!*

She made a mixture of cress juice and *habrotonus*,* washed my genitals with it, picked up a bunch of green nettles and began slowly and gently to hit me beneath the navel with it

*

The little old ladies were sozzled with drink, and inevitably as horny as hell, and tried to chase me down the road. They followed me through several streets. "Stop, thief!" they shouted. But I escaped, though I ran so fast that all my toes were bleeding

*

"Chrysis, who thought you were totally not good enough for her before – she's now determined to follow you, even if it means risking her life"

*

"Was Ariadne as beautiful as she was?* Was Leda? Could Helen have competed with her, or Venus? Even Paris, who acted as umpire in the contest between the goddesses, would have given up Helen for her, and the goddesses too, if his gleaming eyes had been able to compare them all. If only I could steal a kiss, if only I could put my arms round that heavenly, divine breast – maybe my body would regain its strength and the parts of my body that were, I believe, made flabby by poison would be their old selves again. I'm not put off by insults. I was given a flogging? That's all in the past. I was chucked out of doors? That was merely a game. Just let me get back into her good books"

*

139. I writhed on the bed, twisting and turning, as if seeking the ghostly shape of my love

*

"Not me alone do god and implacable Fate pursue!
Before me, the Tirynthian* was driven from the Inachian shore!*
He had to bear the whole weight of heaven.*
Before me, Laomedon was punished by *two* gods until they were
                                            done with him!*
Pelias felt Juno's* might
Telephus* took up arms in ignorance;
Ulysses was scared stiff of Neptune's kingly power.*
Me also over the earth, over the waters of white-haired Nereus*
The Hellespontine Priapus's wrath tracks down, implacable"

*

So I asked darling Giton whether anyone had been asking after me.

"No," he replied, "not today. But yesterday, there *was* this woman, rather attractive, walked in at the door, and had quite a long talk with me. After a while I got a bit tired of her endless chatter and she finally got round to saying that you thoroughly deserved to get it in the neck and you'd be tortured like a slave if whoever it was you'd offended persisted with their complaint"

*

I was still grumbling when Chrysis appeared. She ran in, flung her arms round me and hugged me

139

"Now you're mine!" she said, "just as I'd always hoped! I yearn for you, I want you, I'm hot for you – and you won't put out this flame unless you quench it in my blood"

*

One of the new slaves suddenly came running up and informed me that my master* was mad at me as I'd been skiving off work two days now. Best thing I could do was have some suitable excuse ready for him. He was absolutely furious, and unlikely to be satisfied with anything less than a flogging for me

*

140. There was a highly respectable married woman, Philomela her name was, who'd managed to extort a fair number of legacies when she was still young, and now, as an old woman, faded and wrinkled, was planning to push her son and her daughter into the arms of childless old men, hoping to continue practising her art by proxy. So up she trots to Eumolpus and starts telling him she commends herself and her children, her dearest hopes, to his wisdom and kindness [...] He was the only man in the whole world, she added, who could inculcate decent principles into young people on a daily basis. In a word, she'd leave her children with Eumolpus in his house, so they could hear him holding forth [...] This was the only inheritance she could bequeath on them. She was every bit as good as her word. She left her daughter, a ravishing young thing, with her handsome young brother in Eumolpus's bedroom and pretended she was going out to the temple to give thanks for prayers granted. Eumolpus was pretty unassuming about sex, ahem: actually, he reckoned that I was just an innocent babe in arms in comparison with him. Result: he didn't waste any time, but invited the girl to a lesson in the sacred art of rumpy-pumpy. Anyway, he'd always told everyone he suffered from gout and general flabbiness in the groin area, and if he couldn't keep up the pretence, the whole thing risked toppling over into tragedy. So, to save appearances, he implored the girl to climb on board his goodness gracious. But he also told Corax to climb into the bed he himself was lying in, brace his hands against the floor, and give his master a good rub with his arse. Corax obeyed the order, nice and slow, and rewarded

the girl's skilful movements by keeping in time with her thrusts. When Eumolpus saw that things were about to come to the desired climax, he started urging the dutiful Corax to go faster. So, sandwiched between his servant and his lady friend, the old man swung, as it were, too and fro. He did it once. He did it again. Roars of laughter (including his own).

And me? Use it or lose it, as they say. While her brother watched his sister's antics through the keyhole, I went over and asked if he'd like me to do it to him. He's a smart boy, and was not averse to my sweet-talking. But that divine power that was still intent on persecuting me found me out even here

*

"But there are greater gods and they have restored me to my full strength. For Mercury, whose task it is to lead our souls into and out of life, has kindly given back to me what angry hands had taken away. So you can count me as more well-favoured than Protesilaos* or any other hero of antiquity."

So saying, I lifted my shirt and displayed myself for Eumolpus's approval. All of me. At first, he recoiled in horror. Then, not trusting his eyes, he took in both his hands the benevolent gifts of the gods

*

"Socrates, wisest of gods and men, used to brag that he'd never even glanced into a shop, nor allowed his gaze to wander when there was a crowd of any size. So the best idea is: always converse with wisdom" [...]

"All that," said I, "is true, and nobody deserves to fall into misfortune more quickly than those who envy other people's belongings. But how would cheats live, or pickpockets, if they didn't have little boxes or purses filled with clinking coins that they sent out like bait into the crowd? Dumb beasts are snared by food, and men are no different – they'd never be caught unless they could bite on the hook of hope"

*

141. "You promised a ship would come from Africa, with the money and your household of slaves. It hasn't turned up. The fortune-hunters

are tired of waiting, and they're less and less prepared to be generous. Either I'm very much mistaken, or our luck is starting to revert to its default position: lousy"

*

"All those to whom I have bequeathed something in my will, with the exception of my freedmen, will receive it – on one condition. They must cut my body into pieces and, in the presence of the people, eat it"

*

"We know that there are countries where this law is still observed: the dead are devoured by their own relatives. As a result, sick people are often told off for spoiling their own flesh. So let me warn my friends not to disobey my orders, but to consume my body as heartily as they cursed my spirit" [...]

His enormous reputation for wealth blinded the eyes and minds of the poor [...]

Gorgias was ready to carry out the instructions

*

"Your stomach will turn? I don't have any anxieties on that score. It'll follow your orders if you promise to repay it for one hour of unpleasantness with a heap of good things. Just close your eyes and imagine you're not eating the innards of a human being but hundreds of sesterces. As well as that, we'll find some tasty condiments to disguise the flavour. After all, no flesh tastes nice by itself, it needs to be artificially spiced up if it's to be accepted by the reluctant stomach. You want an example or two? Just look at history. The people of Saguntum were besieged by Hannibal; *they* ate human flesh, and they weren't even expecting to come into an inheritance.* And the Petelians, who were on the brink of starvation, did the same – and the banquet didn't bring them any advantage except that of keeping hunger at bay.* When Numantia* fell to Scipio, some mothers were found clutching the half-eaten bodies of their children to their breasts"

Poems

For these poems attributed to Petronius I have used the text and numbering of the Loeb edition. Whether the poems were originally part of the *Satyricon* (in which case they would have been produced by one or other of the characters, and thus often deliberately poor), or whether they are even really by Petronius, is in doubt (though metrical and lexical similarities suggest that some, at least, are authentic and belong in his novel).

1

Everyone will find what he's looking for.
Nothing pleases everyone:
this man gathers thorns, that one
roses.

2

Already autumn had cast its chill shades
and Phoebus now turned his gaze to winter,
tightening his frosty reins;
now the plane tree had begun to shed her leaves,
and the vine to count her grapes,
her young shoots now being withered:
we gazed our fill at all the year had promised.

3

It was dread that first created gods in the world,*
when the steep lightning bolts fell from the sky
and the world's ramparts were shaken by flame and
Athos was set ablaze by their impact. Soon Phoebus
rose and sailed over the land, and sank, and the moon

grew old and renewed her glory; then the star signs
were spread over the world
and the year divided up into changing months.
The nonsense gained ground, and soon inane superstition
was ordering farmers to dedicate the first fruits of harvest
to Ceres, and to garland Bacchus with ripe vine branches,
and Pales* to exult in the shepherds' handiwork;
Neptune [...] wholly sunk in the water, and Pallas
protects the inns, and the man whose prayer has been answered,
and who has sold the world for gain,
now avidly contrives to create gods for himself.

4

I don't want to be always suffusing my head with the same sweet scent,
nor coaxing my stomach with familiar wine.
A bull likes a different valley to graze in,
and a wild beast enjoys a change of food now and then.
Even the draughts of light we wash in each day
are welcome only because the hour gallops on
with a fresh team of horses.

5

A wife should be loved like lawfully gotten property.
But I wouldn't like to love my property for ever.

6

Leave your old home, young man, and head for distant shores:
a widening horizon stretches out to greet you.
Don't give up when the going gets tough. Faraway Hister,*
icy Boreas* and the happy realms of Canopus* will make your
                                    acquaintance,
and the men who see Phoebus rising again and falling:
the man who sets foot on distant sands grows.

7

For nothing is altogether useless to mortals;
when things are against us, what we rejected helps:
so, when a ship founders, yellow gold weighs you down,
but the lightness of oars bears up your shipwrecked limbs.
When the trumpets blare, barbarian steel is pressed
to the rich man's jugular:
ragged clothes are a badge of safety.

8

My little house is covered by a safe roof
and wine-swollen grapes hang from the fecund elm.
The branches put forth cherries, and the woods red apples,
and Pallas's grove collapses under its heavy-laden branches.
And now where the light soil drinks from the channelled springs,
Corycian kale* springs up, and sprawling mallows
and the poppy that will send sweet restful sleep.
And if I've decided I want to entwine snares for birds,
or prefer to catch the shy quiet deer
or pull up the quivering fish on a slender line,
these are the only stratagems known in my humble fields.
Go now, and spend what time remains of fleeting life
on lavish banquets. If the same end awaits me,
here, I pray, it may find me,
and ask for an account of how I have used my time.

9

Mad youth overwhelms us;
our good name is drowned;
we are swept away by a tide of obloquy.
Isn't that all enough?
But no: even slaves and the mob that wallows in shit
luxuriate in the wealth amassed by us!
The common slave owns a kingdom's riches, and the prisoner's cell
shames Vesta and Romulus's humble home.

Therefore virtue lies buried in the depths of the mud,
and the fleets of injustice put out white sails.

10

So too the limbs hem in the belly's winds.
When, buried within, these winds struggle to emerge,
they probe and thrust their way out, and the cold shiver
which rules over the cramped bones shivers on
until a warm sweat has trickled through the weakening body.

11

O shore, than life to me more sweet, o sea!
O happy me,
enjoying this my earth without delay!
For long ago, in this soft land,
I roused the Naiads with alternate hand!*
Here is the spring's sweet pool, and there the bay
has washed ashore its seaweed. O bright day!
A haven safe for silence, peace and pleasure.
I've lived life to the full; Fortune can never
what once the hour has given us take away.

12

So he spoke, and tore the white hair from his head with trembling
hand,
and rent his cheeks; his eyes were filled with rain,
but as the unruly river sweeps down the valleys,
when the frozen snows have perished and the languid south wind
will not allow the ice to live on the thawed earth,
so his face flowed in a raging flood, and his heart
echoed with the turbulent murmur of deep groans.

13

For mortals will hold fire in their mouths rather than
keep a secret. What you utter casually in your hall

dashes out and batters the town walls with sudden rumours.
And it is not enough to have bruited forth a secret. The work of
betrayal grows
as it hurries out and strives to add weight to report.
So, fearing to unlock the knowledge entrusted to him, the greedy
servant
dug into the soil and betrayed what he knew of the king's hidden
ears.
For the earth conceived sounds, and the speaking reeds
sang of Midas, that he was just as the informer had told.

14

There the sea and air batter and brawl with each other,
here the soil laughs as it gently guides the streamlet.
There the sailor sheds tears for sunken ships,
here the shepherd washes his flock in the gentle river.
There death confronts and throttles the greedy maw,
here Ceres rejoices to be cut by the curving sickle.
There, in the midst of water, parching thirst burns the throat,
here, even to a faithless man, many kisses are given.
Let beggar Ulysses set sail and weary the waters,
on land she will live, Penelope, pure, white-shining.

15

The man who does not wish to dash to his doom,
or compel the Fates to snap the delicate threads
with a sudden hand, should know the sea and its rage
just this far and no further. Look,
the sea swirls back and the unharming wave
gently washes his feet. Look,
the mussel is cast up in the green seaweed
and the slippery-smooth shell
is rolled along,
whorled with a hoarse-hollow sine-echo breast of a wave.
Look,
where the flood turns over and over the scurrying sands,

from the sea-humped beach emerges a bright-streaked pebble.
Whoever can tread these things under his feet,
should play safely on the shore
for *this* is the sea. Why wish for anything more?

16

Beauty is not enough, and the woman who wishes to appear a *belle*
must not be content with common ways:
bons mots, piquant remarks, playfulness, grace of speech, laughter,
surpass the work of mere innocent nature.
For beauty requires expense of art,
and grace unadorned by a touch of pretence will perish.

17

So, against the functions of familiar nature,
the raven lays her eggs when the fruits of the field are ripe.
So the she-bear, when she has given birth to her cubs, licks them
                                        into shape
and the fish produces young even though conjoined in no love.
So Phoebus's tortoise with her humid nostrils keeps warm the eggs
delivered in a clutch thanks to the favour of Lucina.*
So the bees, stirred to life, without sex,
from woven cells of wax
hum-seethe and fill the camp with soldiery.
Nature does not flourish, is not content with one tune,
but rejoices in ever changing harmony.

18

In Indian lands, there was I born
on a red and sandy shore,
where, shining-bright, the days return
and the noontime sun does soar.
There I, conceived in godly pomp,
swapped barbarous squawks for Latin:
so turf out the swans from your temples, old chump:
I'm a jolly sight better at singin'.*

19

The shipwrecked sailor, staggering around naked, seeks
some comrade likewise afflicted to whom he may lament his fate.
The farmer, his whole year's crops destroyed by a hail storm,
weeps over his fate on the shoulder of a fellow sufferer.
Death brings together the unhappy, and bereaved parents
groan with others: one hour has made them alike.
We too will try to move the stars with our mingled words;
it is said that prayers are stronger when they rise in unison.

20

You send me golden apples, my sweet Martia,
and you send the fruit of the shaggy chestnut tree.
They would all be welcome – but if, instead, *you* would come
in person, then your beauty, my dear, would adorn your gifts.
Perhaps you will press astringent apples to my palate,
but their sourness will be sweet as honey when I bite.
Yet if you tell me you will not come, my darling,
send kisses with the apples; then I will gladly devour them.

21

If you are Phoebus's sister, then, Delia, I will entrust my cause to you:
surely you will carry my prayers to your brother:
"I have built for you, god of Delphi, a temple of Sicilian marble,
and I have played you lovely songs on my slender reed pipes.
Now: if you can actually hear me,
and really *are* a god, Apollo – well, sonny,
just tell me this: where can a bloke
who's currently stony-broke
ever manage to lay hands on some money?"

22

Whatever can put an end to our wretched lamentations
is close to hand, as a candid god ordained.

Your ordinary cabbage, for instance, and berries on rough brambles
satisfy the hunger of your gnawing stomach.
If there's a river nearby, and you're still thirsty,
like, how dumb is that?
If you freeze in the east wind while the warm hearth crackles with
                                                    hot flames,
ditto.
Dread law awaits at the door of a faithless bride:
the girl in a legal bed need know no fear.
Nature bountiful gives us all to be satisfied;
what ravening hubris teaches us is endless: desire.

23

Doves have builded a nest in the warrior's helmet.
Lo, how Venus loveth Mars!

24

The Jew may worship his piggy god
and raise his cry to the ears of high heaven,
but unless he has taken a knife to the region of his groin
and artfully removed the knotted head of his putz,
he shall be cast out from amidst his people,
he shall be thrust forth from the holy city,
and shall break the commandment
that biddeth him to fast upon the sabbath day.*

25

There is one nobility
and one proof of freeborn blood:
your hands have never been timid.

26

I was lying in bed
and starting to enjoy the first quiet of the night

and to yield my shattered eyes to sleep,
when savage AMOR seized me,
and pulled me up by the hair on my head
till it hurt. "You must watch until day.
You are my slave," he said.
"You love *mille e tre*,
And you can lie here alone?
You're a hard man! Get with it! Come on!"
I leap out of bed,
my nightshirt fluttering around my feet,
I try out every street;
each street is a dead end;
now I run; now barely walk;
now I've gone too far to turn back,
and I can't just stand out there,
and I can't go home again.
Listen.
Hushed are the voices of men
and the hubbub of the town;
silent the songs of the birds
and the bark of the faithful hound.
I alone of all men dread
sleep, and when it's time for bed,
I'd rather just not go.
No...
Your wish is my command,
O mighty CUPIDO.

27

That night, Nealce, which first laid you on my breast –
may it long be cherished by us.
The bed too, and the guardian spirit of the bed, and the secretive
lamp.
They saw you gently come to our love's pleasures.
So come, let us persevere, even if older now,
and enjoy the years that soon will wear away.
It is right and proper to prolong an old love.

What we began in haste,
may it not end in haste.

28

Screwing is nasty, its pleasure is brief,
and once it's all over it seems such a bore.
We rut like the beasts, blindly seek some relief,
but the flame soon dies down and we're left feeling sore.
And yet
Yes… yes…
just like that,
not for work, just for play
with you, let's lie here kissing.
Easy now, let yourself go…
God that was good.
It's good.
It's going to be good
for ages yet.
It never fails.
Jouissance,
always a new beginning.

29

To love and at the same time to accuse?
A task too hard even for Hercules.

30

Our eyes deceive us
and our wandering senses
stymie reason with their lies.
The tower that stands four-square
when seen up close
has its corners blunted and seems round
from a distance.
When you're full, you turn away from the honey of Hybla*

And the nose often hates the odour of sweet cassia.
One thing couldn't please us more or less than another
Unless the senses were locked in combat, and the outcome uncertain.

31

The dreams that play tricks on the mind
with their flitting shadows
are not sent forth from the temples of the gods,
or by the powers that dwell in the sky:
no, everyone dreams them up for himself.
When quiet rest holds in thrall
limbs prostrate in sleep, and the mind, unburdened, can play,
in the dark it pursues the same activities as in the day.
The man who makes towns quake in war
and overruns cities with horror and fire
dreams of weapons of war, and armies in disarray,
and the deaths of kings,
and fields filled with pools of blood.
Those who plead cases in law
gaze at the statutes and courts
and are filled with terror at the sight of the judge's seat
and the throng surrounding it.
The miser hides his treasure and unearths hidden gold.
The hunter beats the woods and the meadows with his dogs.
The sailor rescues his ship from the waves or clings to its wreck,
                                        drowning.
The whore writes to her client, the adulteress grants her last favour:
and, in his sleep, the dog
sniffs after the tracks of the hare.
The pain of the suffering lingers all night long.

From the Fragments

These fragments attributed to Petronius are found in several places: Servius's commentary on Virgil, Boethius on a translation of Porphyry, Fulgentius's compendium of *Mythologies*, Isidore's *Etymologies*, etc. They occur in the context of discussions on the meaning of words, or the use of an unusual poetic metre, or a grammatical remark. I gather them here, out of these contexts, for the oddly characteristic Petronian poetry they make, even as *disjecta membra*.

...bath-woman...

...his thumb bitten to the quick...

...the soul locked in our breasts...

...the morning sun has smiled on the rooftops...

...Albucia...*

...he wanted to feel horny, so he drank a myrrhine cup...*

...the barrister was a Cerberus of the law courts...

...after the dish of flesh was brought in...

...lips twisted as if to throw up...

...as the mosquitoes were bugging my companion...

...so many regal ornaments, found in a runaway's possession...

...I hurled myself into the privy...

...what, m'learned friends, is tort? I put it to you that the answer is obvious: it is when something is done to dis*tort* the law. There you have tort: well, now take a bad...

...now raised high, at the see-saw's whim...

...it was pretty certainly their habit not to go through the grotto of Naples unless their backs were bent...

...bring us an alabaster jar of Cosmus* ointment...

...the girls of Memphis, ready for the gods' rituals
the boy, dyed the colour of night,
with eloquent gestures...
Egyptian dances...

...the cornfields have lightened my labour...
you see how Trivia's fire*
rotates from her triple rising
and Phoebus on his winged wheel
crosses the swift globe...

...an old woman, soused in wine, with trembling lips...

...this Roman citizen...

...the straits of the Nereids...

...if you always smell good, you don't smell good...*

...the vulture which delves deep into our liver
and yanks out our hearts and innermost fibres
is not the bird our fastidious poets mention
but the soul's evils: envy and lust...

Servius, glossing Virgil's phrase *auri sacra fames* ("the sacred hunger for gold") points out that the word "sacred" could also mean "accursed" (*execrabilis*), and tells the following story, which he says occurs in Petronius. (This suggests that lost episodes of the *Satyricon* may well have taken place in Massilia, modern Marseilles):

"Sacred" means "accursed". This phrase is taken from a custom of the Gauls. Whenever the people of Massilia were attacked by plague, one of the poor would volunteer to be maintained for a whole year at public expense, fed with especially pure food. Then, draped with sacred herbs and robes, he would be led through the whole city while the people showered curses on him, so that the sufferings of the whole city would fall onto this one man: and so he was made an outcast. This account is found in Petronius...

This haunting story is an example of the mechanism of scapegoating, as found in the *Azazel* of the Israelites and the *pharmakos* of the Greeks. The sacred is also accursed, and vice versa. Thus Trimalchio the clown is Thrice King, the Lord of Misrule, the Master of Revels at the summer Saturnalia – and then again, a clown. Some traditions claim that Eumolpus was to be killed as a scapegoat after the manner of Massilia – our inspired poet hurled off the top of a cliff in Croton by its angry citizens.

Finally, a poem by Sidonius Apollinaris (Carmen XXIII):

Why should I sing of you, eloquent Latins,
Of Arpinum, Patavium and Mantua?
And you, Arbiter, who in the gardens of the Massilians
worship the sacred tree trunk
as an equal of Hellespontine Priapus?

Petronius is named in the same verse as Cicero (born in Arpinum), Livy (from Patavium, modern Padua) and Virgil (of Mantua). Even though this Sidonius may be staging a certain aloofness from "pagan" writings ("Why should I sing?..."), it is a nice tribute to the author of the *Satyricon* from a man whose lifetime included the official ending of the Western Empire under its last emperor, the boy Romulus Augustulus, in AD 476. Sidonius Apollinaris seems from his letters to have shared Petronius's love of pleasure and luxury, and like him, he was a man of high rank. Franks and Goths were pouring into Gaul, but Apollinaris could count himself an Urban Prefect of Rome, a patrician and a senator. He was part of Petronius's old world. But he was part of the new world, too – a bishop and a saint.

Appendices

Appendix 1:
Before our Text Begins

The following episodes from the lost books of the *Satyricon* have been pieced together from indications in the text. They are highly speculative, but may be of some help in indicating some of the activities our heroes may have been engaged in before we meet them:

Encolpius, in Massilia, is engaged to Doris. He offends the god Priapus and flees the city; he meets Lichas, whom he robs, and his wife Hedyle, whom he seduces, as he does Tryphaena, a friend of Lichas. Among Tryphaena's circle is a slave boy called Giton, whom Encolpius also seduces. In "the porch [or portico] of Hercules", Encolpius is prosecuted, and flees again. He has murdered (or assaulted and left for dead) a man called Lycurgus, and he and his companions have burgled Lycurgus's house. They meet Ascyltos, who joins the gang and becomes Encolpius's rival for the love of Giton. Somewhere in Campania they come across a ritual in honour of Priapus being celebrated by the priestess Quartilla; they desecrate this mystery, perhaps merely by witnessing it. At about the same time, they steal a fine cloak, but lose a shirt in which they have sewn some gold coins (from Lycurgus's house, perhaps).

Appendix 2:

The Main Characters in the Satyricon

(In each case I also give the number of the chapter in which the character first appears.)

AGAMEMNON: teacher of rhetoric (ch. 1); has the same name as the leader of the Greeks against Troy. Greek *agan* = "very", *memnon* implies "the steadfast". Agamemnon-the-teacher's deputy Menelaus fittingly/ironically has the same name as King Agamemnon's brother.

AGATHO: a perfumer (ch. 74). Greek *agathos* = "good".

ASCYLTOS: the friend, and rival, of Encolpius (ch. 6). Greek prefix *a-* = "not", and *skullo* = "to trouble" or "annoy", so he is "Untroubled" or maybe "Indefatigable".

BARGATES: landlord or caretaker ("*procurator*") of the apartment block where Encolpius and Giton stay (ch. 96), and a friend of Eumolpus. The *Bar-* prefix indicates a Semitic name.

CARIO: one of Trimalchio's slaves (ch. 71). Latin *Cario* = "Carian", i.e. from Caria in Asia Minor; the name Cario was often given to slaves.

CARPUS: Trimalchio's meat-carver (ch. 36, translated here as "Hackett"). A common slave name. Greek *karpos* = "fruit", but also, in Homer (and perhaps more appositely here – cf. our adjective "carpal"), "the wrist".

CHRYSANTHUS: recently deceased member of Trimalchio's circle (ch. 42). Greek *chrusos* = "gold", *anthos* = "flower": "Goldflower".

CHRYSIS: handmaid of Circe (ch. 128). Greek *chrusos* = "golden": so "Golden Girl".

CINNAMUS: Trimalchio's steward (ch. 30). Ultimately from Greek (and even more ultimately Phoenician) *kinnamomon* = "cinnamon".

CIRCE: woman who embarks on an abortive affair with Encolpius (ch. 127): named after Circe the witch and transformatrix of men into swine, in the *Odyssey*.

CORAX: a manservant hired by Eumolpus (ch. 117). A common slave name. Latin *corax* = "raven".

CORINTHUS: Trimalchio's supplier of Corinthian copperware (ch. 50); the name is obviously linked to that of the Greek city.

CROESUS: Trimalchio's "darling boy" (ch. 64), named after the millionaire king of Lydia.

DAEDALUS: Trimalchio's cook (ch. 70), named after the Greek Daedalus who built the labyrinth and made himself a pair of wings (and is mentioned in ch. 52). The Greek name meant "cunningly wrought" or "cunning worker", and sometimes "variegated", from which it evolved into the Anglo-Saxon *tāt* = "gay" – in the old sense.

DAMA: friend of Trimalchio (ch. 41). Greek *damazo* = "to tame", hence, fittingly, *damar* = "wife".

DIOGENES, Caius Pompeius: friend of Trimalchio (ch. 38). The Greek name suggests "born of God" or "sprung of Zeus".

DIONYSUS: slave boy of Trimalchio's (ch. 31). The Greek name (of uncertain origin) is that of the god of wine.

DORIS: one of Encolpius's exes (ch. 126). The Greek name means "a Dorian woman".

ECHION: friend of Trimalchio's, dealer in old clothes (ch. 45). Despite this, the name had heroic-mythological resonances: "son of the viper", from Greek *echis* = "viper".

ENCOLPIUS: narrator of the work (we do not learn his name until one of the fragments assigned to ch. 20). Other characters with this name (e.g. in Martial) are often homosexual favourites. Greek *kolpos* = "lap, groin", so *en* + *kolpos* suggests "in the groin", and what is found in that general area: "Crotchet", perhaps, given his occasional querulousness (not least over the misbehaviour of his crotch). A more positive meaning can be derived from the way the word *kolpos* also means "womb", "fold", "hollow" (as between waves), "bay" "vale"; swerves of shore and bends of bay. See also POLYAENUS.

EUMOLPUS: poet(aster) and critic(aster), associates himself with Encolpius (ch. 90). Greek *eu* + *molpe* = "good song/dance/chant", so Eumolpus is "Good Singer" (an example of the name as antiphrasis). Eumolpus was also the name of a priest of Demeter who introduced the Eleusinian Mysteries to Attica; he was a fine musician and singer.

FORTUNATA: Trimalchio's wife (ch. 37). An ex-slave like him (and a former prostitute). Latin = "fortunate" and thus, often, "wealthy".

GAIUS (same name as CAIUS): see TRIMALCHIO.

GANYMEDES: guest of Trimalchio's (ch. 44). The mythological Ganymede was ravished by Zeus and turned into his cup-bearer. The Greek name *Ganymede* (of uncertain etymology) gave us the English "catamite".

GITON: boy loved by Encolpius (ch. 9). Greek *Giton* = "neighbour".

GORGIAS: a man from Croton who is always on the lookout for legacies (ch. 141). Greek *Gorgias* was the name of the Sophist who appears e.g. in Plato's dialogue of that name; the name has grim resonances (with the Gorgon, with Greek *gorgos* = "fierce, terrible").

HABINNAS: friend of Trimalchio's and stone mason (ch. 65). An ex-slave; a man of some local distinction. The name is Semitic.

HEDYLE: Lichas's wife (ch. 113). She seems to have run off with Encolpius in a part of the story we no longer possess. Greek *hedus* = "sweet"; she is "Sweetie".

HERMEROS: guest of Trimalchio's (ch. 59); an ex-slave. Also the name of a historically attested gladiator of the Neronian period (ch. 52). The Greek name = "lover of Hermes" or "Hermes as lover".

JULIUS PROCULUS: guest of Trimalchio's (ch. 38).

LICHAS: sea captain from Tarentum in S. Italy; enemy of Encolpius, who probably cuckolded him in a missing episode (ch. 100). The Greek root *lich-* is linked with licking: he is "Licker".

LYCURGUS: an enigmatic character, cruel in nature (ch. 83); if it is the same character, Encolpius and friends rob his villa (ch. 117). Also the name of several ancient rulers and mythical characters, including the austere and militaristic semi-mythical law-giver of Sparta. The name suggests "wolfish" (Greek *lukos* = "wolf", *ergon* = "work").

MANNICIUS, Marcus: owner of the building in which Encolpius and Eumolpus stay (ch. 95).

MASSA: a favourite slave of Habbinas (ch. 69). Latin *massa* = "mass", "lump".

MENELAUS: a rhetoric teacher, assistant to Agamemnon (ch. 27).

MENOPHILA: female partner of Philargyrus (ch. 70). Greek name = "lover of strength" (Greek *menos*).

NICEROS: guest of Trimalchio's (ch. 61). The Greek name includes *nike* = "victory" and *eros* = "love, passion": "lover of victory".

OENOTHEA: priestess of Priapus at Croton (ch. 135), hired to cure Encolpius of his impotence. Greek *oinos* = "wine", *thea* = "goddess".

PANNYCHIS: very young slave girl (about seven years old) of Quartilla's (ch. 25). Greek "*pan* = "all", *nux* = "night": she is the "All-night Girl".

PETRAITES: a gladiator – the name of at least one historical gladiator of the Neronian period (ch. 52). Greek *petra* = "rock, stone": he is "Rocky".

PHILARGYRUS: one of Trimalchio's slaves (ch. 70). Greek *philos* = "friend, lover" and *arguros* = "silver, money", so he is "Lovemoney".

PHILEROS: Guest of Trimalchio's (ch. 70). Greek *philos* = "friend, lover", *eros* = "love", so he is "Friendlove".

PHILOMELA: "highly respectable" woman at Croton who sells her children for legacies (ch. 140). The Greek word means "nightingale".

PLOCAMUS: Guest of Trimalchio's (ch. 64). Greek *plokamos* = "lock of hair".

PROSELENOS: an old witch (ch. 131); her name suggests that she is older than the moon (Greek *selene*).

PSYCHE: maid of Quartilla (ch. 20); her name is Greek for "soul" (and "butterfly").

QUARTILLA: priestess of Priapus (ch. 16). Her name suggests "fourth" in Latin, but may also allude to the "quartan fever" (i.e. malaria) from which she claims to suffer.

SCINTILLA: Habinnas's wife (ch. 66). Her name is Latin for "Spark".

SCISSA: A friend of Habinnas (ch. 65). His name means "cut up".

SCYLAX: Trimalchio's great mutt (ch. 64). In Greek, *skulax* = "puppy".

SELEUCUS: Trimalchio's guest (ch. 42). The name is oriental (as in the Seleucid Empire, which – following Alexander the Great – at one stage extended from the Mediterranean to the Indus).

SERAPA: Trimalchio's astrologer (ch. 76). Serapis was a Babylonian and then Egyptian god.

TRIMALCHIO: full name Gaius Pompeius Trimalchio Maecenatianus, with allusions to Pompey the Great and to Maecenas, Octavian/Augustus's wealthy patron of the arts; ex-slave; he throws the banquet that dominates the *Satyricon* as we have it (ch. 26). The name Trimalchio is of Greek and Semitic origins: Greek *tri* as prefix = "three", and the root m-l-k (*melech* in Hebrew or *malik* in Arabic) signifies "king": "Thrice King".

TRYPHAENA: a prostitute and now woman of leisure from South Italy (ch. 100). In Greek, her name suggests "luxury".

Appendix 3:

Tacitus on Petronius

Here is Tacitus's account of the man called Caius Petronius to whom the *Satyricon* is traditionally attributed:

I mentioned C. Petronius. Here are a few more details. He spent his days in sleep, his nights on the duties and amusements of life; hard work raises some to greatness, he idled his way to fame. He was not viewed as a debauchee and profligate, like most spendthrifts, but as a connoisseur of excess. And his words and deeds had a certain freedom, displaying a degree of unselfconscious negligence that made them all the more acceptable, with their air of simplicity. And yet he was proconsul of Bithynia and later consul, and showed himself to be energetic and up to the job. Then he relapsed into the habit – or the affectation – of vice, and was taken up into Nero's elite inner circle, as Arbiter of Elegance [*elegantiæ Arbiter*], for the Emperor deemed nothing to be enjoyable or pleasurable unless Petronius had recommended it to him. Hence the envy of Tigellinus for this apparent rival, one who seemed more expert in the science of pleasures. So Tigellinus played on Nero's cruelty, the chief of the Emperor's lusts, intimating that Petronius was a friend of Scaevinus; he had already bribed one of his slaves to turn informer, withholding any means of defence from Petronius, and arresting most of his household.

The Emperor happened to have moved to Campania. Petronius travelled as far as Cumae, but was then stopped; he decided to waste no more time in hope or fear. He did not rush to end his life, but cut his veins, and then, at his own whim, had them bound up and then opened again, and began to chat with his friends, saying nothing that was serious or might leave behind a reputation for stoicism. And he listened as they talked, not of the immortality of the soul or the maxims of philosophers, but cheerful ditties and light verse. He gave some of his slaves generous presents, and others a beating. He went into dinner and drowsed awhile, so that death, though forced on him, might appear natural. He did not add codicils to his will, as did many when at death's door, flattering Nero or Tigellinus or some other powerful figure, but detailed the Emperor's debaucheries, first giving the names of the catamites and women involved, and the novel features of each fornication; then he sealed the document and sent it to Nero. And he broke his signet ring so that it could not be used to imperil other people.

Tacitus's marvellous portrait was written fifty years after the events he was describing, making it at least as historically accurate as, say, the earliest gospel. Tacitus may have been ambivalent about Petronius: his *sine ira et studio* stance makes it difficult to tell. But his view of court life under Nero, in which Petronius long played a considerable part, was one of icy disdain.

Appendix 4:

Some Later Mentions of Petronius's work

The *Satyricon* circulated widely in antiquity: it is mentioned by Saint Jerome and Boethius, Bishop Fulgentius and Isidore of Seville. John of Salisbury may have brought a copy from France to Canterbury.

Ben Jonson told Drummond of Hawthornden that "Petronius, Plinius Secundus and Tacitus speke best Latin" (*Conversations with Drummond*, 1619). Robert Burton, echoing Justus Lipsius, thought the *Satyricon* was "a fragment of pure impurities", and *The Anatomy of Melancholy* includes some seventy quotations from Petronius. Burton mistrusted the satirists, among whom he numbered our Arbiter: "they that laugh and contemn others, condemn the world of folly, deserve to be mocked, are as giddy-headed, and lie as open as any other". Saint-Évremond, the seventeenth-century *libertin* writer, praised Petronius for depicting vice with grace (instead of being a mere moralist) and lauded his suicide as "the most exemplary" death in all antiquity. Giambattista Vico wrote an account of the dining customs of the Romans (*Delle cene sontuose de' Romani*, 1698) which drew largely on the *Cena Trimalchionis*. During Carnival time in Hanover, in 1702, a "Trimalchio Celebration" was organized; guests at the dinner had to enter with their right foot raised; the role of Trimalchio was played by the Raugrave (who was, aptly enough, a heavy drinker). He made a grand entrance "carried on a machine, preceded by huntsmen, drummers, musicians, slaves, and it all made a considerable din". A "Eumolpus" figure recited verse in honour of his military and amorous exploits – and the whole scene was reported, in a letter to the Princess Luise von Hohenzollern, by the philosopher Leibniz.

Thomas Love Peacock was an admirer, and mimicked something of the *Satyricon*'s conversational style in his own works. For Nietzsche, Petronius was untranslatable into German: the "tempo" of the two languages was so different. Petronius was "master of the presto", who swept along "on the feet of the wind"; he was on a par with Aristophanes and Machiavelli. (Nietzsche was, as often, interestingly wrong: there are several excellent, vigorous versions of Petronius in German, not least the eighteenth-century *Begebenheiten des Enkolp* or *Deeds of Encolpius*.) Nietzsche contrasted the *Satyricon* with the New Testament, full of the stink of "bad instincts" (resentment, slave rebellion, dishonesty):

> Everything in it [the N.T.] is cowardice, everything in it is a shutting of the eyes and self-deception. Every book becomes pure in comparison, once you have read the New Testament: to give an example, immediately after reading [Saint] Paul, I just read with delight that most graceful, most high-spirited of mockers, of whom one could say what Domenico Borgia wrote to the Duke of Parma about Cesare Borgia: *è tutto festo* – immortally healthy, immortally cheerful and achieved.

Huysman's 1884 novel *A Rebours* (*Against Nature*) tells the story of the jaded, misanthropic, world-weary Jean Des Esseintes, who seeks escape from the tedium of modern (i.e. late-nineteenth-century) life in France by seeking the refined, the delicate, the recherché. Naturally his tastes include our author:

> The author he truly loved, who led to his banishing once and for all from his reading the sonorous ingenuities of Lucan, was Petronius.
>
> What a perspicacious observer he was, what a delicate analyst, what a marvellous painter! Calmly, without prejudice or hatred, he described everyday life in Rome, and in the short, alert chapters of the *Satyricon* he recorded the customs and manners of his day.
>
> Noting the facts as he went along, setting them down in a definitive form, he revealed the ordinary lives of the people, their adventures, their bestial appetites, their couplings.
>
> Here you see the inspector of furnished lodgings asking after the names of the recently arrived guests; there you see the brothels, with men prowling round the naked women standing between the boards with their names and prices – while, through the half-open cubicle doors, you can glimpse the couples writhing together. The society of the time swarms through the villas with their insolent luxury in a mindless revel of wealth and ostentation, or in the poor hostelries that follow each other through the book, with their

rough, rumpled, bug-ridden beds. Dirty crooks like Ascyltos and Eumolpus keep their eyes open for the main chance; old incubi with their skirts hoicked up and their cheeks plastered with white lead and red acacia gum; sixteen-year-old catamites, plump and curly-haired; women on the edge of a nervous breakdown; legacy-hunters offering their boys and girls to the debauched tastes of testators – they all scurry across the pages, quarrel in the streets, fondle each other in the baths, and give each other a good drubbing, as in some pantomime.

And all of this is narrated in a style of strange and racy vigour, precise in its colour, drawing on every dialect, borrowing expressions from all the languages imported into Rome, pushing back all the limits, breaking all the shackles of the so-called Golden Age, making everyone speak in his own idiom: the uneducated freedmen speak in vulgar Latin and street slang; foreigners in their barbarous patois, peppered with African, Syrian and Greek; inane pedants, such as the book's Agamemnon, in a rhetoric of verbose artificiality. All these people are drawn in swift strokes, lounging round their tables, exchanging tasteless, drunken commonplaces, proffering senile maxims and inept proverbs, their boorish faces turned towards Trimalchio as he picks his teeth, offers chamber pots to the company, entertains them with details of his innards and breaks wind, inviting his guests to let it all out.

This realist novel, this slice of quivering Roman life, with no desire – in spite of what is commonly said – to reform or satirize this society, with no need of any fussy moral aim; this story, without plotline or action, setting before our eyes the adventures of those denizens of Sodom, the hunters and the hunted; analysing with even-handed subtlety the joys and pains of these couples and their *amours*; depicting, in a splendidly wrought language, without the author showing himself once, without him indulging in a single comment, without approving or decrying the deeds and thoughts of his characters, the vices of a decrepit civilization, of an empire breaking apart – all this went straight to Des Esseintes's heart. And in the refinement of the style, in the acuteness of the observation, in the firmness of the method used, he caught a glimpse of strange similarities and curious analogies with the few modern French novels that he could bear to read.

To be sure, he bitterly regretted the fact that the *Eustion* and the *Albutia*, those two works by Petronius mentioned by Planciades Fulgentius, were for ever lost, but the bibliophile in him consoled the scholar, as, with devout fingers, he turned the pages of the superb edition of the *Satyricon* that he possessed, the octavo bearing the year 1585 and the name of J. Dousa of Leyden.

D.H. Lawrence decided (in a letter to Lady Ottoline Morrell) that Petronius was "a gentleman", "straight and above-board" – someone who didn't do the dirty on sex. But the text, of course, always had a whiff of scandal about it. "Homosexuality" (the complex of proclivities and activities later subsumed under this word) was for long a burning issue. The interest in the *Satyricon* taken by the great scholar and humanist Joseph Justus Scaliger (1540–1609) attracted suspicion: perhaps his interest in this depraved text was a sign of his own love of men? He had already converted to Protestantism, so any obloquy was deserved. We still lack a proper, scholarly, annotated edition of the *Satyricon* in English: at the end of the eighteenth century, one was attempted in French, by La Porte du Theil, in three great volumes. It was about to be published, in 1800, when panic set in: the work was pulped, and now exists only as a set of corrected proofs in the Bibliothèque nationale.

The lacunary nature of the text has often led to forged interpolations. A Frenchman, François Nodot, filled in all the gaps and circulated a "complete" edition of the *Satyricon*, ostensibly from a full manuscript that had turned up in Belgrade: the forgery was unmasked by, among others, Leibniz. But the desire to provide prequels and sequels is deeply rooted, and Nodot's addenda were incorporated into many later editions and translations. In the 1800s, a Spaniard by the name of Marchena published an ending to the Quartilla episode that outdid the original in indelicacy: having gone over to the French side, he dedicated his work to Napoleon's Army of the Rhine. Perhaps some of the *grognards* carried Marchena's forgery around Europe in their knapsacks, just as the soldiers of Crassus had insisted on taking their copies of the *Milesiaka* with them on the Parthian campaign.

The work has been translated into many languages. It is a pity, given their extraordinarily vivid reaction to Petronius's style (as we have seen above) that neither Nietzsche nor Husymans ever actually translated Petronius. Perhaps their minds were on higher things? Alas, Charles

Baudelaire never carried out his own planned translation. There is, however, one French version which captures the campy elegance of parts of the original: that by Laurence Tailhade. A dandy, a minor poet praised by Mallarmé, a friend of Verlaine (and of Wilfred Owen), an opium addict, he drifted from anarchism via socialism to extreme right-wing royalism. His loose-cannon impertinence made him a typical French Bohemian, a *provocateur* – even an inciter to terrorism. In 1901 he published a violent attack on the visit to France of Tsar Nicholas II: the autocrat of all the Russias was a tyrant who should be assassinated. It was during Tailhade's subsequent detainment in La Santé prison that, although working with a faulty edition, and unable to consult the reference works he needed, he produced his great, anachronistic, querulously mannered version of the *Satyricon*. He probably imported much of its language straight from the mouths of his fellow inmates: as Jean Genet was to point out, the most elegant French is that spoken in prisons.

Appendix 5:

Two Earlier English Versions of the Satyricon

Don't get cross with the poor translator, viz. me! I could hardly make this Satyricon *any better than it actually is; and you know what our art critics are like!*

The translator of the eighteenth-century German version published as *Begebenheiten des Enkolp* (*The Deeds of Encolpius*).

The earliest English translation of the *Satyricon* was by the dramatist William Burnaby (author of *The Double Gallant, Love Betray'd*, the *Modish Husband*, the *Reform'd Wife*, etc.), published in 1694. It was reissued in the early years of the twentieth century with a very interesting introduction, "On Reading Petronius. An Open Letter to a Young Gentleman". This began by alluding, tenebrously, to the things "too infamous to be named" that were mentioned in Petronius's novel, before going on to bring out the fascinating parallels that existed between the first-century world depicted in it and more modern times. Lichas, the author of the introduction opined, was very like Steerforth.

> Dear old Eumolpus, with his boring culture and shameless chuckle, no school is complete without him... Ascyltos is generally the Captain of the XV or XI, sometimes of both, and represents the unending war of muscle against mind. Encolpius is, of course, the hero of every school story ever written [...] Agamemnon is the sort of form-master whom it is conventional to rag.

The "young gentleman" being addressed in this introduction is told to be on his guard against Eumolpus in particular: he will find many examples of his type in London, whether he visits the National Gallery or the Turkish Baths. In short, Petronius's novel turns out to be a reliable guide to Victorian-Edwardian public-school-trained culture; furthermore, it had at least one close contemporary parallel: although the text we have is fragmentary, "we may assume [...] that the whole satire was immensely long, a life work, like Marcel Proust's *A la Recherche du Temps perdu*, and like that work, perhaps, fatal to its author". There are many parallels between Petronius and Proust, the author points out, not the least being that they were both *lucifugæ*, fleeing the daylight and living at night.

The author of this introduction knew that whereof he spoke: he was the great Scott Moncrieff, translator of Proust. He goes on to make two interesting points about the Burnaby translation he is introducing. First: "He is not always scholarly – you can safely leave scholarship to others – but he uses an excellent colloquial English with a common sense in interpretation which carries him over the many gaps in the story without any palpable difference in texture". So scholarship (meaning what, exactly – semantic accuracy? a sense of historical context? a knowledge of origins and influences?) is not a prerequisite for, but rather the opposite of, translation. And, rather alarmingly, we find "common sense" smoothing over the gaps and homogenizing the texture: the contrary of what might seem desirable these days, when an attention to the many-voiced nature of the text (its woof and *warp*, precisely) is a primary concern for the translator. But second, as against the levelling-out and completing tendencies, the sellotaping and sandpapering job that the first point seems to promote, we find a wish to keep the text's rough edges, and respect those moments when the pieces of the jigsaw refuse to stick together: for "the reading of fragments has a fascination for the curious mind".

Here, as an example of an earlier translation, is a section of the one which Scott Moncrieff was introducing: *The satyr of Titus Petronius Arbiter, a Roman knight: with its fragments, recover'd at Belgrade; made English by Mr Burnaby of the Middle-Temple, and another hand*, published in 1694. Unfortunately, all the juicier bits of the text remained in Latin. So here is the speech made by one of the guests at Trimalchio's dinner:

A freeman of Trimalchio's that sate next above me grew hot upon't, and, "What," said he, "thou sheep, what dost thou laugh at? Does not this sumptuousness of my master please you? You're richer (forsooth) and eat better every day; so may the guardian of this place favour me, as had I sate near him, I'd hit him a box on the ear ere this: a hopeful cullion, that mocks others; some pitiful night-walker;

not worth the very urine he makes, and should I throw mine on him, knows not where to dry himself. I am not (so help me Hercules) quickly angry, yet worms are bred even in tender flesh. He laughs! What has he to laugh at? What wool did his father give for the bantling? Is he a Roman knight? I am the son of a king. How came I then, you'll say, to serve another? I did it of myself, and had rather be a citizen of Rome than a tributary king, and now hope to live so as to be no man's jest. I walk like other men, with an open face, and can show my head among the best, for I owe no man a groat; I never had an action brought against me, or said to me on the exchange, pay me what thou owest me. I bought some acres in the country, and have everything suitable to it: I feed twenty mouths, besides dogs: I ransomed my bond-woman, lest another should wipe his hands on her smock, and between ourselves, she costs me more than I'll tell ye at present. I was made a Captain of Horse gratis, and hope so to die, that I shall have no occasion to blush in my grave: but art thou so prying into others, that thou never considerest thyself? Canst thou spy a louse on another man's coat, and not see the tick on thy own? Your master then is ancienter than yourself, and it please you, but yet thou, whose milk is not yet out of thy nose; that canst not say bo to a goose; must you be making observations? Are you the wealthier man? If you are, dine twice, and sup twice; for my part, I value my credit more than treasures: upon the whole matter, where's the man that ever dunn'd me twice? Thou pipkin of a man, more limber, but nothing better than a strap of wet leather, I have served forty years in this house, came into it with my hair full grown; this palace was not then built, yet I made it my business to please my master, a person of honour, the parings of whose nails are more worth than thy whole body. I met several rubs in my way, but by the help of my good angel, I broke through them all: this is truth; it is as easy to make a hunting horn of a sow's tail, as to get into this company. What make ye in a dump now, like a goat at a heap of stones?"

Another English translation of the *Satyricon* appeared in Paris two centuries later, in 1902. It shows an acquaintance with the Burnaby version, but some interesting new renderings too. Some have a more nineteenth-century feel, almost American at times: "Isn't my master's elegant hospitality to your taste? You're a mighty fine gentleman, I suppose, and used to better entertainment", or "You! with your mammy's milk scarce dry on your lips..." while others are more daring in their coarseness: "a night-raker, that's not worth his own piddle! Just let me piss round him, and he would not know where to save his life!". There is the ring of up-to-date cliché here and there: "I was made a sevir, free gratis and for nothing". And the end of the passage is strikingly different from Burnaby. "And I had enemies in the house, let me tell you, quite ready to trip me up on occasion, but – thanks to his kind nature – I swam the rapids. That's the real struggle – for to be born a gentleman is as easy as 'Come here'. Whatever are you gaping at now, like a buckgoat in a field of bitter vetch?"

This second translation was signed by one Sebastian Melmoth – the pseudonym, of course, of Oscar Wilde. It is, alas, unlikely that Wilde actually penned it; Dorian Gray, as well as being a devotee of Huysmans, was tempted to become the Petronius of his own day – "yet in his inmost heart he desired to be something more than a mere *arbiter elegantiarum*, to be consulted on the wearing of a jewel, or the knotting of a necktie, or the conduct of a cane". In Wilde and Husymans, the dandyism they found in the author of the *Satyricon* lived on in the Europe of the late-imperial era – despite the ironizing of any such pose, any such claim to "elegance", that is evident on every page of Petronius.

Appendix 6:

Fellini-Satyricon

Federico Fellini became aware of the sometimes humdrum reality behind the myth as a boy. He was born in an area of Italy through which the river Rubicon flows. When he visited it, this turning point in European history turned out to be "hardly more than a stony creek that dries up in summer" (Baxter, 13).* The young Fellini would jump into it, screaming, as he put it "like a damned soul" the words of Julius Caesar as he headed towards his destiny: "*Alea jacta est!*"

Fellini followed Caesar to Rome, and his love affair with the city produced *La dolce vita*, *Roma*, and, of course, *The Satyricon*, or as his own inimitable flair for self-promotion had it, *Fellini-Satyricon*, the two words welded together as if to hug Petronius's work to himself, insisting that it was *his* vision, maybe not for everyone. (A rival director was planning his own version of the work, so Fellini's use of his own name as a prefix also had pragmatic reasons.) He is cavalier with his original, screening episodes that have nothing to do with Petronius's work, being derived from Apuleius, Suetonius or from Fellini's own dreams. He had read the book (I do not know in what version, expurgated or not) while at school. In 1942, Marcello Marchesi suggested turning the story into a musical. A publisher also asked Fellini, in his capacity as an illustrator, for a book cover, as he planned to issue a version of the text that would be, as it were, expurgated in reverse: all the boring bits taken out, only the sex retained, with suitably raunchy illustrations.

It was while convalescing in a *pensione* at Manzania from a dangerous and almost mortal illness, as he reflected on his recent brush with death (the nuns in the hospital praying for his recovery, the room filling with flowers, the telegrams from all over Italy), and leafed through a copy of Petronius's text that the idea of filming the *Satyricon* returned to his mind. Tackling that death-obsessed work would help him to restore his flagging powers and come to terms with the sense of mortality that had recently assailed him. It would also enable him to celebrate the pleasures of the flesh in which the novel also rejoices. His

179

rebirth occurred, suitably enough, near his own origins: Manzania is near Rimini, Fellini's birthplace. And by the 1960s Rimini had become the sleaziest resort in Italy. Fellini, lover of hippies, obsessed by the Age of Aquarius (his own birth sign), and intent as usual on projecting his own complexes onto the contemporary world (he once said that *Satyricon* was more autobiographical than *Otto e mezzo*), decided that his *Satyricon* would hold up the mirror of first-century antiquity to the swinging Sixties. In the fateful month of May 1968, he signed a contract with the producer Alberto Grimaldi.

The process of casting his film was immense fun. Early possibilities included the seventy-six-year-old Mae West as Oenothea and Groucho Marx as "a philosophical pimp" (Baxter, 240) – and, as Trimalchio, Boris Karloff. Danny Kaye was tempted by the offer of Lichas's role, but was uncomfortable with the idea of portraying the thuggish, gay transvestite, imperial pimp and murderer into which Fellini had transformed Petronius's sea captain. Fellini, forced to go for younger actors, suggested Terence Stamp as Encolpius, and Elizabeth Taylor, Richard Burton, Brigitte Bardot, Peter O'Toole, Jerry Lewis, the Beatles (whose spokesman turned him down with some acerbity – a shame: they could have provided the music at Trimalchio's feast), the Maharishi Mahesh Yogi, Marlon Brando, Lyndon Johnson and President de Gaulle. If he could not secure the services of these stars of stage and screen, he preferred to go for nobodies, for people who were unknown, in order "to increase", as he put it, "the sense of foreignness" (Baxter, 240).

Eventually, on a trip to London, he found his Encolpius: the sultry-innocent Martin Potter, who – said Fellini – reminded him of the Emperor Trajan's beloved Antinous, and his Giton, seventeen-year-old Max Born, whose sexually ambiguous, knowing-child, *gamin/gamine* looks haunt the film, all the more effectively because this object of the desires of Encolpius and Ascyltos (played by the sneeringly predatory, handsomely brutish Hiram Keller) never speaks. Giton can thus assume the role of silent angelic transcendence found in many other of Fellini's films (the girl at the end of *La dolce vita*: nothing but a smile – but what a smile!). The sex therapist (or rather witch-woman) Oenothea was played by Donyale Luna, a woman whose immense height had made her one of Salvador Dalí's muses. Luna had already appeared in films by Andy Warhol: the character she plays in Fellini would be able to kindle fire from her loins (literally). She would die within a decade of appearing in *Fellini-Satyricon*, of an accidental drugs overdose. And Trimalchio, last but not least, was played by the proprietor of Fellini's favourite restaurant.

Fellini, as closely attuned to the spiritual realm as were Petronius's characters, also prepared for shooting by taking a friend along to consult the ageing psychic Penus ("fine name he's got", as Molly Bloom would have muttered: add the word "trio" and you've got "Petronius"). The seance, on the Via Appia, was somewhat inconclusive.

The sense of foreignness Fellini thought would imbue his film because of the relatively unknown actors was, in the event, to be crucial. Fellini wanted to shoot his film on the slopes of Vesuvius (with its obvious Pompeiian associations) and in North Africa. A lot of it has an almost Saharan feel to it; the music, by Nino Rota, often sounds Middle Eastern (or even Chinese), and a sense of exotic splendour was obtained by using "the drums for the Niegpadouda dance", taken from an anthology of Black African music. Inevitably, a considerable part of the movie was actually filmed in Cinnecittà. The scenes in the bathhouse at the beginning, in the theatre of the lascivious actor Vernacchio and in the streets of the city create an atmosphere of Piranesian nightmare more consonant with Rome than with the novel's probable main urban setting, the much more provincial Puteoli. Wisps of smoke and steam hang in the air, tiny characters dwarfed by their eerie cubist surroundings wander through the gloom, scuffling on the edge of infernal abysses and emerging, as often as not, into surreal and artificial deserts or arid, rocky coasts rather than into the clear light of Campania. Another alienation effect created by the final film was the odd dubbing. Depending on their nationality, the actors spoke in their own English or Italian, and were then dubbed into Italian; the English subtitles added a further weird poetry of their own, since they often relate rather obliquely to the original English (or Italian). Luca Canali, a classicist from the University of Pisa, advised on the Latin language, and the Italian dialogue is often remarkably close to the Latin of Petronius's characters. Sometimes the English subtitles read merely "vulgar Latin" (i.e. colloquial Latin, not always rude), and we hear voices uttering what is presumed to be the everyday language of first-century Italy – which is not translated. But why should one understand everything? Fellini clearly thought we should not: some of his characters speak no language that I recognize. Life is such a babble, after all.

Fellini knows that art needs the right ambiance to flourish. His beautiful, delicate, vulnerable hermaphrodite, who has brought healing to so many, is stolen by Encolpius and company, and trundled in a little wagon across the desert, where he-she soon dies of thirst and exposure to sunlight. In *Roma*, the Petronian frescoes unearthed by the archaeologists from under the capital start to fade as soon as they are exposed to the air of modern life.

Some elements in the novel are ignored, others magnified. The short sequence in which Encolpius meets Ascyltos in a brothel (to which neither of them – it appears – has come willingly) becomes, in the film, a prolonged saunter through the sexual phantasmagoria of the vast Lupanare, in which Encolpius and Giton gaze in wonder at the lubricious scenes being staged around them. The character of Eumolpus, already vividly delineated in Propertius, assumes centre stage in many scenes: perhaps Fellini took a somewhat sadistic fancy to this poor (in every sense) poet. He has him being tortured by Trimalchio for plagiarizing his verses.

The Roman Emperor is never named and rarely alluded to in Petronius's novel. He is no doubt there, as part of the atmosphere: but in practical terms, imperial power is distant, and local magistrates count for far more. In Fellini's film, we see one young emperor (an albino) being killed on the beach: a shot of marching soldiers suggests a civil war. A gentleman is seen freeing his slaves before "they" come to confiscate his land. He then slits his own wrists and waits, with his wife, for death. Who are "they"? Presumably the henchmen of the new emperor. Perhaps Fellini is alluding to the Stoic suicides of Seneca and so many other victims of imperial power. Petronius's own suicide, if we are to believe Tacitus, was almost a parody of this – while turning into yet another aestheticized ritual. This filmic episode, imbued with nobility and melancholy, is – together with the first appearance of the fey and vulnerable hermaphrodite – a celebration of the values that are so easily destroyed by violence and rapine. But there is something bleached and anaemic about them, as if Fellini is criticizing a world in which only suicide or a semi-divine withdrawal into childlike ambiguity can escape the general corruption. Both Petronius and Fellini are getting us to think about art and power, in first-century AD as in 1968, and now.

The film *Ciao Federico*, a kind of "making of *Fellini-Satyricon*", shows Fellini imposing his own imperial (or Trimalchian) will on actors who can be attentive and pliable but are more often reluctant, bored, bewildered or stroppy (even when the cameras are rolling, a lot of them seem as fazed, zomboid or just plain stoned as they do in the final film). Sometimes he waves his hand metrically, benedictionally, over his cast, like an actor conducting them very slowly. When not filming, he flirts with the actresses. (He is particularly fascinated by long tongues.) He asks one, "Did you make love last night?" When she replies "No," he shakes his head: "So you've lost a night." *Vivamus, mea Lesbia! Carpe diem! Nox est perpetua una dormienda! Eheu nos miseros...* Sometimes the actors voice their dislike of being filmed for this documentary: "Encolpius" and "Giton" have a conversation about money and then complain about such mercenary chatter being recorded on film. But even when not being filmed (for *Fellini-Satyricon*), they are being filmed (for *Ciao Federico*): perhaps, even when they are not being filmed for *Ciao Federico...* but that is something we cannot know. Sometimes Fellini, floppy black hat tipped rakishly on his head (he has clearly copied his style from Toulouse-Lautrec's Aristide Bruant), wanders around the set in something of a bemused daze, as if himself perplexed at the *grande machine* he is creating ("what the fuck are they doing?" he asks at the "*Madeia, perimadeia*" sequence, which turns into a sexy-grotesque dance routine). Roman Polanski and Sharon Tate pass by, adding an odd frisson. This apparent documentary "about" *Fellini-Satyricon* is, like the film itself, "suspended between fantasy and reality". Everything is "just to make images". When the "Homeristas" perform their party piece, he chortles "Fakers! Fakers!" (but he seems to know their texts by heart).

Fellini's film begins with a wall covered in graffiti, and a voice in mid-sentence. It ends with Encolpius again in mid-sentence, about to set sail on adventures that we shall never know. On the cliff top we see the ruined wall of some Roman villa, decorated with frescoes of the film's main characters, exposed to the four winds, with the wide-open sea as background, glittering in the sunshine.

Notes

p. 3, *Crazy… reckon*: The speaker is our narrator, Encolpius. He is criticizing contemporary courses in public speaking.

p. 3, *hamstrung knees… body*: Prisoners of war were often hamstrung to prevent their escape.

p. 3, *A college education… or more*: Public speaking courses were destined not only for law students: rhetoric was prized so highly that it constituted the core curriculum of higher education – even though the centralization of power under the Empire led to a decline in its impact on real life. Highly artificial or outdated subjects continued to be set as practice themes (e.g. pirates were no longer the threat to Roman shipping that they had once been).

p. 3, *you… culprits*: He is addressing Agamemnon, the peripatetic professor of rhetoric.

p. 3, *Pindar… Homer*: The nine lyrical poets were usually Bacchylides, Sappho, Anacreon, Stesichorus, Simonides, Ibycus, Alcaeus, Alcman and Pindar: sometimes (as here, presumably), Pindar would be replaced by another poet (e.g. Corinna).

p. 4, *Asia… students*: The Asian style ("Asia" here, as later in the *Satyricon*, means "Asia Minor") was seen as baroquely self-indulgent, the Attic as classically restrained. Encolpius's criticisms were commonplace: many public speakers had already denounced over-elaborate rhetoric.

p. 4, *Hypereides*: Hypereides was a fourth-century BC orator, praised for his plain but elegant style.

p. 4, *Egyptians… Painting Made Simple approach*: It appears that the people (perhaps Greeks?) in Egypt had introduced quick-and-easy methods of painting.

p. 4, *Cicero… empty halls*: See Cicero, *Pro Cælio*, XVII, 41: those who insist on hard work from their students "are now left to lecture in empty lecture halls".

p. 5, *Lucilius*: Caius Lucilius lived in the second century BC: he was the first Roman satirist of whom we know. He was famed for his facility, and claimed that he could rattle off 200 lines of verse per hour, while standing on one foot. Horace disapproved.

p. 5, *Tritonis*: i.e., the Acropolis of Athens. Athene's birth had a connection with Lake Triton in North Africa.

p. 6, *Lacedaemonian settler... Sirens sing*: Lacedaemonian (i.e. Spartan) farmers had settled in southern Italy, e.g. at Tarentum. The Sirens sang off the coast of Naples.

p. 6, *Maeonian spring*: The Maeonian spring (aka Pierian, as at the end of the poem), in Thessaly, was sacred to the Muses.

p. 6, *Socratic school... Demosthenes... Romans... history... Cicero resound*: This is Agamemnon's ideal syllabus. First to be studied is Homer, then "Socrates's school" (e.g. Plato's or Xenophon's dialogues), then the orator Demosthenes: only after these Greek propaedeutics have been mastered can the Latin writers be studied. Rhetoric is initially to be neglected in favour of history, but by studying the great republican Cicero, the young aspirant will learn about both public speaking and politics.

p. 6, *Agamemnon's set piece*: Agamemnon's "set piece" is a *suasoria*, a "persuasive" speech on a given theme, generally recommending a course of action to a noted figure (real or fictional), delivered by a rhetoric teacher as a model for his students.

p. 6, *I didn't have the foggiest... our lodgings were*: The text does not state where these episodes actually take place; Encolpius and his friends have clearly only just arrived. There is some evidence that it is Puteoli (modern Pozzuoli), a major port in Roman times, at the heart of the Phlegraean Fields, an area of volcanic, gaseous and hypothermal activity, and the home of Vulcan. Puteoli was very close to Lake Avernus, the entrance to Hades. These numinous associations add a frisson to the image Petronius creates of a typically bustling and seedy Roman port. (St Paul stayed here on his way to Rome, in the late 50s AD – roughly contemporary with the action of the *Satyricon*.)

p. 7, *satyrion*: The aphrodisiac *satyrion* is mentioned in Pliny's *Natural History*, II, 26.10. Derived from several kinds of orchid, some of whose tubers resemble testicles (Greek *orcheis*), it was usually ingested in a rough wine (*in vino austero*). *Satyrion* also meant any kind of aphrodisiac: according to Pliny, Theophrastus had mentioned another such plant potion which, simply by being held in the hand, enabled a man to climax seventy times. (It is unfortunately not clear which plant he meant.)

p. 7, *bro*: Petronius seems to use the word *frater* ("brother") to refer to a male homosexual partner. This usage is apparently not attested outside the *Satyricon*. I translate it as "bro". This usage is apparently not attested much outside the pubs of Soho's Old Compton Street (but it is gradually spreading).

p. 8, *This bro... whatever he is*: Ascyltos.

p. 8, *Shut your face... arena*: The text here is corrupt: another reading has Encolpius being a suitable gladiator for "a midday crowd" in the arena, when unarmed murderers were dispatched. Or else he evaded having to fight in the amphitheatre when it collapsed (as amphitheatres did – see Tacitus *Annals* 4.62).

p. 8, *Shut your... our digs*: This paragraph contains several allusions to lost episodes of the book.

p. 10, *begging bowl*: Strictly, a wallet (here *pera*), the emblem of Cynics who begged for a living to show how much they despised money.

p. 10, *apart from... lupines with*: The text here is corrupt: another reading is: "apart from one shekel and a couple of counterfeit coins". Lupine seeds were used as fake money, especially on stage.

p. 12, *Nobody... away with it*: Encolpius and companions seem to have disturbed Quartilla and her companions while they were celebrating the cult of Priapus (who, as we shall see, takes his revenge on our narrator). The cult of Priapus was, in the Roman world, usually relatively informal and rustic; statuettes of him sometimes resemble a garden gnome with an erection. It is interesting, given his "castratory" pursuit of Encolpius through the *Satyricon* (one that possibly parodies similar persecutions in myth, notably that of Odysseus by Poseidon), that the lusty Priapus himself was cursed from the womb by Hera with ugliness and impotence, a problem that continued to dog his amorous pursuits.

p. 16, *Falernian*: This sweet white wine (produced from vines grown on Mount Falernus, south of Naples) was highly praised in Ancient Rome.

p. 17, *capons of Delos*: The catamites are compared to capons, as found on Apollo's island of Delos.

p. 18, *bender*: The word that I have translated as "bender" is *embasicœtas*, which meant both a "drinking cup" and a "catamite".

p. 19, *Juno*: The guardian spirit of a man was often referred to as his *genius*, while a woman had her *Juno*.

p. 20, *last supper*: Not the dinner at Trimalchio's which actually follows, but the preface to some ordeal: a *libera cena* was a "free dinner" given to *bestiarii*, gladiators who would be facing wild animals in the arena the following day – like the last meal given to a prisoner before execution in the US. Despite the slightly jumbled nature of the text here, the words "So the third day had come" traditionally mark the start of the long and relatively self-contained episode of Trimalchio's dinner, the *cena Trimalchionis*.

p. 20, *water clock… temps he's perdu*: "Ordinary" people would usually just send a slave to the forum to find out what time it was. Trimalchio is obsessed with time's passing.

p. 20, *different games*: It was usual for dinner to be preceded by exercise and a bath.

p. 20, *Menelaus*: Another rhetoric teacher, Agamemnon's assistant, and graced, like him, with a heroic name.

p. 21, *drinking a toast… of him*: Wine was spilt as an offering to the gods; Trimalchio imagines, or pretends, that here it is a (probably funeral) libation for him – the first of a long sequence of references to death throughout the *Cena*.

p. 21, *Four runners… of him*: This is one of the details of Trimalchio's lifestyle (having bemedalled runners in his service) that echoes the pretensions of Nero.

p. 21, *DANGER! DOG!*: *Cave canem*, of course: such dogs, in paint or mosaic, were common.

p. 21, *caduceus*: The herald's wand, with its two serpents twisted into a figure-of-eight, associated with Mercury, god of roads, boundaries, luck, commerce, thieves, interpreters, tricksters and translators. Mercury is also the *psychopompos* who leads souls to the Underworld. Even though he was originally a slave, Trimalchio has himself depicted in great style, entering Rome as if in triumph.

p. 22, *by the chin*: The chin seems to have been a part of the body symbolizing power.

p. 22, *Lares*: The Lares, originally farmland deities, had by this time become guardian spirits of the household. There would be a *lararium* in the atrium of every house, containing small images of these spirits.

p. 22, *first beard… deposited*: The whiskers from a teenage boy's first shave were preserved as an offering to a god (Nero dedicated his to Jupiter Capitolinus).

p. 22, *Laenas*: Laenas was presumably a magistrate who courted popularity in the time-honoured way, by laying on games for the populace.

p. 22, *rods and axes*: The usual insignia of a consul, which Trimalchio, of course, is not.

p. 22, *beak of a ship*: Similar trophies of war would usually be displayed in the *vestibulum* of prominent Romans.

p. 22, *SEVIR... AUGUSTUS*: The *seviri Augustales* were given various privileges in return for supervising the cult of the Emperor. There were six of them (originally *sevir* was *sexvir*) and they were each allowed, on important occasions, to sit on a throne and wear a *toga prætexta*, i.e. a white toga with a wide purple stripe on its border. The grand title was actually quite commonplace – being *sevir* was a typical job for a wealthy freedman in the provinces.

p. 22, *II DAYS... OUT*: I.e. Trimalchio is due to dine out on 30th and 31st December – a long time ahead, as the present events are taking place in summer. The subtext is perhaps that he is so generous he usually dines at home, where he can invite guests to his meals.

p. 22, *the seven stars*: Or "heavenly bodies" – here, Sun, Mercury, Venus, Earth, Mars, Jupiter, Saturn.

p. 22, *studs*: From here onwards, Trimalchio's "superstition" (or interest in astrology) is frequently mentioned in the text, though he was probably no more *religiosus* than many Romans, as the next passage suggests.

p. 23, *break the rules... threshold*: Boundaries and thresholds were objects of proper respect to the Romans: to stumble over them was rightly considered a bad omen. Trimalchio insists on the right form.

p. 23, *steward... client... Tyrian purple... him*: It was unusual for a steward to have clients of his own; Trimalchio's steward seems to live in some style. Tyrian purple was the height of posh: Nero restricted its use (Suetonius, *Nero*, 32).

p. 24, *unusually... top place for himself*: Usually kept for the latecomer, rather than the master. To anticipate: the eventual seating arrangements at the dinner party (where each guest, unusually, has a small table of his own) seem to be as follows. The tables are arranged around three sides of the room, with the opening for servants to bring in the food. If Trimalchio is at the top-left corner, to his right reclines Agamemnon: then Hermeros, Encolpius (bottom-left corner),

Ascyltos, Habinnas (bottom-right corner), Scintilla and Fortunata (sharing), Proculus and Diogenes (top-right corner). Of course, the text, with its babble of voices criss-crossing through space, and its endless and chaotic parade of slaves and performers, makes the scene much more crowded than this neat arrangement suggests.

p. 24, *damsons with pomegranate seeds*: "Syrian plums with Punic apple seeds", as the Latin puts it. These are presumably meant to look like hot coals.

p. 24, *shaven head*: Common in slaves or in recently freed slaves.

p. 24, *broad purple stripe*: Perhaps alluding to the *latus clavus*, the purple stripe appropriate to a Roman senator – though that would be on a cloak, not a napkin, and a purple stripe also adorned the ceremonial garb of a *sevir*, which Trimalchio is.

p. 24, *solid gold... soldered on*: A gold ring would have been appropriate to a Roman knight (*eques*), an iron ring to freedmen.

p. 25, *long-haired Ethiopian slave boys*: Ethiopians are usually curly-headed: Trimalchio's are possibly wearing wigs, or are even blacked-up Roman slaves (Ethiopians were rather exotic and therefore desirable).

p. 25, *a table of their own*: This was very unusual.

p. 25, *FALERNIAN... YEARS OLD*: Opimius had been consul in 121 BC (so the label, if genuine, would have been added in the reign of Augustus). If Trimalchio's wine really was that ancient – and some bottles *were* kept until the mid-first century AD, according to Pliny – it would presumably have been good only as vinegar.

p. 26, *cheers... hatch*: The Latin here is the mysteriously alluring phrase, *tangomenas faciamus* (repeated below in ch. 73) and speculatively interpreted to mean "let's drink our fill". "Let's do the 'I touch anchovies'" or "Let's do the 'I touch the Manes (i.e. the dead)'" are other possible readings, as well as a Greek phrase meaning roughly "let's wet our whistles".

p. 26, *Orcus*: Another name for Dis, god of the underworld.

p. 26, *signs of the zodiac... two mullets*: In each case, the food is associated with a sign of the zodiac, sometimes in shape, sometimes less obviously. The garland on Cancer may be because Cancer is the sign associated with success, or simply because this is Trimalchio's own sign; the "sea horse" placed on Sagittarius is in Latin an *oclopeta*, a difficult word – perhaps something which seeks (*petere*) with its eyes (*oculi*); the goaty Capricorn has horns, while a lobster has claws and antennae; geese were associated with rain. Apicius gives several recipes for the uterus of a barren (or spayed) sow in Book VII of his *De re coquinaria* (*How To Cook*): one includes pepper, celery seed, dry mint, laser root, honey, vinegar and broth, though the womb can also be wrapped in bran and cooked in brine.

p. 27, *Silphium Gatherer*: Silphium, now extinct, was a highly-prized and expensive plant that grew along a narrow coastal strip near Cyrene in what is now Libya: it was used as a seasoning and a contraceptive.

p. 27, *Marsyas*: The satyr who challenged Apollo to a musical contest; he lost, and was flayed alive.

p. 27, *garum sauce*: Garum was a highly nourishing fish sauce used in the cooking of both rich and poor; it was made by fermenting the innards of various fish.

p. 27, *Hackett… hack it… vocative… imperative, see*: The meat-carver's name in Latin is "Carpus": "Carpe!" can be a verb form ("seize!" etc.) or a form of address ("O Carpus!"). Nero too owned a slave named Carpus.

p. 28, *beat any… cocked hat*: The Latin *in rutæ folium coniciet* means "will throw into a leaf of rue". This is obscure expression, though "a leaf of rue" may be proverbial for "a small space". The implication is clear: the "other fat cats" would rue trying to compete with Trimalchio.

p. 28, *eight hundred grand*: 800,000 sesterces was twice what you needed to enter the equestrian order.

p. 28, *Incubo's hat… hidden treasure*: Incubo was a gnome who protected hidden treasure. If you took his hat off, he was obliged to tell you where the treasure was hidden.

p. 28, *slapped free*: A slave being manumitted was given a ritual slap (*alapa*) by his master. Another reading here: "he's a bit touched".

p. 29, *KALENDS JULY*: The 1st of July.

p. 29, *freedman's place*: Apparently a special place reserved for a freed-man, though most of Trimalchio's guests fall into this category.

p. 29, *Is that… you know*: A quotation from Virgil's *Aeneid*, book II line 44.

p. 30, *Virgo… convicts*: Virgo was traditionally depicted with a bow round her feet.

p. 30, *Sagittarius... bacon*: Sagittarius looks cross-eyed as he aims his arrows; thieves pretend to look the other way while surreptitiously eyeing up your property.

p. 30, *Capricorn... heads*: The equation of horns with cuckoldry can be traced back to remote antiquity.

p. 30, *innkeepers*: They water their wine.

p. 30, *Pisces... rhetoricians*: Mouths always open, like fish? Always fishing for students?

p. 30, *Hipparchus and Aratus*: Aratus was the third-century BC author of a book on astronomy, the *Phænomena*. Hipparchus, active in the following century, wrote a critique of this. Hipparchus's work was translated by Cicero, who unkindly described Aratus as a *homo ignarus astrologiæ*.

p. 31, *Bromius... Lyaeus... Euhius*: These were all alternative names for Dionysus (the slave's "real" name) meaning, respectively, "Roarer" (or "Reveller"), "Loosener" (or "Deliverer") and "Sayer of *euoi*", (or "Inspirer" – *euoi* was the Bacchic chant). The man presiding over a Bacchic ritual was often identified with the god himself. Trimalchio goes on to use another name, "Liber" ("Free" – a Roman god identified with Dionysus, whose gift of wine frees us from our cares, as the folk etymology had it), and makes a complicated joke about himself having "Pater Liber" as his father (although he was born to a slave).

p. 32, *fuck off*: The Latin *læcasin dico* (from Greek λαικάζειν = "to fuck") is apparently the one really forceful swear word in Petronius's text, so I have reserved the F-word for this momentous occasion.

p. 32, *Bubbled... soul*: A colloquial phrase for "he snuffed it".

p. 32, *freed... slaves*: Probably in his will, so that they would put on a suitably doleful act as mourners: a common custom.

p. 33, *old dog*: Alternatively, or as well, the text may allude to his having taken hound's tongue, or *kunoglōssos*, the fragrance of which improved a person's hearing – enabling Phileros to pick up all the gossip.

p. 33, *bought... parrot*: Literally, "plucked a bad *parra*". *Parra* seems to have meant a bird of ill omen.

p. 33, *market officials*: Ædiles – in charge of many tasks, including corn distribution, the monitoring of weights and measures, etc.

p. 34, *flour… Sicily… standard*: The text is conjectural here. The flour from Sicily was of very high grade.

p. 34, *guess-how-many-fingers*: Similar to *morra*, still played in Italy – and indeed throughout the world; the name seems to come (though Italian etymologists have cast doubt on this) from the Latin verb *micare* ("to quiver, to move quickly from side to side") used by Petronius here. In Roman times, one version of the game was called *micatio*. There was a proverb: *dignus est quicum in tenebris mices* – "anyone you can play *morra* with in the dark is OK".

p. 34, *Caunian figs*: Caunus, in Caria (Asia Minor) was actually celebrated for its fine figs.

p. 34, *hundred grand*: 100,000 sesterces would have qualified him to be an *ædile*.

p. 36, *Norbanus*: We will meet this character again in ch. 46: he is a wealthy lawyer.

p. 36, *pint-sized… killed off*: Or "horsemen off a table lamp" – it was common to have lamps with the miniature figures of gladiators on them.

p. 36, *the Thracian*: Not necessarily from Thrace: rather, a gladiator who wore light Thracian armour (scimitar, oblong shield, greaves and often a fine crest on the helmet).

p. 36, *young nipper's*: The Latin word is *cicaro* – perhaps an adopted son rather than a biological son.

p. 36, *Greek… Latin… way*: Here again we see that the study of Greek preceded that of Latin.

p. 37, *master of ceremonies*: The *nomenclator*, a slave charged with reminding his master of people's names.

p. 37, *an old man*: Or "six": the text is uncertain.

p. 38, *mincemeat… Pentheus*: The daughters of Cadmus made mincemeat of Pentheus when they caught him spying on their Dionysian rites.

p. 38, *division*: I.e. of slaves.

p. 38, *between Tarracina and Tarentum*: A vast area, since the two towns are over 300 miles apart. Of course, Trimalchio may not have much grasp of geography, or he may just be indulging in boastful exaggeration. Or he may really be fantastically rich, as when he voices the desire to buy the whole of Sicily – he is, after all, a fiction.

p. 38, *casebook speech*: *Controversia* – as the Latin word suggests, a speech on a controversial and usually fictitious subject presented as an example to students.

p. 39, Σίβυλλα, τί θέλεις... αποθανεῖν θέλω: Greek: "'*Sibulla, ti theleis?*' – '*Apothanein thelo.*'" "'Sibyl, what do you want?' – 'I want to die.'" Trimalchio's garbled account of mythology rises to a tragic climax (the Sibyl's words are the epigraph to *The Waste Land*, and are misquoted in Ezra Pound's *Canto* 64). The Cumaean Sibyl (from Cumae, the Greek colony north-west of Naples) presided over the local cult of Apollo. It was she who led Aeneas into the underworld, and who prophesied, in Virgil's *Pastoral Poems*, a new age. Having cheated Apollo of her virginity, she was doomed to waste away until she would be nothing but a voice (see Ovid, *Metamorphoses*, XIV, 153). Cumae was also, according to Tacitus, the scene of Petronius's suicide.

p. 39, *executioners*: Guards/torturers/executioners – at all events, *tortores* were usually State officials. The fact that Trimalchio has his own suggests that his domain is an *imperium in imperio*.

p. 40, *Corinthian bronze... alloy*: There was indeed a tale (told by Pliny in the *Natural History*) that this alloy of copper, gold and silver was discovered when different metals fused while Corinth was being burnt down by the Roman general Lucius Mummius. But Trimalchio mixes Hannibal and Troy into the story.

p. 40, *craftsman... invention*: A version of this story is told about the Emperor Tiberius (again reported by Pliny: *Natural History*, XXXVI, 198).

p. 41, *Cassandra... Trojan horse*: The mythology in the last two sentences is wonderfully jumbled (or, of course, comes from traditions otherwise unattested).

p. 41, *Hermeros and Petraites*: Trimalchio here refers to two real, and celebrated, gladiators.

p. 41, *cordax*: The *cordax* was a lewd dance from Old Greek comedy, for women. It involved a lot of arse-waggling (according to Juvenal, who also notes the playing of castanets). Some have claimed improbably that it evolved into the fandango.

p. 41, Μάδεια, πεϱιμάδεια: Greek: "madeia, perimadeia" – it sounds like a chant, but its reference is uncertain.

p. 41, *Town Gazette*: Trimalchio has his own version of the *Urbis acta*, the Roman daily. The numbers quoted in it are extraordinarily high. It is probably mostly made up (unlike real newspapers).

p. 41, *VII sextile Kalends*: The 26th of July.

p. 42, *porter... Baiae*: Lucky porter! Baiae, near Puteoli, was a notorious pleasure resort for the seriously wealthy, a "whirlpool of luxury" (Seneca) and "a den of lust and vice" (Propertius).

p. 42, *Atellan farces*: These were plays (originally improvised in the Oscan language: Atella was a city in Campania) that were performed after tragedies, rather like the satyr plays of Greece. They were coarsely humorous, dealt with lower-class life, and were based on stock characters (similar to those of the much later *Commedia dell'arte*).

p. 43, *Mopsus of Thrace*: Mopsus was the name of the soothsayer of the Argonauts, though the reference here is probably not to him.

p. 43, *Cicero and Publilius*: Publilius Syrus was a first-century BC writer of moral aphorisms ("a rolling stone gathers no moss", "when vice is advantageous, it's a sin to be virtuous") and farces. The lines Trimalchio professes to quote are almost certainly not by him: they wag a finger at contemporary decadence. The subtext is that it is silly to compare Publilius with Cicero, since the latter was not much good at farces (and incapable of writing decent poetry).

p. 44, *duck meat*: Very good for the digestion, this helped protect Mithridates VI of Pontus from poison, according to Pliny.

p. 44, *tickets... party bags*: These tickets with their crossword-style or rebus-like allusions to takeaway gifts were common. The Emperor Augustus enjoyed playing this game. The slave's (i.e. presumably Trimalchio's) puns are too complicated to explain in English (they are also textually corrupt); I have replaced them by simpler, but equally bad ones.

p. 45, *one of... next to mine*: Presumably Hermeros, who enjoys using Greek turns of phrase. The words in parentheses may be a later explanatory gloss.

p. 45, *eques*: I.e. a knight – not a member of the aristocracy, more a member of the upper middle classes.

p. 45, *Roman citizen... tax-payer*: Hermeros, as a free non-Roman, may have sold himself to a patron on the understanding that he would then be set free and could claim Roman citizenship.

p. 45, *partner*: "Partner" in the sense of wife, though slaves were not allowed to be officially married.

p. 46, *Saturnalia*: At this festival, slaves were allowed to let off steam, and Giton is here pretending to be the slave of Encolpius.

p. 46, *5% freedom tax*: This could be paid either by the master or the slave when the latter was manumitted.

p. 46, *my fellow freedman*: Trimalchio – even though Hermeros had only nominally been a slave, he sees Trimalchio as having risen in society, like himself.

p. 47, *I am... grows apace*: One answer to all these riddles (it is not clear if they are separate riddles or one) is "time". Another (apparently) is "a penis"; another, "a shadow".

p. 47, *Occupo*: Perhaps some popular deity, not known outside Petronius; maybe a goblin who fosters people's business plans.

p. 48, *wearing my toga... front*: As a magistrate did when pronouncing sentence of death.

p. 48, *And... anarchy*: At nunc mera mapalia – "But now, mere African huts". Or *quel bazar!* as the French say.

p. 48, *Homeristas*: I.e. professional reciters of Homer.

p. 48, *drove Ajax mad*: Another rhapsody on a theme by Homer (or rather from the much fuller version in Sophocles's play *Ajax*). Ajax, jealous that the arms of the dead Achilles were given to Odysseus, went mad and slew a herd of farm animals: the meat-carver in the next scene mimics him.

p. 49, *this ritual liquid*: Saffron was used in religious rituals, though the messy ejaculation here seems more like a practical joke (by Trimalchio? by Priapus?).

p. 49, *Hireling... do the same*: It was traditional to sacrifice to the household gods during dinner; less common for the image of the host to be kissed.

p. 51, *every hair... stand up*: Despite his baldness.

p. 51, *Chian ease*: Chios was famous for its wine; the Chians were notorious for their shameless self-indulgence. They were, so to speak, Trimal-Chians.

p. 52, *Apelles*: Not the painter; a tragic actor of the first-century AD.

p. 53, *lictor*: An attendant who would walk (usually with several other lictors) in front of magistrates or certain priests, and attend them as bodyguards.

p. 53, *praetor*: An important magistrate.

p. 53, *place of honour*: Middle couch, lowest seat.

p. 54, *5%... reckon*: Scissa would have paid 5% tax on the value of the dead slave.

p. 54, *pax Palamedes*: *Pax* is "peace", and the expression may mean "if you don't mind my saying so". Palamedes was the man sent by Agamemnon to lure Odysseus into his army against Troy. Odysseus later killed Palamedes in revenge. On the positive side, Palamedes was the mythological inventor of jokes, and of certain letters of the alphabet.

p. 55, *I owe Mercury*: Offerings (here a tenth of a per cent per month) would be made by wealthy Romans to Mercury, god of commerce.

p. 55, *second courses*: The Latin for "courses" here is the same as that for "tables" (*mensæ*), so Trimalchio is playing an extravagant little joke.

p. 56, *Meanwhile... to sea*: Aeneid v, 1.

p. 56, *Cappadocian... short*: The reputation of Cappadocian slaves was not high – they were always on the make.

p. 57, *Daedalus*: The old artificer who devoted his mind to the unknown arts, built the labyrinth, learnt to fly and gave his name to jacks-of-all-trades.

p. 57, *Noricum*: Noricum was a territory that stretched from the Danube to the Alps – roughly Styria.

p. 58, *Scintilla... she could speak*: It was usually vulgar to dance in public.

p. 58, *Philargyrus... greens*: Philargyrus the slave was a supporter of the Green team in circus competitions – the other colours were Blue, White and Red. Rivalry between the Blues and the Greens would later cause fierce civil strife in the Byzantine Empire.

p. 58, *Ephesus the tragedian*: Not otherwise known.

p. 59, THIS MONUMENT... HEIR: *Hoc monumentum heredem non sequitur* – often abbreviated on tombs to h.m.h.n.s.

p. 59, *lay on a big public feast... head*: Laying on a feast for the populace was one way of earning the right to wear gold rings, which otherwise were usually the prerogative of an *eques*.

p. 60, *ELIGIBLE... ALL DOWN*: I.e. he decided not to go to Rome even though, as a freedman, he could have joined the decuries (guilds of lower-ranking public servants).

p. 60, *leftovers... him*: Giton is still acting as their slave. Here, he cleverly throws a sop to Cerberus.

p. 61, *they come in... out another*: Another hint that Trimalchio's house is like Hades (with its gate of horn and its gate of ivory).

p. 61, *Menecrates*: Menecrates of Ephesus was a Greek poet, though there was also a Menecrates whose harp-playing was commended by Nero (see Suetonius, *Nero*, 30).

p. 61, *wine... wine*: If anyone mentioned fire at a banquet, it was usual to pour water (rather than wine) as an offering under the table, to avert the evil omen. A crowing cock was a bad omen, too. Changing rings from one hand to the other was a common gesture for averting such threats.

p. 62, *spit... bosom*: You spit in your bosom when you are lucky.

p. 64, *joint heir with Caesar*: A wealthy man would commonly mention the emperor in his will; that way the emperor was less likely to override the will and confiscate the entire estate.

p. 65, *Scaurus*: Apparently a famous maker of fish sauce, from Pompeii.

p. 66, *a messenger... turned up*: The text in this and the next sentence is corrupt – it may be a messenger (*tabellarius*), from Trimalchio (in at least one rather enigmatic reading), or the tavern-keeper or a shop-keeper (*tabernarius*) who lets our heroes in.

p. 67, *a Theban tragedy*: The tragedies associated with the family of Oedipus are set in Thebes; most pertinent here is the story of how his two sons Eteocles and Polynices fought for the kingship of the city.

p. 67, *The players... onstage*: John of Salisbury quoted these lines ("*grex agit in scæna mimum*") in the mid-twelfth century; the words – admittedly a commonplace – are echoed in the "*Totus mundus agit histrionem*" motto of the Globe theatre, and "All the world's a stage" of melancholy Jacques in *As You Like It*.

p. 69, *Zeuxis... Protegenes's... Apelles's... μονόκνημον*: Zeuxis, Protegenes and Apelles were all famous Greek painters; the μονόκνημον ("*monoknemon*") was presumably a one-legged figure, since this is the meaning of the Greek.

p. 70, *the boy from Ida*: The shepherd Ganymede; Zeus assumed the shape of an eagle and ravished him up to heaven from Mount Ida.

p. 70, *Hylas... him*: Hylas had been loved by Hercules; he went on the

Argonauts' quest for the Golden Fleece and, while bending down to draw water, he was pulled under by an over-amorous Naiad.

p. 70, *Apollo... flower... lyre*: Apollo accidentally killed his beloved Hyacinthus by a poorly judged discus throw; the boy's blood became a hyacinth.

p. 70, *Lycurgus*: Lycurgus was the notoriously austere law-giver of Sparta; but the Lycurgus of the *Satyricon* seems to be a different character: in earlier episodes he *may* have been the host of Encolpius who then mistreated him and was killed by him. There is certainly a Lycurgus whose villa our heroes have burgled, or plan to burgle (mentioned in ch. 117).

p. 70, *white-haired old man*: Eumolpus.

p. 71, *quaestor*: A Roman magistrate or financial official.

p. 72, *a slow comfortable screw*: "*Plenum et optabilem coitum*" – a phrase Byron used in a letter to refer to his congress with young boys.

p. 74, *Democritus... Eudoxus... Chrysippus... Lysippus... Myron... line*: These are all examples of great scientists and artists of antiquity. Democritus contributed to the early development of atomic theory; Eudoxus was an astronomer and geometer (he did not actually retire to a mountain, but went into politics); Chrysippus was a Stoic; Lysippus became personal sculptor to Alexander the Great; Myron sculpted athletes, a Minotaur, and various animals including a celebrated heifer and dog.

p. 74, *In verse*: What follows, known as the *Halosis Troiæ* or *Capture of Troy*, is a rewrite of the second book of the *Aeneid*. It may be meant to show up Eumolpus as a poetaster, whose work is a clumsy pastiche of Virgil – more halitosis than *halosis*.

p. 75, *Calchas's*: Calchas was the priest of Apollo, the god of Delos, who urged the Greeks to build the wooden horse.

p. 75, *Sinon's*: Sinon pretended to be a deserter from the Greeks, and told the Trojans the Wooden Horse was a Greek offering to the gods; they should install it in Troy to protect the city.

p. 80, *If it's... us*: Eumolpus is speaking.

p. 80, *Colchis... Phasis*: Now the River Rioni in Georgia, the Phasis was seen as the easternmost known navigable body of water in Petronius's day. Its Greek name "Phasis" gives us the word "pheasant". Colchis, on the same shore of the Black Sea, was similarly exotic.

p. 80, *Syrtis*: Syrtis was a name applied to two stretches of the North African coast that were notorious for their dangers.

p. 81, *Blessed... exclaimed*: Eumolpus is addressing Giton.

p. 83, *My girl... me*: Probably Bargates to Eumolpus.

p. 84, *made like Ulysses... to avoid detection*: This is a parody of the famous episode in the *Odyssey* (book IX, lines 420ff).

p. 85, *I have... return*: Eumolpus is usually taken to be the speaker here.

p. 86, *It really... boy*: Encolpius is soliloquizing.

p. 89, *a trick like this... one occasion*: Plutarch relates how Cleopatra had herself rolled up in a carpet and delivered to Caesar.

p. 89, *No... escape*: Encolpius is still speaking.

p. 90, *last sacrifices... ship*: People threatened with shipwreck would offer cuttings from their hair or beard to the marine deities.

p. 90, *In my... ship*: The speaker is Lichas. Priapus's persecutions of Encolpius gather pace.

p. 91, *it was decided... us*: They have not yet been recognized.

p. 92, *Ulysses's nurse*: Eurycleia, in the *Odyssey*, book XIX, 467ff. This encounter between Lichas and Encolpius is a nice parody of such scenes of *anagnorisis* ("recognition") in epic and tragedy. The scene in which Eurycleia recognizes Odysseus from his scar is taken as exemplary of one style of realism by Erich Auerbach in *Mimesis*.

p. 92, *his wife... Hercules*: One of the lost episodes of the *Satyricon*.

p. 93, *I believe... friends*: Eumolpus is speaking: his words are a pastiche of forensic speeches.

p. 94, *poisonous bastard*: The insult he uses here is the Greek word "*pharmakos*": poisoner, magician and scapegoat.

p. 95, *mad Medea... foes*: When her father, Aeëtes of Colchis, was pursuing her by sea, Medea chopped up her brother and scattered the parts into the waves, so that the sorrowing father, pausing to gather his son's limbs, would be delayed.

p. 98, *There was... Ephesus*: This story was already well known, as one of the "Milesian Tales" in general circulation by Petronius's time. This title covered a whole genre of episodic, ribald narratives, often containing stories-within-stories: those by Aristides (second century BC) were set in the pleasure-loving city of Miletus and hence known as *Milesiaka*. When the billionaire Crassus was crushingly defeated by the Parthian general Surena at the Battle of Carrhae in

53 BC, the Parthians ransacked the baggage of their Roman prisoners: they were shocked to discover that, even on campaign, the Romans had brought copies of the *Milesiaka* with them (Plutarch, *Crassus*, 32). The tale of the Widow of Ephesus was quoted or mentioned by many later writers, notably Robert Burton in his *Anatomy of Melancholy*. Maupassant tells us that Flaubert dreamt of writing "a sort of modern Matron of Ephesus". The narrative has been set to music many times; a comic opera, called *The Ephesian Matriarch, or The Widow's Tears* (music by Charles Dibdin, libretto by Isaac Bickerstaff) was premiered at the Ranelagh Gardens in London in 1769; it parodied operatic conventions; Petronius might well have approved.

p. 99, *Dost think... feel*: A slightly modified version of *Aeneid*, book IV, line 34.

p. 99, *Would'st fight... thee*: *Aeneid* IV, 38.

p. 100, *Hedyle... eloped*: Another lost episode – Hedyle was perhaps Lichas's lover or wife.

p. 101, *He*: Lichas? So some mss indicate.

p. 101, *If you've... tart*: Sources attribute these words to Tryphaena's maid, addressing Encolpius, but this is far from certain.

p. 102, *goddess's robe... sistrum*: Encolpius appears to have stolen these sacred emblems of Isis, the patron goddess of the ship. The *sistrum* was a rattle.

p. 105, *Croton*: Originally a Greek colony; today's Crotona.

p. 105, *the mother of the gods*: Cybele. Her cult was introduced from Asia into Rome, where she was worshipped as the Great Mother, *Magna Mater*.

p. 107, *I hate... hence*: The celebrated opening line of Horace's poem (*Odes*, III, 1, 1).

p. 107, *example... polish*: The following poems, full of mythological allusions and uncertain textual *cruces*, is best enjoyed as a poetic parody of, or homage to, a certain epic style, maybe Lucan's, the material of whose great poem (*Pharsalia*) it draws on. If it is indeed an aesthetic disaster, it also portrays with crude vividness the Civil War as a cosmic calamity.

p. 109, *Lucrine Lake*: Near Puteoli; it was famous for its oysters. This part of the poem bewails, yet again, the expensive tastes of the Romans – in this case those of a generation before Petronius's own.

p. 109, *Phasis... birds*: Pheasants.

p. 109, *Even Cato... from Cato*: Probably a reference to an election which Cato (of Utica) lost to Vatinius, a colleague of Julius Caesar.

p. 110, *Enyo*: Greek goddess of war.

p. 110, *Crassus... The Great... Julius*: The first triumvirate: Crassus was killed by the Parthians, Pompey "the Great" was assassinated on the shore of Egypt while fleeing Julius Caesar after losing the battle of Pharsalus, and Caesar himself was assassinated in Rome.

p. 110, *Parthenope*: One of the Sirens, and also a name for Naples.

p. 110, *Dicarchis*: The old Greek name for Puteoli.

p. 110, *Dis*: An early name for Pluto or Hades, god of the underworld.

p. 111, *Tisiphone*: The Fury who punished murderers.

p. 111, *Sulla's sword supped full*: Sulla was appointed dictator of Rome in 82 BC and proscribed thousands of his enemies.

p. 112, *APOLLO... enter in*: Apollo was said to have sided with Octavian, later Augustus Caesar, at the battle of Actium against Antony and Cleopatra.

p. 112, *Porthmeus*: Another name for Charon.

p. 112, *his brother*: Jupiter.

p. 112, *the Titan's*: The Sun's.

p. 112, *Cynthia*: The moon.

p. 113, *He threw... Bello Civili*: I.e. Caesar, his war against the Gauls having been successfully prosecuted, now took up arms in the Civil War against Pompey. He wrote accounts of both campaigns.

p. 113, *Hesperia*: Here, Italy, the western land, after Hesperus, the evening star (Italy is also called "Saturn-Land" a few lines down, after that agricultural deity). The poem tells of Caesar's crossing of the Alps, and then the Rubicon, from Gaul into Italy, which precipitated the Civil War; Caesar reminds his soldiers of Rome's "ingratitude" for their victories over her enemies, of the many reasons for his resentment against the Republic, etc.

p. 115, *Amphitryon's fierce son*: I.e. Hercules, who had also mythically crossed the Alps, as well as rescuing Prometheus from Mount Caucasus.

p. 116, *Mr Big*: *Magnus*, i.e. Pompey the Great, whose triumphs and tribulations are now detailed.

p. 116, *earthquake for Pontus*: Pompey defeated Mithridates of Pontus in 63 BC.

p. 116, *Hydaspes... repertoire*: The river Hydaspes was in India, and Pompey (unlike Alexander the Great) did not in fact reach it.

p. 117, *Erebus*: God of darkness.

p. 117, *Erinys*: A Fury.

p. 117, *Bellona*: Goddess of War.

p. 117, *Megaera*: A Fury.

p. 118, *Dione*: The mother of Venus (her name, rather vaguely, just means "the goddess"): here used for Venus herself. Caesar claimed kinship with Venus.

p. 118, *Cyllene kid*: Mercury, born on Mount Cyllene in Arcadia.

p. 118, *Tiryns*: Tiryns in the Peloponnese was the birthplace of Hercules.

p. 119, *Marcellus*: Probably the consul who proposed that Caesar be recalled.

p. 119, *Curio*: Tribune of the people; one of Caesar's supporters; here he is urged to rouse the rabble and monger war.

p. 119, *Lentulus*: Consul in 49 BC, in favour of civil war.

p. 119, *hero-from-heaven*: Julius Caesar, posthumously deified as *divus Julius*.

p. 119, *Epidamnus*: For a while, Pompey's base on the Adriatic.

p. 120, *Just because... cash*: Chrysis, the maid of Circe, is talking to Encolpius (though, as we shall see, he has adopted a pseudonym since arriving in Croton).

p. 120, *first fourteen... theatre*: The first rows in the theatre were allotted to the senators; the fourteen rows behind these were reserved for the *equites*.

p. 120, *She... picture*: We now meet Circe.

p. 122, *sis*: I.e. girlfriend, with *soror*, "sister", apparently being used (like *frater*) to mean "sexual partner".

p. 122, *the-daughter... Circe*: I.e. not the Circe of Homer's *Odyssey*. But the name still evokes that dangerous enchantress.

p. 122, *Polyaenus*: Encolpius has adopted this name, from the Greek adjective πολύαινος: it is one of the epithets of Odysseus in Homer (given to him by the Sirens), and means "much praised", or "many-storied".

p. 123, *in lawful love*: Actually to distract her from the Trojan War.

p. 123, *Tell me... now*: Circe is questioning her maid.

p. 124, *Well, thank you*: Giton is talking to Encolpius, claims one source.

p. 124, *You've got... man*: Encolpius then replies to Giton.

p. 125, *The women... sky*: I.e. they are witches, quite able to dislocate the moon – or put a hex on a man where it hurts.

p. 126, *an old woman*: This is the sorceress Proselenos. Her name is associated with the moon ("Selene").

p. 127, *Daphne*: Daphne was turned into a laurel to escape Apollo.

p. 127, *Procne*: Procne was turned into a swallow, her sister Philomela into a nightingale, after their sufferings at the hands of Tereus, the former's husband.

p. 128, *What a beautiful body*: This fragment may be out of place: the sex of Encolpius's lover is undefined in the Latin, and a scribal note reads: "Encolpius refers to the boy Endymion". Or the fragment is not out of place at all; in any case, our ignorance of the identity of Encolpius's lover need not affect his (fleeting) bliss.

p. 128, *The lady... revenge*: This seems to refer to Circe, disappointed again at Encolpius's flop of a performance.

p. 129, *It looked... stalks*: These lines include a mosaic of words and phrases from different works by Virgil.

p. 130, *τέλος*: Telos, aim, end (Greek).

p. 130, *on the threshold*: Probably of a shrine to Priapus, to whom the following prayer is addressed.

p. 130, *Dione*: Venus, again.

p. 131, *Hypaepa*: A small town in Lydia.

p. 132, *What... away*: Proselenos is the "old woman" we have just met, now talking to Encolpius.

p. 132, *priestess*: This is Oenothea, priestess of Priapus.

p. 132, *Oh... said*: Proselenos is discussing Encolpius with Oenothea.

p. 134, *Lyaeus*: Another reference to Bacchus as "releaser".

p. 134, *Hecale*: Hecale was an old woman who gave hospitality to Theseus. The text of this little poem ends in a flurry of corruption and conjecture.

p. 134, *son of Battus's city*: A reference to the poet of Alexandria, Callimachus, here called a "son of Battus's city" because Battus (seventh century BC) was the founder of Callimachus's birthplace, Cyrene.

p. 134, *She*: Proselenos.

p. 135, *She*: Oenothea, presumably.

p. 135, *birds of Stymphalus... them*: Hercules drove away the Stymphalian birds (brass-winged, metal-feathered man-eaters whose shit was poisonous) by banging metal pots and shooting an arrow at them; this is traditionally counted as number six in his Labours.

p. 135, *Phineus's... poison*: Phineus (or Phineas), blinded by Zeus for revealing the gods' secrets, was also harassed by the Harpies because he had in turn blinded his sons: these women-faced birds stole or mucked up his food (hence "tantalizing") whenever it was laid out for him on his table.

p. 137, *Acrisius... Danaë*: Acrisius was the father of Danaë. He was told that a son of hers would kill him, so he locked Danaë up in a bronze tower. Zeus came to her in the form of a golden shower: she gave birth to Perseus. Perseus later killed Acrisius, apparently quite unintentionally.

p. 137, *Cato... Servius... Labeo*: Three famous lawyers of the first century BC (the Cato indicated here was son of Cato the Censor).

p. 138, *The old woman*: Presumably Proselenos.

p. 138, *habrotonus*: A bitter, aromatic herb mentioned by Lucretius (IV.125) and Lucan.

p. 138, *Was Ariadne... was*: Encolpius is speaking.

p. 139, *Tirynthian*: Hercules. This poem is filled with *exempla* of divinities persecuting mortals.

p. 139, *Inachian shore*: I.e. from Greece: Inachus was in one story the first king of Argos.

p. 139, *He had... heaven*: When he (Hercules) held up the sky for Atlas.

p. 139, *Laomedon... two gods... him*: Laomedon commissioned Apollo and Poseidon to build Troy for him; then he refused to pay them.

p. 139, *Juno's*: Pelias, king of Iolcus, desecrated the altar of Hera/Juno.

p. 139, *Telephus*: Telephus fought against the Greeks during the Trojan War; Bacchus made him trip over a vine root.

p. 139, *Ulysses... Neptune's kingly power*: Neptune (Poseidon) was the deadly enemy of Ulysses (Odysseus).

p. 139, *Nereus*: A sea god – the fabled Old Man of the Sea.

p. 140, *my master*: Eumolpus.

p. 141, *Protesilaos*: Protesilaos, the leader of the Thessalian contingent, was the first soldier to be killed fighting in the Trojan war. His widow begged to see him again, and he was allowed by Hermes to revisit the earth just once more. His "resurrection" signals the restoration of Encolpius's virility.

p. 142, *Saguntum... inheritance*: Now Murviedro, in Spain. Hannibal sat down before it for eight months and took the town in 219 BC. This signalled the commencement of hostilities between Rome and Carthage.

p. 142, *Petelians... bay*: Petelia, in south Italy, fell to Hannibal's deputy Himilco.

p. 143, *Numantia*: Now Garry in Spain; it fell to Rome in 133 BC after a siege of eight months.

p. 145, *It was dread... the world*: This view of the origins of religion is Epicurean.

p. 146, *Pales*: Goddess of herds and shepherds.

p. 146, *Hister*: The Danube.

p. 146, *Boreas*: The north wind.

p. 146, *Canopus*: An ancient port in the Nile Delta.

p. 146, *Corycian kale*: Corycus was the home town of a contented old man praised in Virgil's *Georgics*.

p. 148, *I roused alternate hand*: I.e. I swam (in the fresh water, where Naiads belong).

p. 150, *Lucina*: The goddess of childbirth. She brings the child to light (*lux*).

p. 150, *I'm a jolly sight... singin'*: The speaker is a parrot, addressing Apollo.

p. 152, *The Jew... sabbath day*: In a typical anti-Semitic transposition, the divine prohibition on eating pork becomes an identification of the Deity with a pig. Jews are not in fact enjoined to fast on the sabbath.

p. 154, *Hybla*: A town in Sicily famous for its honey.

p. 157, *Albucia*: The source claims this was the name of a randy woman in Petronius's work.

p. 157, *myrrhine cup*: I.e. one that gave wine a special flavour; here, apparently, a reference to an aphrodisiac.

p. 158, *Cosmus*: A manufacturer of cosmetics in the first century AD.

p. 158, *Trivia's fire*: Trivia is a name for Diana as the moon.

p. 158, *if... don't smell good*: This line is also found in Martial (*Epigrams* II, 12, 4), and there are variants on the theme in other writers.

p. 181, All page references are to John Baxter, *Fellini* (London: Fourth Estate, 1993), whose excellent account I follow closely.

ONEWORLD CLASSICS

ONEWORLD CLASSICS aims to publish mainstream and lesser-known European classics in an innovative and striking way, while employing the highest editorial and production standards. By way of a unique approach the range offers much more, both visually and textually, than readers have come to expect from contemporary classics publishing.

∽

ANTON CHEKHOV: *Sakhalin Island*
Translated by Brian Reeve

ANTON CHEKHOV: *The Woman in the Case*
Translated by Kyril FitzLyon

CHARLES DICKENS: *The Haunted House*

D.H. LAWRENCE: *The First Women in Love*

D.H. LAWRENCE: *The Second Lady Chatterley's Lover*

D.H. LAWRENCE: *Paul Morel*

D.H. LAWRENCE: *Selected Letters*

JAMES HANLEY: *Boy*

JAMES HANLEY: *The Closed Harbour*

JACK KEROUAC: *Beat Generation*

IVAN BUNIN: *The Village*
Translated by Hugh Aplin

FYODOR DOSTOEVSKY: *Humiliated and Insulted*
Translated by Ignat Avsey

FYODOR DOSTOEVSKY: *Winter Notes on Summer Impressions*
Translated by Kyril FitzLyon

ÉMILE ZOLA: *Ladies' Delight*
Translated by April FitzLyon

BOILEAU: *The Art of Poetry* and *Lutrin*
Translated by William Soames and John Ozell

CECCO ANGIOLIERI: *Sonnets*
Translated by C.H. Scott and Anthony Mortimer

STENDHAL: *Travels in the South of France*
Translated by Elisabeth Abbott

GOETHE: *Elective Affinities*
Translated by H.M. Waidson

BÜCHNER: *Lenz*
Translated by Michael Hamburger

DROSTE-HÜLSHOFF: *The Jew's Beech*
Translated by Lionel and Doris Thomas

POPE: *The Art of Sinking in Poetry*

For our complete list, please visit
www.oneworldclassics.com